Surprises on

Lilac Mills lives on a Welsh mountain with her very patient husband and incredibly sweet dog, where she grows veggies (if the slugs don't get them), bakes (badly) and loves making things out of glitter and glue (a mess, usually). She's been an avid reader ever since she got her hands on a copy of *Noddy Goes to Toytown* when she was five, and she once tried to read everything in her local library starting with A and working her way through the alphabet. She loves long, hot summer days and cold winter ones snuggled in front of the fire, but whatever the weather she's usually writing or thinking about writing, with heartwarming romance and happy-ever-afters always on her mind.

Also by Lilac Mills

Summer on the Turquoise Coast
Love in the City by the Sea
The Cosy Travelling Christmas Shop

Tanglewood Village series

The Tanglewood Tea Shop
The Tanglewood Flower Shop
The Tanglewood Wedding Shop
The Tanglewood Bookshop

Island Romance

Sunrise on the Coast
Holiday in the Hills
Sunset on the Square

Applewell Village

Waste Not, Want Not in Applewell
Make Do and Mend in Applewell
A Stitch in Time in Applewell

Foxmore Village

The Corner Shop on Foxmore Green
The Christmas Fayre on Holly Field
The Allotment on Willow Tree Lane

Coorie Castle Crafts

Surprises on the Scottish Isle

LILAC MILLS

Surprises
ON THE
Scottish Isle

CANELO

First published in the United Kingdom in 2025 by

Canelo
Unit 9, 5th Floor
Cargo Works, 1–2 Hatfields
London SE1 9PG
United Kingdom

A CIP catalogue record for this book is available from the British Library.

Print ISBN 978 1 80032 888 4
Ebook ISBN 978 1 80032 887 7

This book is a work of fiction. Names, characters, businesses, organizations, places and events are either the product of the author's imagination or are used fictitiously. Any resemblance to actual persons, living or dead, events or locales is entirely coincidental.

Cover design by Head Design

Look for more great books at www.canelo.co

Printed and bound in Great Britain by Clays Ltd, Elcograf S.p.A.

Prologue

Tara snuggled deeper into the crook of Calan's arm and draped one leg over his. The sheet was a tangled mess of damp cotton, and she pushed it down, too warm for even a light covering in the rare heat of Glasgow in early May.

Her fingers idly stroked the auburn hairs on his chest, and she thought what a lovely chest he had, all firm and muscley, the skin soft and gleaming from their exertions. He appeared to be half asleep, his eyes closed and his breathing even. The only thing that gave him away was the twitch of his lips as he held in a laugh.

She knew her light touch tickled him, but those hairs were incredibly strokable. To be honest, *all* of him was strokable. There wasn't an inch of Cal she didn't love.

Finally, he let out a snort and opened his eyes, turning his head to look at her. 'If you keep doing that, I won't be responsible for my actions.'

It was a promise not a warning, and it sent a shiver of desire through her. Wickedly, her fingers went to work again.

With a low growl, he sat up and flipped her onto her back, pinning her down.

'Want some of your own medicine?' he murmured, his lips on the delicate skin below her ear. He nibbled her neck, and she squirmed with delight.

I

His mouth moved lower, and he licked along her collarbone.

'I haven't got time,' she said, her breath hitching as his hands did some wandering of their own. 'I've got a lecture this afternoon that I can't miss.'

He stopped what he was doing and propped himself on an elbow to look deep into her eyes. 'I wish you didn't have to go.'

'So do I, but it's the last one before my exams. It's all right for you, you've finished yours.'

The reminder killed her mood. Cal had just sat his finals. This was his last year at university and soon he would be heading home to Inverness, leaving her in Glasgow.

Tara was only in her second year of her degree course, and she dreaded having to wait another year before they could move in together. Where that would be was unclear, but Calan's degree was in Business and Management, and with his love of the great outdoors he hoped to land a job working for one of the large country estates in the Highlands.

As for Tara, she hadn't decided what she wanted to do after she finished uni, but it would be something to do with art. In quieter moments, she daydreamed that Cal would manage the grounds of some lofty mansion, whilst she curated its paintings, tapestries and statues. They would make a brilliant team.

Cal was watching her. 'I love you.'

No matter how often he told her those three little words they always made her hum with happiness. 'And I love you,' she replied softly.

He was her soulmate, and she couldn't believe how lucky she was to have found him. People could go their whole lives without experiencing love like this. But there were only three short days left before he returned to Inverness, and the thought of him going made her heart ache. She wished he could stay in Glasgow and move in with her, but she still lived at home with her mum and stepdad, so that was out of the question. The only thing making their imminent separation bearable was the knowledge that the long summer holidays were just around the corner and she would be able to visit him soon. She was looking forward to meeting his parents and seeing where he lived.

Her movements were slow and reluctant as she got dressed, kissed Cal, then headed out the door. Her thoughts were already on this evening and Tara was absolutely determined to make the most of the next three days, because it might be a while before she could be with the man who had stolen her heart.

–

The first thing I'm going to do when I get a job is buy a car, Cal vowed, as he lugged his ginormous rucksack off the train and made for the taxi rank. Thankfully he wasn't the type of guy to acquire loads of stuff, and he'd managed to cram everything he'd wanted to bring to Inverness in it. The rest had either been donated to other students, or disposed of because it was knackered, such as the chipped mug he'd used for the past seven months, or the duvet whose stitching had come undone.

Nevertheless, he was surprised that neither his mum nor his dad had offered to fetch him from uni. Even a lift from the railway station would have been nice, he thought, as the taxi slowed when it neared the bungalow and he saw that both their cars were on the drive.

Barrelling through the front door, he clattered into the hall and dumped the over-large rucksack at the bottom of the stairs. 'Mum? Dad? I'm home!'

The house was strangely silent. Usually there would be the radio or the TV on, and one or the other of his parents would have hurried to greet him.

'Mum?' He poked his head into the kitchen. 'Dad?' The living room was empty. He glanced out the window, but they weren't in the garden.

Sighing, Cal returned to the kitchen and opened the fridge. Was it too early for a beer? He could certainly do with one. Saying goodbye to Tara this morning had been awful. She'd been in tears, and he'd felt like crying himself. The thought of not seeing her for the next couple of weeks was excruciating. He felt as though his heart had been ripped out of his chest.

Cal never imagined he could feel this way about anyone, but leaving her in Glasgow had felt like he was leaving his right arm behind. He'd undoubtedly left his heart. It belonged to Tara, and he prayed she would take care of it.

Prising the top off a cold brown bottle, he necked half the contents in one go, then took out his phone.

> Home safe. Missing you already. Love you x

Her response was immediate.

> Missing you more. LU2 xxx

A thud overhead caught his attention and he stashed his phone in his pocket, wondering which one of his parents was upstairs and why they hadn't heard him shout.

When he reached their bedroom, he discovered that the reason they hadn't responded to his calls was because his dad was sitting on the floor at the foot of the bed, staring absently at the wall and rocking back and forth, being comforted by his mum who had tears streaming down her face.

What's wrong? How long has he been like this? and *Why didn't you tell me?* were the first questions Cal asked his mother after he'd helped her persuade Dad to get into bed and swallow a tablet out of a blister packet whose box had a long name written on it.

She was sitting at the dining table, shoulders hunched, cradling an untouched mug of tea. 'The doctor says your dad has had a breakdown.'

'When did it happen?'

She dashed the back of her hand against her pale cheek. 'I should have seen it coming. He hasn't been right for weeks. That *bloody* job of his. He never should have gone for that promotion. It was too much for him. I should have tried to talk him out of it. *Oh God!*' She burst into tears again, and Cal scooted his chair closer and put an arm around her.

'How long has he been like this?' he persisted.

'Three weeks, give or take. He woke up one morning and refused to go to work. He wouldn't tell me why. He just sat on the edge of the bed in his pyjamas and wouldn't move. I couldn't get any sense out of him for ages. He won't speak to me for hours on end, and he won't eat. Keeps saying he doesn't want to be here.'

Cal struggled to hold back tears. 'Why haven't they admitted him?'

His mother bit her lip and blinked furiously. 'You *know* why.'

'Granny Fraser?' he guessed and she nodded. 'It's not like that these days,' he assured her. 'I don't think they do electric shock treatment anymore.'

'Your dad isn't taking the chance.'

'What did the doctor say?'

She pulled a face. 'Not a lot. Gave him a prescription for antidepressants and sent him away.' She banged a fist down on the table. 'Your father wouldn't let me go in with him – he saw the doctor alone. God knows what he said to him, but I bet it wasn't the truth about how he's feeling. Your dad was never one to discuss his feelings.'

'He needs help, Mum.'

'Don't you think I'm aware of that!' she yelled. 'But if anyone sees him like this he'll be sectioned.'

'He won't, Mum.'

'Do you know that for a fact?' she demanded.

He didn't. He knew absolutely nothing about mental health provision. 'What's he told them at work?'

'He hasn't spoken to them. *I* had to. The doctor signed him off with exhaustion, would you believe, so that's what I told them he's suffering from. Your father is terrified they'll find out. He doesn't want anyone to know.'

'They'll find out eventually.'

'Not if we don't tell anyone.'

'Mum, you can't hide it forever,' Cal insisted.

'I can and I will. He doesn't want anyone to know. He doesn't need to be in hospital. What he needs is peace and quiet, and his family around him. We can make him better ourselves.'

'Does Fliss know?'

'No! And you can't tell her.'

'She'll want to know. I would, if I was her.'

'If you say anything to your sister she'll be home like a shot. Felicity has worked hard to get where she is, and I don't want her to jeopardise that.'

Fliss lived in Manchester and worked in television – behind the screen, not in front of it – something to do with the production side of things but he wasn't sure what.

'I'll make you a deal,' he said. 'I'll not say anything to anyone for now, but if he gets worse…'

The tears he'd been holding back nearly escaped when he saw the relief on his mum's face. Thank goodness he'd come home, because she never would have coped on her own.

'Calan, promise me you won't say anything to anyone,' she begged. 'I'm scared of what your dad will do if people find out. It's the shame, you see. He's never got over the way he was picked on at school when the other kids found out his mother had been in a mental institution.'

'They're not called that these days, Mum, they're—'

'I don't care. It's what your dad wants. Please, I beg you, don't tell a soul. He'll get better on his own. I *know* he will.'

What his mother didn't appreciate, and neither did Calan, was just how long that would take.

–

Tara anxiously stared at her mobile phone. Cal had been gone almost seven weeks. Forty-seven days and thirteen hours to be precise, and she had felt every second of it.

She didn't know what it was, but something was definitely wrong.

It had begun as soon as he'd returned to Inverness. Tara knew long-distance romance wasn't easy and that it had to be worked on, but it seemed she was the one making all the effort. Cal said the right things when she managed to get him on the phone, and wrote the right things in his messages, but the passion they'd shared in Glasgow was lacking. The promised visit to Inverness hadn't materialised, and neither had he come to see her. The summer was slipping by but so far, she'd been unable to pin him down.

Tara had a horrible fear Cal didn't love her anymore, and it was tearing her apart. She wished she had the courage to ask him outright, but she was terrified of the answer. As long as she didn't know, she could pretend everything was all right.

When her phone finally rang, relief swept through her. 'Cal, hi. How did the interview go?'

'I got the job.'

'Wow, that's fantastic news! Congratulations! When do you start?'

'As soon as they've obtained references and done the necessary employment checks.'

Tara's sixth sense prickled. He didn't sound thrilled. He should be over the moon, considering this job was exactly what he wanted – an assistant estate manager, working for a large manor in the Highlands, not far from his home town. It was perfect. So why wasn't he more enthusiastic?

'We should celebrate,' she said, then lowered her voice, because although she was in her bedroom with the door closed, her mother was downstairs. '*Properly*.'

'Um, Tara—'

'Shall I come to you? We could stay in a hotel or a bed and breakfast, and maybe you could show me around the estate. I'd love to see where you'll be working. *If* we can drag ourselves away from the bedroom for long enough.' She uttered a throaty laugh, her pulse quickening as she thought about what she intended to do with him as soon as she got him alone.

'Tara, I don't think that's a good idea.'

'Oh, OK. Anyway, we'll probably be too busy for you to show me around, if you know what I mean.' She giggled. 'God, I miss you so much. I can't wait to see you. I love you, Cal.'

She waited for him to tell her he loved her too. But he didn't. He didn't say a word.

'Cal? Are you still there?'

'Yes.'

Then it struck her. He didn't say 'I love you' back, because he *didn't*.

'You don't love me any more, do you?' she blurted.

She heard a noise that sounded like a sob, but realised Cal was clearing his throat.

'It's not that,' he said, and the heaviness in her heart lifted for a split second. Then he continued, 'It's just that we're so young. Too young for a serious relationship.'

His voice was stilted and staccato; there was no emotion whatsoever, and she stuffed her fist into her mouth to hold back the scream that threatened to break free.

'My mum and dad agree,' he said. 'They think we're too young to settle down, especially when you've got another year of uni left. You need to enjoy it and have fun, not mope around waiting for me. And with my new job, I'm not going to have much free time, and—' He took a breath, and she heard him exhale slowly. 'It's not going to work, Tara. Everyone knows long-distance relationships don't work.'

He didn't mean it. He *couldn't* mean it.

'You don't *want* to make it work,' she accused, pain stabbing her in the chest. It felt like her heart was being torn from her ribcage and she couldn't breathe.

'I'm sorry, Tara, I—' He gulped. 'I'm sorry.' And before he ended the call she heard him whisper, 'Be happy.'

As if she could ever be happy again…

Tara's mother found her sobbing on her bed, her heart broken into a thousand pieces, her dreams of a future with Cal shattered on the rocks of her unrequited love.

Chapter 1

10 Years Later

Sod Dougie, he could have the lot as far as she was concerned. Tara McTaigh was done. If he wanted to move his mistress into the house that he and Tara had once lived, loved and laughed in, then let him. But he was going to have to pay dearly for the privilege.

Personally, she didn't care if the damned house burnt to the ground, but she *did* care that *Dougie* wanted it. Since he'd informed her that he wanted a divorce, making his life difficult was what had kept her going. These past few months had been hard – seven years of marriage down the drain and very little to show for it: just this house and her memories.

Was she bitter? Yes, absolutely.

But her bitterness had finally run its course, as evidenced by her decision to let him have the house. She was simply too weary to fight any more. Anyway, what was the point? Dougie would get it one way or another, whether he bought her out as part of the divorce settlement or bought it on the open market when it was put up for sale. Dougie had always managed to get what he wanted. He had a knack for it.

Tara made the call. 'You can have the house. Just give me my half of the proceeds.'

'I've changed my mind.' Dougie's tone was mocking.

She didn't rise to the bait. 'In that case, I'll contact the estate agent in the morning.'

Her soon-to-be ex-husband hesitated. 'What's the catch?'

'There isn't one.'

His incredulous laugh made her wince. 'I find that hard to believe.'

'I don't care. Believe what you like. Let's get this over with.'

'It didn't have to be like this.' His voice had softened.

Tara recognised the tactic. He was worried she might change her mind, so he wanted to keep her onside. 'You made certain that it did,' she retorted, but she sounded weary and resigned, rather than bitter and angry.

She hoped it was a step in the right direction. For her own sake, she had to move on, and it wasn't as though she still loved him. He'd killed that particular emotion when he'd informed her that the woman he'd been cheating on her with was pregnant. What a bloody cliché! Tara felt like a poorly written character in a badly scripted film.

Cheating husband? Tick.

Younger woman? Tick.

Pregnant mistress? Tick.

Unsuspecting, heartbroken wife? Tick, tick, *tick*!

But that wasn't strictly true, she acknowledged, after the call ended and a sum for her share of the property and its contents had been agreed. She'd experienced true heartbreak once, and this wasn't it. She had loved Dougie, and what he'd done had hurt, but he hadn't been the love of her life. Which was just as well, really.

For quite some time Tara had suspected he was being unfaithful. And she was pretty certain that The Pregnant

One hadn't been the first. She also suspected The Pregnant One wouldn't be the last. Leopards, spots, and all that jazz.

However, she had a feeling Dougie might find it more difficult to extricate himself from his newest relationship once children were involved. Yes, *children* – his mistress was having twins.

Tara thanked God that she and Dougie hadn't had any kids. It would have made an awful situation completely unbearable.

In some ways, she blamed herself for allowing their marriage to go on for as long as it had. She should have ended it the first time she'd suspected him of cheating. But it had been just a suspicion, no concrete proof. He had slickly and convincingly talked his way out of it, until Tara believed she must have imagined the smell of unfamiliar perfume on his skin, and accepted his flimsy excuses for not being home when he'd told her he would be, et cetera, et cetera, et cetera.

Bored with going over the same old thing, Tara made her way up to the large attic which she'd converted into her workroom. Now that the decision to move out of the marital home had been made, she urgently needed to start thinking about where she was going to live.

Wherever it was, it had to be big enough for her huge collection of doll's houses and all the paraphernalia that was used to make them. The upside was that properties in Edinburgh were expensive, so her portion of the divorce settlement would be substantial. The downside was that properties in Edinburgh were expensive, so her portion of the divorce settlement wouldn't buy her the space she needed.

Maybe it was time to look further afield, for a new home for McTaigh Miniatures?

Tara leaned back in her chair and raised her arms above her head, clasping her fingers together and arching her spine to ease out the kinks. She'd been hunched over her laptop for what felt like hours, searching for the perfect property. Needless to say, she hadn't found it.

To be fair, she wasn't entirely sure what she was looking for. She had no fixed idea in her mind, apart from it needing to be large enough, not too expensive, and available soon. She'd looked at houses, flats, and even commercial properties, all within a twenty-mile radius of Edinburgh.

Nothing.

An expanded search had produced equally dreary results.

None of them were quite right, although there were plenty that would do. But Tara didn't want to *make do*. This move was important if she intended to grow her business, and without anything else in her life to focus on, she was going to give it her best shot.

She'd show him.

Dougie used to call her doll's houses her 'little hobby'. The sarcastic, patronising git! Her *little hobby* brought in enough to pay the bills and then some, a fact he used to conveniently forget because his job was *so much more important*. As far as Tara could tell, it was also far less fulfilling, although working in fiscal management had provided him ample opportunity to play around, so he'd clearly got his *fulfilment* in ways other than from his job.

She glanced around the attic, feeling sad. She didn't mind leaving the house, but she did mind having to vacate her attic. Apart from the structural work, such as putting in a proper staircase and having Velux windows fitted to flood the top floor of their terraced Victorian villa with loads of natural light, Tara had kitted out the attic herself. She'd done everything from cladding the walls and ceiling, to laying the floor and installing the shelves and workbenches. This was her space, her sanctuary. This was where she created miniature models of other people's houses, and everything to go in them. She would miss this space far more than she would ever miss Dougie.

Getting to her feet, Tara wandered around the room, trailing her fingers along the shelves, stopping every so often to open up one of the houses or to peer through the little windows.

The wall opposite the staircase was lined with the miniatures she'd created, ranging from tiny plates of cakes, to elaborate four-poster beds and planters of tiny flowers for the garden. These were her bread-and-butter items, which didn't take an age to make and were easily sold online, either from her own website or from sites special-ising in unique handmade items.

Thankfully, she didn't have an actual physical shop to worry about. Her business was fully portable. As long as she had a suitable space in which to work, she could carry on earning a living. The only other requirement was a local post office, a collection service for the bulkier items and decent Wi-Fi.

Returning to her desk, Tara resumed her search, but it was rather desultory and she found herself going down a rabbit hole of looking at properties in places like the Western Isles or the Outer Hebrides, before reining herself in. Ideally, what she wanted was—

She froze. She'd left the popular property search sites behind and had been reading local online newspapers in the hope that something would jump out at her, when something *did*.

An article featuring Coorie Castle and its associated craft centre caught her eye, and as she read it, excitement bloomed in her chest. It sounded perfect, and from examining the photos accompanying the article, she thought its location on the Isle of Skye was stunning. But what really sent the butterflies in her tummy into a fury of fluttering, was reading that the craft centre had a vacant studio to fill.

With trembling fingers and a stern admonishment to herself to not get too excited because the chances of it leading to anything were slim, Tara typed the words Coorie Castle into the search bar.

Bloody hell! It *was* perfect. This was exactly what she'd been looking for, even if she hadn't realised it.

Could she?

Dare she?

Tara *could* – after all, nothing ventured, nothing gained – and a polite enquiry didn't commit her to anything, did it?

With great care and the attention to detail that she was gaining a reputation for, Tara typed out an email and attached several photos of her work, along with a link to her own website. The castle looked impressive, the craft centre even more so, and as she pressed send, she crossed her fingers. If, by the remotest chance, she was lucky enough to be able to rent the studio, it would be a fresh start, a new beginning.

Tara didn't get much sleep that night. She was too busy imagining a whole new life away from Dougie, Edinburgh, and a slew of bad memories.

Chapter 2

Tara had never visited Skye, and as she drove across the bridge which connected the mainland to the island, she felt apprehensive. On paper (or rather, on the internet) the castle and the craft centre looked absolutely perfect. But looks and photos could be deceiving, and she prayed she wasn't about to be disappointed.

With the best part of another hour to go before she reached the village of Duncoorie and its castle, she settled into the drive to enjoy the scenery. For some of the way, the road skirted the eastern edge of the island, with the incredibly blue sea to her right and views of the smaller islands of Scalpay and Raasay.

She passed isolated houses and small hamlets, and there were so many motor homes and caravans on the road that she lost count. Despite the castle's website hinting at a thriving craft centre with a gift shop on site, Tara had wondered whether there would be much in the way of visitors. Not that a lack of footfall would affect her unduly, because she did all her business online, but it would nevertheless be nice to display her creations in the flesh, so to speak. And she might be interested in running a workshop or two once she'd settled in.

'Don't get ahead of yourself, Tara,' she muttered, her words whipped away by the breeze from the half-open window.

The weather was unseasonably warm for May, and her little car's air conditioning had never worked properly. Her blouse clung stickily to her back and she couldn't wait to park up and get out. She debated whether to have a quick pit stop in Portree to check out the town but decided against it. There would be time enough to have a look around if she managed to secure the studio. She'd want to scout around the estate agents and see what was for sale. Tara had looked online yesterday after she'd received the reply to her email, but it had only been a quick look because she'd been too busy selecting samples to bring along to her meeting this morning. Although she'd sent them a few photos of her work, there was nothing like seeing it in person, and she hoped they would be impressed. After all, both Tara and Miss Gray, who owned the castle and who she was meeting this morning, had to be convinced that they were a suitable match for each other.

Tara was forty-five minutes early for her eleven thirty appointment, but she didn't mind. Better to be too early than too late, and it would give her the chance to take a look around the place beforehand.

After parking in the ample car park, she clambered stiffly out and cricked her neck from side to side. The five-hour drive from Edinburgh to Skye had felt more like ten, and she'd been on the road since half past five this morning.

Thirsty and in need of a wee, Tara gazed around to get her bearings. If anything, the location was even more stunning than in the photographs.

Perched on a hill above a loch with the open sea in the distance and a backdrop of impressive peaks, the castle proudly rose out of the rock to tower over the landscape, white and gleaming in the morning sun. Its mullioned windows glinted and glittered, and a flag fluttered from the top of a crenellated turret.

Tara was impressed. It was grander than she'd envisaged, and she couldn't wait to see inside. But first, she needed to find a loo and then have a coffee, followed by a quick delve into the gift shop.

A wooden signpost indicated the way to the cafe, which was cutely called Coorie and Cuppa, 'coorie' being the old Scots word meaning to snuggle or to be cosy – much like the Scandinavian word 'hygge'. The cafe certainly lived up to its name, she discovered, when she went inside and saw the squashy sofas, the wooden beams in the ceiling, the fairy lights, and the most gorgeously mouthwatering selection of cakes and pastries.

Maybe she would treat herself to a spot of lunch after her meeting, but for now she'd have a quick coffee, then go and explore. She already knew from her research that the individual studios, the cafe and the gift shop had been converted from the castle's extensive outbuildings, and she was keen to have a look around.

Almost scalding her mouth on the seriously good coffee, she gulped it down and then hurried into the gift shop.

Oh, this is simply lovely, she thought, gazing around in delight.

The shop was full of the most wonderful handmade items: silver jewellery, driftwood sculptures, stained glass ornaments, needle-felted figures and quilts, and Tara could easily imagine how well her doll's houses would fit in.

Tingling in anticipation, she went back outside. With fifteen minutes to go until her appointment, she just about had time to check out the rest of the set-up.

The craft centre was laid out at right-angles, with a courtyard in the middle, and the gift shop and the cafe occupying the corner where the two sides met. To either side of them lay the individual studios. Some were quite small – the one where the silver jewellery was made, for instance – but others were larger. The largest by far was the glass-blowing studio, and she lingered for a moment, watching a guy rolling a long stick with a blob of white-hot glass on the end back and forth over the edge of a wooden bench.

It was fascinating and she would have liked to have stayed longer, but she was conscious of the time. Besides, there was one more thing she wanted to do before she made her way to the castle's main entrance, and that was to take a look at the empty studio, if she could.

It was easy to find, being the only one whose door was locked, whose lights were off and whose window was empty. Cupping her hands around her eyes, Tara peered through the window.

Bigger inside than it first appeared, she was relieved to see that there would be plenty of space to display her little houses, as well as sufficient room in which to construct them.

Having seen enough and with five minutes to spare, she hurried back to the car to fetch the wee house she'd brought with her, along with some of the miniatures. Then she made her way to the castle's main entrance and went inside.

At the far end of a wide wood-panelled hall was a reception desk, and as she walked over to it, she couldn't help being impressed by the sweeping staircase, the crystal chandelier, the portraits on the walls and the coat of arms, as well as a couple of large tapestries. The castle smelt of beeswax and old money, and she bet it cost a fortune to run.

'Hi, I'm here to see Miss Gray,' Tara announced, balancing the corner of the large box on the desk and smiling at the woman manning the desk. 'I've got an appointment at eleven thirty.'

'Tara McTaigh?'

'That's right.'

'Great, I'll let her know you've arrived. One second, please.' The woman briefly spoke into the phone, while Tara hovered anxiously.

This place was even grander than she'd thought, and after seeing the craft centre she was even more keen on securing the studio. It was perfect, exactly what she'd been looking for.

'I'll take you through,' the woman said, and as she got to her feet, Tara spotted a name badge: Avril.

'Do you need any help with that?' Avril asked, nodding at the box.

Tara shook her head. 'I can manage, thanks.' She might be short, but she was stronger than she looked.

Following the receptionist, she was led across the hall and into one magnificent room after another through a series of interconnecting doors, and soon she was thoroughly lost. Wondering whether she'd be able to find her way out again, she was relieved to be shown into a small sitting room.

'Here we are,' Avril announced. 'This is Tara McTaigh.'

'Thank you,' Tara muttered absently as she took in the tall, thin woman standing in front of her.

'You can put that down over there, my dear,' Miss Gray said, pointing to a substantial desk in the corner underneath a window.

Tara did as she was instructed, then turned to offer her hand. Miss Gray took it, her handshake surprisingly firm for a woman who, Tara guessed, was somewhere around eighty years old. She'd expected someone younger.

'Thank you for inviting me,' Tara said. 'I've brought some pieces to show you, if you'd like to see them?'

'In a minute, dear. Let's have a chat first. Take a seat.'

Tara sat on one of the two sofas.

'Tea?' the old lady asked. 'I'm having a cup.'

'I'd love one, thanks.'

Miss Gray pressed a buzzer and Avril reappeared. 'Could you ask Cook if she would mind making a pot of tea?'

Miss Gray had a *cook*? Tara wondered how many more staff the castle housed. Quite a few probably, because she knew from trawling through the website that it was also a hotel. But 'Cook' sounded very *Downton Abbey*-ish.

'Tara… May I call you Tara?'

'Please do.'

Miss Gray beamed at her. 'And you can call me Mhairi. How old are you, Tara?'

'Thirty-two.'

'Married?'

'No.' Tara backtracked. 'I mean, I am, but not for much longer. The decree nisi should be winging its way towards me as we speak.'

'I'm so sorry, dear.'

Tara sighed. 'I'm not. It's been over for a while.' More than a while, if she was honest. Her marriage had been on the rocks for the past three years and had totally sunk by the time Dougie announced that he wanted a divorce.

'Children?'

'No.'

Mhairi nodded thoughtfully, her bright blue eyes fixed on Tara. The questioning was interrupted by Avril's arrival with a tray, but it resumed as soon as she left. 'Milk and sugar?'

'Just milk, please.'

'Have you always lived in Edinburgh?'

'No, I'm from Glasgow originally.'

Mhairi handed Tara a cup and saucer and Tara took it carefully, trying to hold the saucer steady so it didn't rattle. It was china, the porcelain so fine it was almost translucent.

'How long have you been making doll's houses?'

A smile crept across Tara's face. 'About ten years.'

'You've had plenty of time to hone your craft,' Mhairi said, with a dip of her head. 'I must say, I was impressed with your photos. And your website. Tell me, could you recreate Coorie Castle?'

Tara took her time answering before she said, 'I *could*, but it wouldn't be easy.'

'Nothing worthwhile ever is. Biscuit?'

'No, thank you.' Tara hadn't felt this nervous in a long time. It was like being grilled by a head teacher after being sent to stand outside their office for misbehaving.

Mhairi was relentless. 'Why Coorie Castle?'

'Aside from the vacant studio, the location is gorgeous, you've got a fair number of visitors for a Tuesday morning, and the range of crafts is excellent.'

'So this is purely a business decision for you?'

'Not entirely. It has to feel right.'

'And does it?' Mhairi peered over her spectacles.

'Yes.'

'Good. You can show me what's in that box now.'

Tara had chosen one of the smaller doll's houses to bring with her. It was a commercial piece, not a bespoke one, but she'd given it the same attention to detail as she did to her commissioned ones. This wasn't a toy for a child, this was a doll's house for an adult who had been bitten by the doll's house bug but was just starting out. Tara referred to it as a 'starter home' in her head.

She'd also brought with her a selection of some of her finest, more intricate pieces of bedroom furniture to go in it. Keen to show them off, Tara carefully removed the house from the box, conscious of Mhairi peering over her shoulder.

'How delightful!' the old lady cried. 'This takes me back to my girlhood. I did love playing with my little house.'

'I think that's part of the allure,' Tara replied, unwrapping each model and putting it next to the house. 'Even if you didn't have one as a child, you probably wanted one.'

As Tara had hoped, Mhairi couldn't resist picking up a tiny bed and placing it in one of the upstairs rooms. This house was very typical and rather basic in design, with a central doorway, windows on either side, and a front opening. It also had two bedrooms, a bathroom, a kitchen and a living room.

Untypically, Tara hadn't brought enough furniture for the whole house. She'd brought four different styles of beds, several wardrobes, a selection of rugs, some night-stands, and a few pairs of curtains.

She wanted Mhairi to see how much fun could be had by changing the look of just one room. Tara's bread and butter was designing and creating the interior pieces.

Her jam was her ability to recreate someone's beloved flat, house, bungalow or garden shed in exquisite detail.

Her most recent project had been an old mill. The new owners were converting it into living accommodation but had wanted a 3D reminder of it in its original state.

Tara had thoroughly enjoyed the challenge, even down to the millstones and empty bags of flour. Her clients had been delighted.

Mhairi was engrossed in rearranging and replacing the furniture, exclaiming over how changing just one rug could alter the look of the room. She was having so much fun that Tara didn't want to interrupt, so she moved aside and examined the old lady without being observed.

Coiffured white hair framed a lean wrinkled face, and high cheekbones and piercing blue eyes hinted at the beauty she might have possessed in her youth. Taller than Tara's five foot one by at least six inches, Mhairi was slim and held herself erect. She was dressed immaculately in a lavender-coloured twin set and a navy plaid skirt. She wore court shoes on her feet, a gold locket around her neck, and a diamond ring on her right hand.

Finally Mhairi grew tired of playing with the doll's house and turned to face her. 'I think you'll fit in very well,' she said. 'Very well, indeed. Shall we talk business?' She indicated a return to the sofa, and Tara resumed her seat.

Folding her hands in her lap to stop them from shaking, Tara tried hard to contain her delight.

'I shall ask Avril to prepare a rental contract,' Mhairi said, reaching for the phone. 'Shall we say from next Monday? Or from the first of next month?'

'I don't mind. Whatever suits you.' Tara was wincing inside at having to pay rent on a studio she mightn't be able

26

to use for a couple of months, but if that meant securing it, she would simply have to bite the bullet. 'I won't be moving in for a while though, as I've got to sell my house in Edinburgh first before I can buy a place on Skye.'

Mhairi's eyes widened, before her expression fell. 'But that could take months.'

'I know, but don't worry, I can afford to pay the rent until I'm ready to move.'

'Paying the rent isn't my concern. Having a studio empty for more than a couple of weeks, is.'

'I see.' Tara frantically considered her options and concluded that the only viable one was to move into rented accommodation on the island until the Edinburgh house was sold and she received her half. Money would be tight for a while, but she had some savings to fall back on. 'No problem,' she declared cheerfully. 'I'll find a place to rent nearby.'

Mhairi pursed her lips. 'I think you'll find there's a distinct lack of properties to rent on the island, unless one is a tourist and only looking for a holiday let. However, I do have a solution. There's an empty cottage on the estate I intend to rent out to visiting artists and crafters who want more of a self-catering experience instead of staying in the castle itself. The renovations are almost complete – it used to be a boathouse – but it should be ready to move into in a week or so. Would that suit you?'

Wouldn't it just!

'That would be brilliant, thank you.'

'Would you like to see it?' Mhairi began to get up.

'No, it's fine.' Tara had no doubt that the standard of the cottage would be as good as the rest of the castle and she was eager to return to Edinburgh and begin packing.

There was so much to do, and she couldn't wait to get started.

The sooner all the loose ends in Edinburgh were tied up, the sooner she could embrace her new life in Coorie Castle.

Chapter 3

'Are we nearly there?' Bonnie asked.

Calan Fraser met his nine-year-old daughter's eyes in the car's rear-view mirror. 'Not quite. Another couple of miles yet.'

'Aw, you've been saying that for ages,' she complained.

It was true, he had. 'Sorry. I mean it this time. Ten minutes and we'll be at Nana and Grandpa's.'

Duncoorie to Inverness wasn't the shortest of journeys, and they had been on the road for over three hours. No wonder Bonnie was becoming restless, despite the pitstop halfway for a snack and to stretch their legs.

'Can we go on the Hogwarts Express? And to the adventure park? And the Raceway?' She bounced up and down in her seat. '*Please?* I'm old enough now.' At only seven years old the last time Calan had taken her to visit his parents, his daughter had been too young to visit the Raceway.

Was it really fourteen months since he'd been back to Inverness?

It must be, he calculated. His mum and dad usually visited him on Skye so he could stay close to Bonnie. Bonnie's mother, Yvaine, could be awkward when it came to his parents, and she often came up with some excuse or another why he couldn't take Bonnie to visit them. His ex-wife and his mother hadn't seen eye to eye from the get-go.

He tried not to feel bitter at Yvaine's change of heart now there was a new man in her life, one who had whisked her off on a fourteen-day holiday to Cyprus, just the two of them. The reason he tried not to be bitter was that he was getting to spend two whole weeks with Bonnie, and he was so looking forward to it. Lenn didn't know what he was missing.

Or perhaps Lenn did. He didn't strike Calan as the paternal type, although according to Bonnie, she seemed to get on OK with him. And that was another thing that got Calan's back up – the thought of a strange man spending more time with Bonnie than he possibly could.

His conflicting emotions about Lenn were a daily battle. On the one hand, Cal felt he should be pleased Bonnie didn't hate him. On the other, an immature part of him wished she did. However, his daughter's happiness meant more to him than anything else in the world, so he'd have to suck up his jealousy for her sake.

Bonnie's squeal of excitement made him jump.

He hadn't expected her to recognise the turning into the road where her grandparents lived, but she did. They owned a bungalow on the outskirts of Inverness with views over Beauly Firth in one direction and the city in the other.

As he aimed the Range Rover at a spot on the drive behind his mother's Nissan, Calan could see his parents peering out of the window. Bonnie was incandescent with excitement, and the car had barely come to a halt before she was unbuckling her seatbelt and launching herself out of the door.

The way granddaughter and grandparents greeted each other brought tears to his eyes. They must miss her dreadfully, he thought, as he followed more sedately behind. His mum's face was glowing and she had tears in her eyes when it was his turn to receive a hug from her. His dad grinned at him over his shoulder as he was dragged inside the bungalow by a very determined little girl, and Calan guessed he'd have to wait a while for a hug from his father.

His mum's embrace more than made up for it. She clung to him for several seconds, then she pulled back and studied his face.

'Let me look at you,' she said. 'Have you lost weight?'

'I don't think so. How's Dad?'

'He's fine.'

'Are you sure?'

His mum stopped and turned to face him. 'I would tell you if he wasn't. There's no need to ask every time you see me.'

Cal only ever asked his mum about his dad's mental health. He was too scared of upsetting his father if he asked him directly. It had been over ten years since his dad had suffered a breakdown, but the shadow of that terrible time continued to linger in Cal's mind. Maybe it was because Cal's life had altered so dramatically because of it.

His mother changed the subject. 'Are you sure you haven't lost weight?'

'I'm sure.'

'Hmm. You tell Mhairi that if she's working you too hard, she'll have me to answer to.'

'I will, but she isn't working me too hard, honest.'

'How is she?'

'The same as always. For such a wee old lady, she hasn't half got some stamina.'

'How old is she now?'

'Eighty, I believe, but I'm not a hundred per cent sure. I know when her birthday is, but she keeps her age a secret. She might be even older than that.'

'I can't believe she manages Coorie Castle all by herself.'

Calan's reply was wry. 'She doesn't, Mum. That's what she employs *me* for.' He threaded an arm through hers as they headed for the front door. 'Anyway, enough talk of work. Mhairi has given me strict instructions not to think about the castle for the next two weeks.'

Once inside the bungalow, his mum went into the kitchen and put the kettle on, saying, 'Hasn't Bonnie grown? She's shot up since we last saw her.'

'She's growing like a weed,' he laughed. 'Always hungry. I swear she's got hollow legs.'

'She looks just like you did at her age.'

'Don't let Yvaine hear you say that.'

His mother's face immediately clouded over. 'How is Yvaine?'

'Oh, you know, same as ever.'

'That's what I'm worried about. Is she still being unreasonable?'

'Now and again.'

Their split hadn't been amicable. Cal didn't know where Yvaine's bitterness came from, but her accusation that he didn't love her had kind of hit home. He *hadn't* loved her: he'd cared for her, but he'd never been *in love* with her. When they'd met, he had been hurting and adrift, reeling from lost love and his father's illness, and she'd helped him forget his troubles for a while. It hadn't been serious, but she'd fallen pregnant and suddenly it was as serious as it could get. At the ripe old age of twenty-three, he'd found himself married with a baby on the way. He'd been determined to make it work though, and to be the best father he could possibly be, and he'd doted on Bonnie from the second she'd been placed in his arms, pink and bawling.

His mother sighed. 'You think she'd be happy that you take such an active interest in Bonnie's life.'

Cal shrugged. He had the feeling Yvaine was jealous of his close relationship with their daughter. In a way, he could understand – he suspected Bonnie saw him as the 'fun' parent, because he tried to make sure she had his complete attention on the weekends they spent together and that they did lots of fun things. He didn't have to nag her to get up in the morning for school, or to learn her spellings, or tidy her room. And he also didn't have to be the day-to-day disciplinarian.

He guessed Yvaine resented him for that, even though she'd been the one to end their marriage. He also suspected she wanted to hurt him, and the only way she could do that was through his love for Bonnie.

When their marriage ended, it had been perfectly reasonable for Yvaine to want to return to Skye to be near her parents, but he felt part of her desire to move was because it would put a hundred miles and three hours between him and his daughter. Her incredulity when he'd found a job in Duncoorie was something he would never forget.

Every so often Yvaine would make it difficult for him to see Bonnie, although she did nothing he could complain about to a solicitor or the courts. It was little things, such as telling him that Bonnie was unwell on the weekend he was supposed to have her, and him finding out afterwards that his daughter had been well enough to go shopping or to a party. Things like arranging a weekend away when it was his turn to have her. Things like 'forgetting' to tell him about parents' evenings. They might be little things, but they added up.

To be fair, his ex-wife hadn't been as bad since Lenn had come into her life, so Cal was quietly hopeful that they'd turned a corner, even though he resented the chap for seeing more of Bonnie than he did.

One thing was certain, Cal wasn't going to do anything to upset the apple cart, and if that meant keeping his resentment under wraps, that's what he would do.

Cal tucked his daughter into bed and kissed her forehead. He especially loved this time of day, when she was warm and sleepy, but he only got to experience it every other weekend when she came to stay with him at the cottage in the castle grounds.

'Can you read me a story?' she asked, snuggling deeper under the covers and peering at him hopefully.

'I can, but Nana has only got baby stories here. They'll be too young for you.' Cal's sister had a two-year-old son who his mum and dad looked after regularly now that she'd moved back to Inverness.

'Make one up,' Bonnie commanded.

'Um…' Making up stories had never been one of his strong points.

'Please?'

He tried to come up with something, but his mind was blank.

'I'm waiting,' Bonnie said. 'I haven't got all night.'

'Cheeky madam.' He smiled as she repeated her nana's words back to him when he'd been tardy in helping with clearing the dinner table this evening. 'Once upon a time,' he began, unsure where his story was going, but at least the start was good, 'there was a handsome prince.'

Bonnie rolled her eyes. 'There's always a handsome prince.'

'OK then, an average-looking prince with a wart on the end of his nose and a squinty eye.'

'The *witch* is supposed to have the wart, not the prince.'

'Can he still have the squinty eye?' Cal screwed his left eye shut and pulled a face.

'Now you're being silly. Is there a princess?'

'Of course there is.'

'A witch?'

'If you want one.'

She nodded. 'Can the witch have a dragon?'

An image of his ex-mother-in-law, Bonnie's other grandmother, popped into Cal's head. She'd been a right old dragon. She still was, but thankfully Cal didn't have much to do with her.

An idea began to form. He mightn't be any good at making up stories, but he could adapt a real-life one. He would have to amend the ending, but that was OK.

He began again. 'Once upon a time there was a prince, who would have been handsome if it wasn't for his squinty eye, but he made up for that with oodles of charm and charisma.'

'What's charisma?'

'Who's the most popular girl in your class?'

'Alisha.'

'Why is she popular?'

Bonnie shrugged. 'I don't know. She just is.'

'That's what is meant by charisma. You don't know why someone is popular, so they call it charisma.'

35

'Can anyone get charisma?'

'Not really. You can't go to a shop and buy some, and it's not catching like a cold or chicken pox.'

Bonnie pulled a face. 'That's not fair.'

'Do you want to hear this story or not?'

His daughter subsided and Calan carried on. 'The prince was very intelligent, so the king and queen sent him away to university to learn how to be the best ruler ever when it was his turn to be king. While he was at university—'

'How do you be a good king?'

'By being just and kind. You also have to be—'

'Just what?' she interrupted.

'Eh?'

'You said he has to be just, but you didn't say what.'

'Oh, I see. In this instance "just" means "fair".'

Bonnie nodded to show she understood.

'Where was I...? Oh, yes, whilst he was studying hard – because he really wanted to be the best king ever – he met a beautiful princess.'

'What did she look like?'

Calan stiffened as a memory leapt into his mind. 'She had long dark hair down to here,' he touched the middle of his chest, 'and grey eyes, like the sea on a stormy day.'

'What was her name?'

'Um, Tara.'

'What was the prince's name?'

'Calan.'

'That's *your* name! You're not a prince.'

'Are you sure I'm not? I live in a castle...'

'You do not.' Bonnie was emphatic. 'You live in a tiny house.'

'It's not that tiny,' Calan objected.

36

'It's not as big as Coorie Castle.'

'True, but not many places are.'

'So you *don't* live in a castle.' Bonnie narrowed her eyes. 'Is Mhairi a queen?'

Calan hid his smile. 'No, Bon-Bon, she isn't a queen. But she does own the castle.'

'She must be very rich.'

Calan wasn't prepared to discuss his employer's finances with his daughter – or anyone else, for that matter.

He began to get to his feet, saying, 'You obviously don't want to hear my fabulous story,' but Bonnie pulled him back down onto the bed.

'I do! I do!' she cried, and he tucked her in once more and continued the story.

'As soon as the prince saw Tara, he fell in love and wanted to marry her. She loved him too, despite his squinty eye, but he didn't know that his good looks and charm had also made someone else fall in love with him. And that someone was a witch!' He paused for dramatic effect.

Bonnie had the covers up to her nose and was peering over the top of them. 'What happened next, Daddy?'

'The witch had a dragon, and the dragon threatened to burn him to a crisp unless he married her instead of the princess. So, do you know what he did? He challenged the dragon to a duel! But this wasn't any old duel, because a mere sword couldn't kill a fire-breathing scaly dragon. The prince suggested a *virtual* duel on a computer, and because he was a modern prince who had played loads of computer games, he won! The dragon was defeated, the witch was banished, and the prince married his princess and they lived happily ever after.' He ended the final sentence on a triumphant note, feeling smug.

'Daddy, that was…' Bonnie had a mischievous twinkle in her eye. 'Awful,' she finished.

Calan pretended to be hurt. 'Are you dissing my story-telling skills?'

She giggled and nodded, and he swept her into his arms. God, how he adored this child! He regretted many things in his life, but Bonnie wasn't one of them.

Later, though, as he sat quietly on the back step enjoying a peaceful few minutes before his own bedtime, he couldn't help thinking back to the story he'd told his daughter.

It hadn't been a complete work of fiction. Tara had been very real. And he had fallen in love with her. But he hadn't married her. He'd married someone else instead, and the happily ever after had ended in divorce and heartache.

After a hectic few days of entertaining Bonnie at the adventure park and go-karting, Cal was more than ready to do something more sedate, so when his tired-looking parents suggested a trip across the city to Whin Park, he was all for it.

While his mother made a picnic (with Bonnie's help), Cal and his dad had a root around in the garage for a ball and a frisbee. To his delight, Cal also unearthed a stunt kite that he'd had when he was around Bonnie's age. His dad must have packed it away because the strings were remarkably tangle free – if Cal had done it, the poor thing would be a messy nest of knots.

'Do you think this still flies?' he asked, holding it up.

His dad peered closely at it and said, 'There's only one way to find out.'

Bonnie was just as excited about the kite and the thought of playing football in the park as she had been about the more high-profile things she'd done this week, and it gladdened Cal's heart to see his daughter able to find a similar degree of enjoyment in simpler – and less expensive – activities.

But he didn't care if he had to spend a fortune, because he was determined that she would have the best time ever to make up for her not going abroad on holiday with her mother and Lenn. Bonnie hadn't said anything, but he suspected she might be disappointed. After all, two weeks in Inverness couldn't compete with two weeks on a Mediterranean island, even if Inverness was experiencing sunny weather.

The sun was high in an azure sky with not a cloud in sight as they arrived at the park, and Cal insisted on smearing more sunscreen on Bonnie's face, arms and legs before he let her loose. Then he helped his dad carry the picnic basket, the cooler box and travel blanket to the spot his mum had decided would be an ideal place to sit and have lunch.

Calan had loved coming to Whin Park when he was a kid. Despite growing up only a stone's throw away from Beauly Firth and within easy walking distance of the Caledonian Canal, the boating lake in the park with its ducks and swans had held a special appeal.

His mum, bless her, had remembered to bring a bag of lawn cuttings for the ducks, and Cal helped her spread the blankets out on the grass while his dad and Bonnie went off to feed them.

Sitting down next to her, his gaze was on grandfather and granddaughter as Bonnie chewed his dad's ear off.

'That child can talk for Scotland,' he observed.

'She's certainly a live wire,' his mum said, her eyes also on the pair.

'You're going to need a holiday after we've gone.' He was only half joking.

'You forget how hard work they are,' she said, adding hurriedly, 'Not that your dad and I mind. We're always thrilled to see her. And you too, of course.'

'Thanks.' He smiled wryly. 'Glad to hear you don't mind seeing me.'

They sat in silence for a while, Cal enjoying the sound of the ducks squabbling and the shouts and laughter of children in the play area. Then his mother surprised him with a question.

'Are you happy, Calan?'

Taken aback, he said, 'I'm not *un*happy.'

'That's not the same thing.'

'Who *is* happy?' he countered.

'Your dad and I are.'

'Yeah, that's because you took early retirement. You wouldn't be as happy if you had to scrape ice off the car in the dark on a winter morning before you went to work.'

She gave him an arch look. 'That's not something you have to do, either. And our happiness isn't because we are retired, although I'm very grateful that we are. It's because we don't just love each other, we are still *in love* with each other.'

Cal didn't know what to say to that, so he didn't say anything.

'I want you to be happy, Cal, like me and your dad.'

'Difficult, considering I'm single and intend to stay that way.'

'I understand, I really do. But not all women are like Yvaine. She was a real piece of work. I remember thinking

40

it the first time I met her, but I never said anything. Well, you can't, can you? You've got to accept your son or daughter's partner and hope it works out.'

Calan was lost for words again.

His mum had enough words for both of them. 'It's a pity you couldn't find someone nice to settle down with.'

'As opposed to someone nasty?' he quipped.

'I'm serious. You don't want to let one bad experience put you off love for life.'

Cal scoffed, 'I'm not "off love". I love you and Dad, and Bonnie.' God, how he loved Bonnie!

'I'm not talking about the love you have for your parents, your children or even your friends. I'm talking about the kind of love that makes your heart sing.'

He knew what she meant. He had felt it himself, years ago.

Once again, an image of a woman with long dark hair and grey eyes floated into his mind.

'Mum, I'm fine as I am,' he replied. 'I'm not looking for love and romance.'

Her response was a dry laugh. 'Be careful it doesn't find you anyway.'

'It won't.' He was certain. Even if he did meet someone who piqued his interest, he didn't intend to do anything about it. With a demanding job and a young daughter, he didn't have the time.

He deliberately ignored his conscience when it suggested that he *could* find the time if he wanted. After all, he didn't have sole care of Bonnie – she spent far more time with her mother than she did with him – and his job, although not nine-to-five Monday to Friday, gave him more than enough free time. So, yes, he would have time to date if he wanted to.

But he didn't. He'd had his fill of love and romance. He didn't need that kind of hassle in his life. All he wanted was to focus on Bonnie and be the best father he could possibly be.

She was his sole priority, and her happiness was his only concern.

Chapter 4

Tara was so exhausted that the only thing keeping her going was nervous excitement and adrenalin. In just ten days (*ten days!!*) she had put the house on the market and had sorted through all her possessions, which had been a mammoth task as she'd had to decide what to take and what to send to the charity shop. The biggest and most important task had been packing up the tools of her trade and all her gorgeous miniatures and houses, and she had closely supervised when they were loaded onto the small removal van earlier today.

As she drove over Skye Bridge towards her new life on the island, it felt symbolic, and she experienced a pang of regret for the death of her old one. She was closing the door on the dreams she'd once had. But what saddened her the most was that she didn't feel sad to be leaving Edinburgh. And she felt no compunction to capture her marital house in miniature. All she felt was relief, and it was rather sobering to think that she had spent seven years and most of her adult life there, yet she had walked away with barely a second glance.

The final part of her journey to Duncoorie and its lovely castle seemed to take forever, but eventually she found herself trundling up the long drive and heading towards the narrow lane behind the castle, which led to the cottage she would be living in until she was able to purchase a house of her own. It irked her slightly that she wasn't moving into her permanent home and that she would probably be moving twice in a matter of months, but she was nevertheless very grateful for Mhairi's kind offer.

The removal van hadn't arrived yet, so Tara took a moment to reacquaint herself with her surroundings and she halted briefly to gaze up at the castle and its impressive ramparts, then she drove down the narrow track towards her new home.

Not knowing what to expect, her first sight of the former boathouse had her squealing with delight.

Situated on the edge of the loch, the single-storey cottage was built out of old stone and had a pitched slate roof. As she slowly got out of the car, Tara was stunned by the amazing views. She was going to be living *here*? Oh my goodness!

Galvanised into action, she hurried to the door and tried the handle. As promised, it was unlocked, and she pushed it open and stepped into a narrow hallway.

Barely glancing through the open doors on either side, which contained a double bedroom and a bathroom respectively, Tara's attention was captured by the glass panel door in front of her and the light that was streaming through it.

Beyond it lay an open-plan kitchen and living area, but she only gave the room a cursory glance. Instead, she focused on the large picture window at the far end and the simply stunning view it framed. It drew the eye and held it, and Tara had to make an effort to look away.

The walls of the living area were devoid of adornment, and Tara could understand why. No photo or painting could compete with the view through that enormous window. Although there was a small TV in the corner, the two squashy sofas were angled so anyone sitting in them would have a perfect view out of the window rather than the screen.

Feeling emotional, Tara checked out the rest of the small house and was delighted to find it had everything she could possibly need. When Mhairi had informed her that the cottage was fully furnished, Tara had been relieved. Apart from a few bits and pieces and her doll's houses and equipment, she'd decided to bring nothing with her to Skye and her new life, not wanting to carry the memories that those things evoked. She'd left them in situ for Dougie to keep or burn. She didn't care which.

Realising that the van would be here shortly, she scooped up the keys to the studio which were sitting on the kitchen counter and hurried towards the car park to meet it. There would be time enough later to settle into the cottage. Right now, her priority was the studio and she couldn't wait to get started.

Tara blew out her cheeks and put her hands on her hips. The flurry of activity this past hour or so had left her feeling drained, but she still had an awful lot to do before she was finished for the day. At least the van was unloaded and everything was in the studio, so that was a start.

As the driver and his mate had ferried box after box inside, under Tara's watchful eye, she'd been conscious of curious faces staring at her from the other studios. She'd smiled at them but hadn't had time to introduce herself. Hopefully she would make their acquaintance later today, but before she attempted to make friends, she really should eat something. It was already four in the afternoon and she was ravenous.

Tara hadn't brought any supplies with her, just a carton of long-life milk and some teabags, which would do for a cuppa in the morning, so her only option was to see whether the cafe had anything left, or drive into Duncoorie.

Not wanting to take time away from setting up the studio, Tara locked up and headed to the cafe.

The heady aroma of coffee wafted up her nose when she stepped inside, and she sniffed appreciatively. Moving towards the counter, she saw a couple of slices of cake under a glass dome, along with a solitary scone. It would have to do.

'What can I get you?' a cheery middle-aged woman asked. She had been wiping down the coffee machine, but she stopped what she was doing when she saw Tara approach.

'A large cappuccino and the cake please.'

'Which one?'

'All of them.'

The woman's eyebrows rose as she repeated, 'All of them?'

'I haven't eaten since this morning, and I'm starving,' Tara explained. She held out her hand. 'I'm Tara McTaigh, and I've just moved into the empty studio.'

The woman's face cleared as she took her hand. 'Gillian. I manage the cafe. Lovely to meet you. I'd heard a rumour that a doll's house maker was about to join us, so I guess that's you.'

'It is. McTaigh's Miniatures.'

Gillian beamed at her. 'How fitting.'

Tara smiled back. It wasn't often someone realised that *taigh* meant "house" in Gaelic. The smile was only slightly forced. If she'd had even the slightest suspicion that her

46

marriage would fall apart, she never would have used her married name for her business. But at the time Tara had thought it fitting and had seen it as a sign. Now she was stuck with it.

'You can't have cake in lieu of lunch,' Gillian said. 'I'm sure we can do better than that. How about I rustle up a sandwich? Is there anything you don't like or are allergic to?'

'I'll eat anything,' she replied gratefully.

Taking a seat to await her food, Tara removed her phone from her pocket. She should let her mum know she'd arrived safely, and she also wanted to see whether she had any new orders.

Pleased to find she had several, she vowed to make packing them up a priority as soon as she had located the items among the multitude of boxes sitting in the middle of the studio.

Tara wolfed her tuna sandwich down hungrily, then finished her coffee, but when she attempted to pay Gillian waved her away.

'It's on the house,' she said. 'Consider it a little welcome to Coorie Castle. You must let me know as soon as you're sorted and I'll pop over for a look. I love a doll's house, and so does my little granddaughter. She isn't old enough for one yet, but when she is— Oh, darn it! Who am I kidding? If I buy one, it'll be for *me*.'

'I'm hoping to have everything ready by tomorrow,' Tara replied. It was going to be tough, but the quicker she unpacked and sorted out her workspace, the sooner she could get some work done. She was halfway through a commission and she'd promised to have it finished in the next four weeks. The move to Skye had put her behind – not by much, but she hated having to rush. In addition, she still had to unpack the car and she would have to do a grocery shop soon if she wanted to eat. She also wanted to pop into the castle and pay her respects to Mhairi, and then there was a visit to the gift shop to be made, plus updating her website…

Tara was already tired, but just thinking about that lot was exhausting.

Mentally rolling her sleeves up, Tara returned to her studio. Thinking about it wasn't going to get it done and she had a long night ahead of her.

Despite being so pooped last night that even her eyelids ached, Tara was up with the dawn chorus the following morning. She leapt out of bed, eager to get going (she still had loads to do) but pulled up short when she entered the living area to make a cup of tea and caught sight of the early morning light on the loch.

The sky was silver, the water calm and flat, and the sun's rays illuminated the distant peaks on the opposite side of the loch.

Mesmerised, Tara made a brew and then perched on the sofa to drink it. On future mornings if she was awake at this time, she would take her tea and drink it at the water's edge. It would be a wonderfully grounding start to any day.

Tea finished, she got ready to face the busy day ahead, thankful that she'd forced herself to put all her clothes away and sort out her toiletries last night, despite feeling as though she'd been walking through treacle because she was so knackered. Then she'd had a quick shower and had fallen into bed, her hair still damp.

This morning, she plaited it and tossed the heavy dark braid over her shoulder, then swiped mascara over her lashes. That would have to do. She had too much to be getting on with to fuss with her appearance, and the first thing was a visit to the supermarket in Portree to stock up on food and other essentials. Then she would visit the post office and send off her latest orders. If she was quick, she could be back at the cottage before the craft centre's opening time of ten a.m. And if she was *really* quick, she might even have time to eat a couple of pieces of toast while she put her shopping away.

The supermarket opened at seven, so Tara was in her car and heading to Portree by half-past six, under no illusion that it would take her a while to find the supermarket, and then have to spend more precious time trundling up and down unfamiliar aisles.

Two hours later, she'd finished her shopping and was back in Duncoorie. Parking outside the post office, she was first in the queue and quickly had her parcels weighed and the postage paid. Making a mental note to check out local delivery and collection services, she hurried back to the boathouse, and by five minutes to ten, she was unlocking the studio door and breathing a sigh of relief. The morning had been hectic, but hopefully things would slow down a bit from here on in, and she could take a breather.

Before she resumed work on her latest commission, Tara took a moment to study her new studio and was quietly pleased with how it looked. The window was large enough to display three decent sized doll's houses and although she hadn't put any furniture in them yet, they looked lovely set at differing heights. Each style and colour was different, which she hoped would draw the eye. The bunting she'd purchased especially for the window was draped along the top of the frame, and she'd used model grass for the houses to sit on. The space in front of the houses held a selection of miniatures, ranging from the cutest nursery scene imaginable, complete with a tiny rattle, a dummy, and a changing bag with miniature nappies and a tub of cream in it, to a swing seat and a picnic basket.

Anything that could be found in a real house or garden, Tara was able to make in miniature.

Many more tiny items were on the shelves next to the display, and a counter separated the shop floor from the work area to the rear where there was another window set quite high up which faced the loch and let in loads of natural light. It was the perfect set-up.

Feeling calmer, Tara settled at the workbench. Laying her tools out next to her on the well-worn surface, she was soon lost in the delicate operation of installing a fireplace in the living room of the house she was currently working on. As she did so, she kept glancing at the photos of the real living room on which the doll's house was based, making sure the miniature one was accurate.

Tara was so engrossed that she only vaguely registered someone entering the studio, and she was startled when she heard her name being called. It was Avril, the castle's receptionist and admin person, checking to see if she was settling in.

'Do you have everything you need at the boathouse?' Avril asked as Tara hurried forward with a smile. But Avril wasn't looking at her. She was too busy examining Tara's stock. 'Oh my God, how cute is that!' she cried, pointing to a fully equipped kitchen, the table sporting cookie cutters, a pink bowl, a wooden spoon, and even a bag of sugar and half a dozen eggs in a box. 'Do you make all this yourself?'

'I do,' Tara confirmed, with more than a hint of pride. 'Thank you for asking, but I've got everything I need. I can't believe how stunning the boathouse is.'

'It's lovely, isn't it? Mhairi sends her apologies. She wanted to be here to greet you yesterday but with the castle's estate manager on leave, she's rushed off her feet. We both are, as I'm having to do some of the things he normally deals with.' Avril bit her lip. 'I hope to goodness I've filled in the contract properly,' she said, then sighed. 'No doubt Cal will tell me if I haven't. He's back on Monday, so you'll probably meet him then. Or maybe before that – he lives in the cottage next to the old boathouse where you're staying.'

Cal? The name sent a shiver through her. Nah, it couldn't be. The Cal Avril was talking about was probably short for Callum, which was far more common. And, the Cal she once knew and loved, lived on the opposite side of the country.

Avril was saying, 'Anyway, I'd better be off. If you need anything or you have a problem, pop up to the castle. Oh, and everyone knows you're here, so expect a flood of nosey parkers throughout the day.' This was said with a smile. 'I'm not serious. The crafters are a great bunch. Everyone is so friendly, and you'll soon get to know them all. Mhairi says we're like one big happy family. Ooh, you've got a customer. See you soon.'

And with that, she breezed out of the door, leaving Tara staring after her with bemusement.

With a bright smile she greeted the two ladies who'd entered the studio, and when she'd made her very first face-to-face sale, Tara knew her instincts had been right – she *was* going to love it here. In fact, she was loving it already.

Chapter 5

At first, Cal didn't notice how quiet Bonnie had become. He was concentrating on the road and reflecting on the lovely couple of weeks he'd enjoyed with his daughter and his parents. He'd had a great time and so had Bonnie.

Driving back to Skye on Sunday morning, Cal felt exhausted – having a nine-year-old was knackering – but at the same time he wouldn't have wanted it any other way, despite suspecting that he needed a holiday to get over *this* holiday. Bonnie was so lively. She rarely sat still and never stopped talking.

She was quiet now, though.

'Have you had a good time?' he asked.

'Uh-huh.' She nodded.

'What was your favourite bit?'

Bonnie shrugged. When he attempted to meet her eye in the rear-view mirror, she was staring out of the window, her face turned away.

'Go-karting? Boating? The adventure park?' he tried. Another shrug.

'Are you tired? I know I am. We've been on the go since we got there. I bet Nana and Grandpa are shattered.'

Silence. Bonnie didn't even acknowledge that he had spoken.

Cal refused to give up. 'You've got loads to tell your mum, haven't you?'

She glanced at him, caught his eye and hastily looked away.

Ah, so that was it. Bonnie was missing her mother. It didn't come as a surprise. This was the longest she'd ever been away from her.

The knowledge stung, nevertheless. Regret that his daughter would rarely have both parents with her at the same time settled over him. It must be hard, and his heart went out to her. It mightn't be his fault that he and Yvaine were no longer together, as she'd been the one to end it, but he felt responsible all the same. If only he'd—

He shook his head to clear it. There was nothing to be gained by recriminations or wishful thinking. And if he had never met Yvaine, then he wouldn't have Bonnie, which was unthinkable.

'I bet you're looking forward to seeing your mum,' he said. 'I expect she's missed you, too.' He met Bonnie's gaze again, before snapping his attention back to the road, dismayed to see the worry lurking in her eyes.

He was about to ask what was wrong when she said, 'You won't ever have a girlfriend, will you, Dad?'

To Cal it didn't sound like a question. It sounded like a plea. 'Probably not,' he replied, keeping his tone deliberately light. He couldn't promise he would *never* have a girlfriend (he had been on several dates over the past few years, although none of them had come to anything), but neither did he want another serious relationship.

'I don't want you to have a girlfriend,' she persisted.

'That's OK, because I haven't got one.'

'I wish Mummy didn't have a boyfriend.'

Cal stiffened. On full alert but trying not to show it, he asked casually, 'Why is that?'

'I think she likes Lenn more than she likes me.'

They'd just driven through the village of Achnasheen and still had well over an hour to go before they reached Skye, so as soon as he was able, Cal pulled over onto the side of the road then scooted around in his seat to face her. 'Your mother *does not* like Lenn more than she likes you. She loves you with all her heart.'

'But she went away without me.'

'Yes, she did. But that doesn't mean she doesn't love you. It just means she wanted to have some grown-up time, doing things you wouldn't enjoy.'

Bonnie scowled.

Cal could tell she wasn't convinced by his explanation. 'Who is your best friend?' he asked.

'Katie, duh!'

'What do you do when you're with her?'

A frown creased Bonnie's brow. 'We play make-up and dolls – but don't tell anyone because Alisha in school says that playing with dolls is lame. And we sometimes play computer games, or we draw, or make stuff.'

'Next time you go to Katie's house, or she comes to yours, it might be nice if you were to ask Mum to play with you.'

Bonnie's expression was horrified. 'But we—' She stopped, realisation dawning. Then she scowled again. 'It's not the same.'

'No, it isn't,' Cal agreed. 'But would you really want to go wine tasting with Mum and Lenn, bearing in mind that you wouldn't be allowed to taste any? Or would you be happy to sit at a table for three hours eating dinner?'

'No.'

'You'd be bored, wouldn't you?'

'Maybe.'

'And you wouldn't want to lie on a sunlounger all day, snoozing, would you?'

'Ugh, no.'

'That's what Mum and Lenn have been doing. You'd have been bored out of your noggin. Besides, if they'd taken you, I wouldn't have been able to spend my holiday with you. We had fun, didn't we?'

Her nod was emphatic. 'Yes.'

Thank goodness for that. He'd tried his hardest to ensure she'd had a good time.

Unfortunately, Bonnie wasn't done with him yet. 'But if you *did* have a girlfriend, you would have taken *her* on holiday and not *me*.'

'I wouldn't.'

'You would. You'd want to do grown-up things with her, the way Mummy wanted to do grown-up things with Lenn. What is wine tasting?'

'It's when— Look, I haven't got a girlfriend, so it's a moot point.'

'What's a moot point?'

'It means it's irrelevant.'

'But you *might* have one.'

'How about if I make you a promise not to have a girlfriend?'

'Never?'

'Never. At least, not until you have a boyfriend. Deal?'

'I'm never having a boyfriend.'

'Never is a long time.'

'So is two weeks.'

Cal started the car. 'Let's get you home. Your mum will be wondering where we've got to.'

Bonnie didn't look quite as anxious, but Cal wasn't fooled. She definitely wasn't happy that her mum was seeing Lenn. He didn't blame her, because he wasn't happy either.

His reason was very similar to Bonnie's: jealousy. Bonnie was jealous of her mum spending time with Lenn and not her, and Calan was jealous that if Lenn moved in with Yvaine, Lenn would get to have breakfast with Bonnie every morning and tuck her in every night. Cal should be doing that, not some strange bloke. Bonnie was feeling pushed out and usurped in her mother's affections, and Cal could wholeheartedly understand because he feared the same thing, that Lenn would become the most important man in Bonnie's life and not him.

Feeling disgruntled, Cal carried on with the journey that would end with his daughter being returned to her mother's waiting arms – and those of Yvaine's blasted boyfriend.

In her usual excited way, Bonnie was out of the car before Cal had even opened the driver's door and she flew into the house, yelling for her mother. Cal lifted Bonnie's case from the boot and followed behind in a considerably more sedate manner.

He hesitated on the step, unsure whether to go on in or wait until he was invited.

To his annoyance, it was Lenn who did the inviting, acting as though it was his house, not Yvaine's. He seemed very much at home, despite having a rather grand home of his own on the outskirts of Portree.

Cal tried not to scowl as he realised Yvaine and Lenn might be living together sooner than he'd hoped. The chap seemed to have moved in already.

'Did Bonnie have a nice time?' Lenn asked, taking the case from Cal's reluctant fingers. It felt symbolic somehow, as though it wasn't just the case he was handing over, it was Bonnie, too.

'She did, thanks. And you?'

'We had a lovely time. Sand, sea, se—' Lenn stopped, but the proprietorial smarmy look in his eye left Cal in no doubt as to what the man had been about to say.

It was a blatant show of possessiveness, Lenn letting Cal know that he was the bloke sleeping with Yvaine now, not Cal. He didn't care. Lenn was welcome to her. His only concern was Bonnie, and he hoped she didn't pick up on any of it.

Yvaine appeared in the hall, Bonnie clamped onto her like a limpet. 'Cal, thank you for taking such good care of her,' his ex-wife said.

Cal bit back a snarky retort. Had she expected him to neglect their daughter? If she had been so concerned, maybe she shouldn't have buggered off to Cyprus for two weeks.

He tried to keep his voice even as he replied, 'I'm her father. It's my job to take care of my daughter.'

It took a monumental effort on Cal's part not to look at Lenn as he said it, his gaze remaining on Yvaine. She was looking good, he noticed, the golden tan suiting her. She appeared to be relaxed and happy, despite the flight landing late last night and the long drive from Glasgow airport. In fact, Yvaine was glowing, radiant even.

Lenn looked good too, and Cal's dislike of the man couldn't detract from the fact that the guy was a handsome chappie. At thirty-five, he was two years older than Cal, slim, dark-haired and sophisticated. The opposite of Cal, who had a bigger build (all muscle, so he claimed), light russet hair and could in no way be described as sophisticated. Lenn was at home in an office. Cal was more at home on a mountain.

He wondered, not for the first time, whether Yvaine had deliberately chosen a man who was as far from Cal as she could find.

'Go say goodbye to your dad,' Yvaine urged, and Bonnie, suddenly realising that her father was about to leave, launched herself at him.

Cal scooped her up, her skinny legs wrapping around his waist, her arms around his neck.

'I don't want you to go,' she muttered into his shoulder.

'I have to Bon-Bon, you know I do.'

'It's not fair!'

Cal couldn't agree more. And when Yvaine followed him to the car and quietly told him the news that she and Lenn were moving in together so that the three of them could be a 'proper family', Cal thought that life was very unfair indeed.

'You're back!' Mhairi exclaimed in delight. She made to rise, age-spotted hands gripping the arm of her chair as she shuffled to the edge of the seat.

'Don't bother getting up,' Cal told her, crossing the room in five strides and bending down to kiss her powdered cheek. As usual she looked immaculate. With her neatly styled hair, rouge, lipstick, and elegant clothes, she reminded him of the late Queen Elizabeth.

Mhairi accepted the kiss, then gestured for him to take a seat. 'How is Bonnie?'

'She's good, thanks.'

'And you? How was your visit to your parents?'

'It was lovely. They were thrilled to have us stay, but I think they're secretly relieved to see the back of us. They forget how lively she can be.'

'You look tired, too,' Mhairi observed. 'I hope you're not thinking of doing any work today. You are still officially on holiday. Go home and have a nap. I'll see you tomorrow for our usual Monday morning meeting.'

'But—'

She held up a hand. 'I refuse to discuss business today, and if I hear you've disobeyed me, you'll get the sack.'

'Surely not. A misdemeanour like that only warrants a written warning.'

'Consider yourself warned.' Her eyes twinkled and he grinned back.

Cal had fallen on his feet when he'd landed this job, and he was thankful for it every day. Mhairi was the best employer anyone could wish for, and in the five years since he'd started working for her, he'd come to consider her a friend.

His job as the castle's estate manager suited him down to the ground. He was Mhairi's second-in-command, answerable only to her, and he thrived on the responsibility. As well as managing the castle itself, he also managed the craft centre and the land. It was challenging and hard work, and he thoroughly enjoyed it. But what had appealed to him the most when he'd applied for the job was that the castle was only a short distance from the village of Duncoorie, where Yvaine had moved after the divorce, so she could be near her parents who lived in the village. If Cal wanted to see as much of his daughter as possible, he'd had no choice but to move from Inverness, where he'd been the assistant manager of a large estate a few miles away, and relocate to Skye.

At the time he hadn't cared what job he did, as long as he was near Bonnie.

Being offered the position at Coorie Castle had been wonderful, and his gratitude knew no bounds.

Giving Mhairi another peck on the cheek, he took his leave.

As he drove the short distance down the lane towards his cottage, his thoughts returned to Yvaine's news. He wondered when she was planning on telling Bonnie. He would like to be there when she did, but he guessed there was little point in suggesting it.

As he reached the turn-off to the old boathouse, he glanced automatically at the loch, but for once the sight of water didn't calm him. However, he did notice a car parked at the top of the track leading to the boathouse and he hoped whoever was renting it was having a better time than he was.

Chapter 6

Tara intended to spend Monday morning replenishing her stock of furniture. She had sold a surprising amount over the weekend to the tourists who flocked to the castle and the craft centre in their droves. But first, she was off to the gift shop with the items she wanted them to sell.

Over the course of the last few days, she'd met the other crafters and had made friends with Jinny who managed the gift shop. Jinny was around Tara's age, tall and curvy, whereas Tara was short and slim, statuesque to Tara's petite frame. Jinny was lively and outgoing, and had the gift of the gab, seeming able to sell heather to a Scotsman.

When Tara first met her, she'd watched Jinny make several sales in quick succession to customers who, to Tara's eye, hadn't appeared to want to put their hands in their pockets to buy anything. All of them had left with a carrier bag and a smile on their face, and Tara had been impressed.

'I've made a space for your stuff,' Jinny announced as Tara pushed open the gift shop door with her bottom, her arms full with a doll's house.

Tara headed towards the empty shelves and placed the house on a wooden crate that would be used as a display stand. This particular house was quite large, with a price tag to reflect its size, but she had two smaller ones in different styles waiting to be brought over.

Several trips later, Tara was happy with the space allocated to her craft and the way everything was displayed. A tall swivel stand held clear cellophane packs of things such as crockery sets and bathroom accessories, as well as lamps, rugs and soft furnishings. On the other shelves were box sets of furniture, with the display-only pieces in front. All in all, she was proud of it.

'Do I have to pop in every day to see if anything needs to be replenished?' she asked, as she was about to head back to her studio.

'That isn't necessary, although I'm always happy to see you for a chinwag. It's all computerised these days.'

'Brilliant. Well, that's me done. I'd better get back before people start arriving. Oh, I forgot, can you hand out one of these with each sale of mine?' Tara gave Jinny a wedge of leaflets containing details of the bespoke side of the business, as well as information about her website. She'd finally got around to updating it last night, having taken some photos of the studio and added the craft centre's address and location, in case anyone wanted to visit her in person.

'Of course, and I forgot to mention something too – a bunch of us are going for a drink and a meal on Friday evening. Would you like to join us? It's only the local pub in the village, but the food is good, the pints are cheap, and it's got a good atmosphere.'

'That would be lovely, thanks.' Tara was looking forward to it already. Mhairi was right – Coorie Castle *was* like one big happy family, and she was thrilled to think she was part of it.

Cal was sitting opposite Mhairi, her desk between them. He had a tablet on his knee and was busy making notes as the old lady brought him up to speed. He'd been up early this morning, keen to have a quick scout around the estate, choosing to walk most of it. Being out in the fresh air as the sun came up was the best possible start to any day, and as he'd hiked around the perimeter and all points between, he had breathed deeply, the fresh cool air filling his nose with the salty scent of the loch and the sweet smell of the heather which had recently come into bloom.

The tide had been going out, exposing wet shingle and rocks covered in seaweed, and he would have loved nothing better than to stand and watch for the next hour or so, but he wanted to check the rest of the estate before his meeting with Mhairi. The estate wasn't large, but it had a variety of landscapes – man-made, such as the maze and duck pond, and natural, like the loch's edge, as well as the woodland, which was managed.

Satisfied that everything was as it should be, although there were plenty of jobs that needed to be done which he had made a note of on his tablet, Cal had turned his attention to the craft centre before he ventured into the castle.

'I see you managed to find a tenant for the empty studio,' he said to Mhairi a short time later. 'Doll's houses – nice.' He'd peeped in through the window as he'd walked past and been impressed by the crafter's workmanship and attention to detail. It was a good addition to the castle's range of crafts and artisan goods.

'I wouldn't have taken you for a man who likes doll's houses,' Mhairi teased, pouring tea into two delicate china cups.

Cal helped himself to a splash of milk from a matching jug. 'I'm not, but I know a certain little girl who will be thrilled.' He could picture the delight on Bonnie's face, and he couldn't wait to show them to her. 'Who's renting it?' he asked.

'A woman by the name of Tara McTaigh. Avril drew up the contract, but I'd like you to take a look at it later today, if you have time. I'm sure she's completed it properly, but it's the first one she's done.'

'No problem, I'll—' Cal was interrupted by the sharp trill of an incoming call. Expecting it to be work-related (it usually was), he was taken aback to see the phone number of the local primary school flash up. 'It's Bonnie's school,' he said. 'I'd better take it.'

Mhairi nodded and calmly sipped her tea.

'Hello, Calan Fraser speaking.'

'I'm sorry to trouble you, Mr Fraser, but could you collect Bonnie from school? She's not well.'

'What's wrong?'

'Headache, feeling sick, complaining of a tummy ache, lethargic. I'm sure it's nothing to worry about, but we do feel she needs to go home.'

'I'm at work. Have you tried phoning her mother?' As he said it, he realised how daft he was being. Obviously, they would have called Yvaine first.

'We have, but we can't get through. We've tried Bonnie's grandmother as well, but no joy there, I'm afraid.'

Mhairi had been listening to the conversation and had understood the gist of it because she flapped a hand at him and mouthed, 'Go.'

Informing the school that he would be with them in ten minutes, he ended the call and began to apologise to Mhairi.

She said, 'Don't be daft. Go fetch Bonnie, and if she doesn't seem too poorly, bring her back here. Otherwise, take her to the cottage and stay with her for as long as you need.'

Worry prodding him in the chest, Cal jumped in the car and drove to the little school. It was so wee and quaint, it made him smile every time he saw it.

When he was buzzed inside, he found his daughter sitting with Mrs Brown, the school secretary. Bonnie's face was pale and she had shadows like bruises under her eyes.

Crouching beside the chair, he said, 'Mrs Brown says you're not well. What's wrong Bon–Bon?'

Bonnie scowled and glanced around furtively before hissing, 'Don't call me that.'

'Sorry. What's wrong, Bonnie?'

'I've got a headache.' She put the back of her hand to her forehead to demonstrate. 'And my tummy hurts.'

'OK. Let's get a dose of medicine into you, and you'll soon feel better.' He straightened and held out his hand. Bonnie slipped her palm into his and gave the secretary a small wave as he led her outside.

Cal expected Bonnie to be wan and listless on the way to the castle, but she seemed upset and annoyed, rather than unwell. And he had an awful feeling he knew what was causing it. However, he decided not to say anything, in case he was wrong and Yvaine hadn't yet mentioned to her that Lenn was moving in with them.

They'd pulled into the castle grounds when Bonnie finally spoke. 'I hate Lenn and I hate Mummy, too.'

Cal drove down the lane and parked in his usual spot outside his cottage. 'You don't mean it.'

'I do!'

'Why? What's happened?'

'Mummy says we have to go live with Lenn, but I don't want to. She can't make me, can she?' Her little face was hopeful, and Cal's heart constricted.

'I think she can, Bon-Bon.' He gave her an apologetic look.

'Well, I'm not going, so there!'

'It won't be so bad—' he began, then he realised what Bonnie had said. '*You're* going to live with *Lenn*?'

'Yes, Daddy. Weren't you listening?'

'I was, but I thought he would move into *your* house, with you and Mummy.'

She pursed her lips. 'No. Mummy says we're going to live in Portree. I don't want to live in Portree. I don't want to go to a new school, and Katie won't be next door.' Then she burst into noisy tears.

His heart breaking for her, Cal scrambled out of the car, lifted her out of her booster seat and carried her inside the cottage, where he gently deposited her on the sofa. After locating a packet of tissues, he sat next to her and held her until she was all cried out.

It took a while.

With a damp patch on his shirt and an ache in his chest, he tried to help her look on the bright side of the move. Which wasn't easy, because he couldn't see any bright side to it, either. Instead of being five minutes away, Bonnie would be a thirty-minute drive away, which meant he would see even less of his daughter than he currently did.

–

Tara looked up as the studio door opened and was surprised to see a girl of about eight or nine step inside. She was on her own, but Tara guessed that a responsible adult would be nearby, so with a quick 'Hello', she returned to her task.

She was fitting mullioned windows to a Tudor-style house, and inserting the tiny pieces of Perspex was fiddly.

'Is it hard to make a doll's house?' the child asked.

Tara glanced up again. 'It can be.'

'Can anyone have a go?'

'Yes, but you might need some help when you're starting out.'

'Will you be running a workshop?'

Tara blinked, surprised that the little girl knew about such things. Then again, Tara reasoned, the child may well have attended one here in the past.

'I might,' she replied cautiously. It was something to be considered for the future, but not right now. She wanted to get her feet under the table first and, let's face it, she hadn't been here a week yet.

'Are all the doll's houses different?'

'Yes and no. I have several standard designs, like that one.' Tara got up, walked towards the counter and pointed to the most basic model she produced.

As she grew nearer, she could see the little girl more clearly. Gosh, she was a pretty little thing, Tara thought. Her hair was the colour of a chestnut, and she had translucent skin with a dash of freckles across her nose and hazel eyes almost the same colour as her hair.

'Are you here with anyone?' she asked, wondering where the child's responsible adult was and whether they were looking for her.

'My dad. He works here. He's the boss.'

'Oh?' Tara's eyes widened.

'I'm Bonnie.'

'Yes, you are.' Wow, the child was precocious as well as pretty.

The girl gave her a long-suffering look. 'It's my *name.*'

'Ah.'

'What's yours?'

'Tara.'

'Like the princess in the story.'

What princess and what story, Tara wondered, but wasn't interested enough to ask.

Bonnie continued, her head tilted to the side, 'You were telling me about the doll's house?'

'So I was. This is a basic house. I make loads of those, so you could say that they are all the same, apart from the colour. But, when people buy them, they like to add their own touches, so no two will have the same wallpaper or the same curtains, for instance.'

'Like the way my house and my friend's house look different inside, even though she lives next door?'

'Exactly.'

'I hope you will run a workshop, because if you do, I'd like to have a go.'

'You'd better check with your dad. What's his name?'

'Cal.'

Ah, yes, the estate's manager, whom she had yet to meet. She hoped he was as nice as everyone else she'd met so far.

'What's that one?' Bonnie asked, pointing to the house Tara was currently working on. It was the commissioned piece.

'Sometimes people ask me to make a special doll's house, one that looks exactly like the house they used to live in as a child, or a house that has very special memories for them.'

Bonnie was listening intently.

'I'll either go visit the house and take lots of measurements and photos so I can make sure that the one I make looks exactly like it, or the customer takes their own photos and sends them to me.'

'Do you make *everything*?'

'I try to.'

'What about...?' Bonnie looked around for inspiration. 'A mug?'

'Yes.' Tara followed her gaze to the mug on the workbench.

'A hairdryer?'

'Yes.'

'A jewellery box?'

Tara smiled. 'Yes, but let's not name everything you can think of, eh? Otherwise we'll be here all day and all night too, and I don't know about you, but I don't fancy missing my lunch and my supper.'

'What's the time?'

Tara checked. 'Twelve thirty.'

'I'm hungry.' Bonnie skipped to the door. 'Thank you for telling me about your doll's houses.'

'Thank you for asking,' Tara said with a smile, thinking what an absolutely delightful child she was. Her parents must be so proud. If she was ever lucky enough to have a daughter, she would be honoured to have one as lovely and as inquisitive as her.

Chapter 7

Calan had only taken his eyes off Bonnie for just one second, and she'd disappeared. He was in the office working through the list on his tablet, and his daughter had been sitting on the floor, colouring. She clearly felt better, but he had no intention of sending her back to school, not when she'd been so upset, and he didn't care what Yvaine said. It was his decision to make because he was the one who'd collected her from school.

He tried to call his ex-wife again, but he got the same message as before. Yvaine was unavailable.

Sooner or later she would see that the school had phoned, as had he, and he knew she would panic and would want to speak to Bonnie herself to make sure their daughter was OK. So he had best go find the child, hadn't he?

Whenever Bonnie was at the castle, she had free rein to go where she pleased, with two provisos: that she didn't stray beyond the immediate castle grounds (no going down to the loch, for instance), and she didn't get in anyone's way. The crafters and the castle's staff were wonderfully tolerant of her, with Gillian in the cafe slipping her hot chocolates or milkshakes depending on the weather, and slices of cake or cookies, but he didn't want her to make a nuisance of herself.

At least by wandering off, Bonnie proved that her illness wasn't physical, so he had no need to worry that she might be sick or have a temperature. However, her emotional distress was another matter, and he wasn't sure how to deal with it, especially since he was so upset himself.

Cal was hoping Bonnie had got the wrong end of the stick and Yvaine wasn't really planning on uprooting their daughter and moving her to Portree, but he guessed the hope was a vain one. He wanted to hear it from the horse's mouth though, before he said anything further to Bonnie.

He was about to step into the hall when he heard his daughter calling him. 'Dad! Dad!' She shot through the door and barrelled into him.

He caught her by the shoulders. 'What's the hurry? How many times have I told you not to run or shout indoors? You'll annoy the guests.'

'Sorry.' She lowered her voice. 'You'll never guess! There's a lady making doll's houses in the craft centre, and she said I could have a go. Can I, Dad? Please?'

'Hang on, young lady, what did she say, exactly?'

'Exactly? Um…' Bonnie screwed up her face. 'Tara said – that's her name, Tara – she said that I would have to ask you if I could join her workshop.'

'When is it?'

'I don't know, she hasn't decided. But when she does, can I? Please? I want to make a doll's house just like my house, so when we move I'll always remember what it looked like. Tara can show me.' Her face crumpled and her chin wobbled. 'I don't want to leave my house, or Duncoorie, or Grandma and Granddad. And I don't want to leave Katie and my school.' She stamped her foot as she began to cry.

As Cal gathered her to him, trying his best to soothe her, he felt a spark of irritation at the doll's house maker for unwittingly upsetting Bonnie all over again. Which reminded him – he should go and introduce himself. After all, he would be the one she'd be dealing with on a regular basis.

But not yet; for now he needed to concentrate on Bonnie. She was his primary concern. His *only* concern.

When Cal's phone rang, Bonnie was in the castle's kitchen scrounging something to eat even though she'd eaten a good lunch. It was Yvaine and she was furious.

'What the hell do you think you're playing at, taking Bonnie to the castle?' she yelled, and Cal winced, holding the phone away from him. When he put it to his ear again, she was saying, 'Can you imagine what was going through my mind when she didn't come home from school?' She paused to take a breath and Cal wasted no time leaping into the momentary void.

'Have you listened to your messages?'

'No, but—'

He cut across her, his ire building. 'I didn't think so. If you had, you'd have realised I had no choice. You weren't answering your phone, and neither was your mother. Or would you have preferred me to leave our daughter sitting with Mrs Brown when she was unwell? She feels better now, thanks for asking.'

Yvaine didn't apologise, but at least she'd stopped yelling when she said, 'I've got a new mobile number. I lost my old phone on holiday. It fell into the sea.'

'You could have mentioned yesterday that you had a new number.' He wasn't at all mollified by her explanation.

'I've only just this afternoon got a new phone. Can I speak to Bonnie?'

'She's pestering Cook for a snack.'

'Please don't let her eat too much rubbish, she won't eat her tea.'

Cal held his tongue. Cook wasn't in the habit of stocking 'rubbish' in her larder. Everything was homemade, using the freshest ingredients.

'Are you at home now?' he asked.

'Where else would I be?'

In Lenn's bed, he nearly said, before coming to his senses. He didn't care whose bed she was in, but he cared about how her actions affected Bonnie. 'We'll be there in ten minutes.'

True to his word, Cal pulled up outside his ex-wife's house within the promised timeframe. Usually when he dropped Bonnie off, he waited by the car until she was safely inside, unless she had a suitcase like yesterday. Today, though, he wanted a word with her mother, so he accompanied Bonnie to the front door, where Yvaine was waiting to greet her.

After checking with Bonnie that she was OK and placing a hand on her forehead to make sure she didn't have a temperature, Yvaine turned her attention to Cal. 'Was there something else?' she asked, with raised eyebrows.

'When you told me that you and Lenn were moving in together, I didn't think you would be living at his place in Portree.'

'Why ever not? It makes perfect sense. His house is twice the size of mine, and there's more to do in Portree than in Duncoorie.'

'Bonnie doesn't want to move to Portree.'

'I know, but she'll get used to it. Children are very adaptable and it's not as though we're moving a hundred miles away.'

'Her friends are here, her school—'

'She'll soon make new friends, and when she's eleven her school will *be* in Portree. That's where the high school is, in case you've forgotten.'

Calan hadn't forgotten. But Bonnie wouldn't be attending high school for another two years. 'Why can't Lenn move in with you until then? She's settled and happy where she is. She doesn't need the upheaval of moving schools and moving houses. She's got enough to cope with getting used to you having a boyfriend.'

Was he being unreasonable? He didn't think so, but Yvaine looked annoyed.

'As I said, she'll soon make new friends. And for your information, Lenn is more than a boyfriend. He's the man I'll be spending the rest of my life with. This isn't about her, is it? It's about you. Don't worry, you'll still have her every other weekend. That won't change.'

Yvaine could be so infuriating.

'This isn't about me. It's about Bonnie, and what's best for her.'

'Are you saying I don't know what is best for my daughter?'

'She's my daughter, too.'

Yvaine lowered her voice and hissed, 'And don't I bloody know it. Get over yourself, Cal. Bonnie and I are moving in with Lenn whether you like it or not.'

With that, his ex-wife shut the door in his face, leaving him standing on her step, his mouth open and an ache in his chest.

The ache intensified when he saw his daughter's pale face peering at him through the bedroom window, as he realised she had probably heard every word.

–

Tara stared at the middle-aged woman standing in front of her and said, 'Did you just ask whether I could make a coffin?'

'Yes. Can you?' The woman's eyes flickered around the studio before returning to Tara. Her mouth was down-turned, her expression sour. She was clutching an over-sized bag to her bosom in a white-knuckled grip, as though she feared Tara might attempt to wrestle it from her.

'I suppose I could.' Tara had never been asked to make a coffin before. There wasn't much call for them in the doll's house industry. Although she supposed she could try branching out into creating Halloween scenes. It was something to consider.

'Good. When can you come to measure up? He's been dead two weeks and frankly I want to get this over with.'

Tara's mouth fell open and her eyes widened. '*Excuse me?*'

The woman peered at her, squinting behind her brown-rimmed glasses. 'I must say, you don't seem keen to have my business.' The accent was pure Glaswegian and the tone was scathing.

'I, er… You do realise I make doll's houses?'

'I do.' The woman scowled and glanced around the studio again. 'Can I speak to your manager? I might have better luck explaining it to him.'

'Sorry, but I *am* the manager. This is my business.'

'Is there someone up at the castle I can speak to?'

'About what?' Tara wished she hadn't left her mobile on the workbench. She had a feeling she might have to call for backup.

Glancing at it out of the corner of her eye, she wondered whether she would be able to reach it in time if the woman decided to cause a scene. When several more people entered the workroom, crowding in behind, Tara didn't know whether to be relieved or alarmed.

Smiling vaguely in their direction, she kept her focus on the decidedly odd woman and her decidedly bizarre request.

'About false advertising,' the woman said.

'Um, I think you'd be better off speaking to an under-taker,' Tara suggested, trying to inject sympathy into her voice. Grief affected people in different ways.

'What on earth for?'

'The coffin.' Maybe it wasn't grief. Maybe the woman was suffering from dementia? Tara's heart went out to her. Should she call someone? She had to do something…

The woman tutted. 'As far as I'm aware, undertakers don't do scale models.'

And the penny dropped.

Tara breathed a sigh of relief. 'Ahh, I see! You want a *model* of a coffin, not a real one. Silly me! When you said he'd been dead two weeks, I thought…' She ground to a halt. No wonder the woman was looking at her strangely. She must think she was a right nugget.

The woman pursed her lips. 'You thought I wanted you to make a *full-sized* coffin?'

'Well, yes.' Tara bit her lip.

'And I suppose you thought I was asking you to measure him up for it?'

'Sorry.'

The woman's bark of laughter made Tara jump and she yelped in surprise.

'Bloody hell, Willie would have found that hilarious.' She was chuckling. 'He always did have a morbid sense of humour. I suppose he had to, in his line of work.'

'What did he do?'

'He was an undertaker, of course. They cremated him in one of his own coffins.'

'I'm sorry for your loss.' Tara was mortified.

'Och, we weren't very close. Willie was my brother-in-law. My sister is a bit upset, though.'

'I expect she is.' Tara felt awful.

'She loves that funeral parlour.'

'Riiight…'

'Which is why I'm here. I want you to make a model of it. Can you do that? Your leaflet says you can.' She flapped it at her.

'Yes, I can do that.'

'She doesn't want to carry on with it on her own. She can't, you see – too squeamish. Can't stand the sight of a dead body. Willie handled that side of things. He used to love laying them out in their Sunday best, powdering their dead faces, combing their hair. Did you know it's a myth that people's hair and nails continue to grow after death?' When Tara shook her head, the woman sighed. 'It's amazing the things you learn when your brother-in-law is a funeral director. *Was* a funeral director. He stocked a lovely line of coffins.' She seemed to gather herself. 'Where was I? Oh, yes, a scale model of the funeral parlour. What do I need to do?'

Tara hastily gathered her own wits and briefly explained how it worked, before making a note of the woman's name and email address. 'Right, Mrs Esplin, I'll send you all the details of the things I'll need from you, and we'll take it from there. Is that OK?'

It was, and Mrs Esplin left, a relatively happy customer, although Tara didn't think either of them had quite recovered from the initial misunderstanding.

A funeral parlour was certainly a first, and her head was still swimming with just how much detail she would be expected to go into, as she turned her attention to her next customer.

He'd been very patient, examining the window display whilst she dealt with Mrs Esplin, and he continued to study it, his back to her.

'Sorry to keep you waiting…' Tara began, then drifted into silence.

Although she could only see his back, there was something familiar about him. She couldn't quite put her finger on it, but whatever it was made her pulse quicken and a shiver go right through her.

It was only when he slowly turned around to face her, that she realised who he reminded her of. Come to think of it, he didn't just *remind* her. It was him, *Cal*. The man she had fallen in love with at university. The man who she had thought loved her. The man who had broken her heart. Calan Fraser.

The total, utter *shite*.

Chapter 8

When Calan saw Tara Shaw in the doll's house studio, his instinct had been to turn tail and run. But knowing that he would have to deal with her at some point, he kept his feet firmly glued to the floor.

At the sight of her, confused and uncertain as she dealt with an awkward situation and a woman who had initially seemed to be off her trolley, his heart had fluttered, before giving an almighty thump as it tried to catch up with itself. Thankfully he'd entered the studio behind three other people and had managed to keep them between him and Tara.

When they left, he'd already positioned himself with his back to the counter and the woman he'd once loved with all his heart. He had loved her so deeply and so totally that he'd been devastated when he'd had to let her go.

She was the one who had got away – and he was the one who had let her.

He hadn't wanted to end it, but at the time he'd felt he had little choice. His dad's breakdown and his mum's insistence that it was kept quiet, on top of Cal finishing his degree and being offered a job near his hometown, had made it incredibly difficult to carry on seeing her.

At first, he'd tried to keep his relationship with her going, but not being able to leave Dad to visit her in Glasgow (his mum had been terrified that Dad would harm himself) and not being able to invite Tara to visit him in Inverness, had inevitably put a strain on their relationship. After one particularly fraught phone call, where Tara had accused him of not loving her any more, Cal had made the heartbreaking decision to set her free. It wasn't fair on her.

He might have tried to hang on to her, but there was no knowing how long his dad's poor mental health would continue, and with him being sworn to secrecy there'd been nothing he could say to make her understand. So he'd told her that they were too young for such a serious relationship and it couldn't possibly last, that his parents kept telling him they were too young to settle down, that she was in Glasgow with another year of her course to complete and he had a job in Inverness and everyone knew that long-distance relationships never worked, and that she should be enjoying university life. He had told her everything but the truth and had ended it there and then.

And had spent the rest of his life regretting it.

Not for the first time he wondered whether things would have been different if he had confided in her, if he'd broken his promise to his mum and had told Tara what his dad was going through. He mightn't have been able to visit her often, nor she him, but at least she would have understood. Their relationship mightn't have survived anyway, but that was something he'd never know.

Cal wondered what had brought her to Skye. Then he remembered that Mhairi had called her Tara McTaigh and the knowledge that she was married gave him an unexpected pang. He wondered whether she was happy, and hoped with all his heart that she was.

Did she even remember him? Ten years was a long time, and so much had happened.

A whole decade had passed, but as Cal glanced at her out of the corner of his eye, it felt like no time at all.

Then, before he was ready, he found himself on his own in the studio with nowhere to hide, and she was speaking to him and he had no choice other than to turn around.

'Hello, Tara.'

He watched the blood drain from her face and her eyes widen in shock, and he wished he'd done something to prepare her. But he hadn't expected her to react like this, and even if he had guessed she might, what could he have done?

'What the—?' she began, then stopped, her eyes narrowing. '*Cal?*'

His mouth twisted in an attempt at a smile.

Her lips became a thin line and her jaw tensed, before realisation dawned on her face. '*You're* Mhairi's Cal.' It wasn't a question. It was an accusation.

He shrugged, almost an apology but not quite, as though it was his fault she'd turned up in Coorie Castle, when it was she who was the interloper, not he. This was *his* home, not hers.

Her mouth dropped open. 'And Bonnie is your daughter.' Again, not a question.

'Yes.'

Tara swallowed, and his gaze was drawn to her throat. The same throat he had kissed countless times. Abruptly, he looked away.

'She's lovely.' Her words sounded forced, as though she was trying to be polite. But surely she couldn't still be upset with him? Not after all this time.

'She is.' His voice was warm, reflecting the pride he had in his daughter.

'She wants to attend a workshop if I hold one,' Tara said, a frown wrinkling her forehead.

'She told me.'

'Good... good.'

'I said she could.'

'If I hold one,' Tara repeated.

'Yes, if you hold one.'

'It's just... I haven't decided yet. I only moved in last week.'

'I know.'

Her laugh was nervous and sharp. 'Of course you do. I, er—' She hesitated. 'I didn't realise... If I'd known, I would never...'

She caught her bottom lip between her teeth, and the familiar habit hit him in the solar plexus. Memories rushed back, surging through his mind like a fast-flowing tide, washing away the years and filling the empty spaces in his head with long-forgotten images of her. Had he truly forgotten? Or had he deliberately not allowed himself to remember?

A silence stretched between them, tense and painful.

Cal broke it. 'Where are you living? In Duncoorie?' The thought of her living so near made his heart constrict.

Her eyes flickered to the door and back to him. 'In the boathouse.'

'In the—?' Damn Yvaine and her bloody boyfriend. If she hadn't decided to move in with Lenn, Bonnie wouldn't have been upset at school and Cal wouldn't have had to leave his meeting with Mhairi before she'd had a chance to tell him who was renting the cottage by the loch. 'I see,' he said.

'That's OK, isn't it? Mhairi offered it to me until my house in Edinburgh is sold.'

'Mhairi is the boss. It's her boathouse to do with as she sees fit.' He sounded churlish, but for pity's sake, Tara was living only a stone's throw away from him.

Tara flinched. 'Hopefully it won't take long, then I can be out of your hair.'

'It's fine,' he lied. Then to try to make up for his appalling lack of manners, he said, 'How do you like Coorie Castle?'

Her expression cleared, the wariness lifting a little. 'It's lovely. The craft centre is fabulous, and everyone is so friendly.' She ground to a halt and Cal could easily guess what she was thinking – everyone except *him*.

He deserved that. 'We're like one big happy family.'

'So everyone keeps telling me.'

Another awkwardly long and uncomfortable silence followed as Cal scrabbled around for something to say. Tara appeared to be equally at a loss.

Eventually he said, 'OK, then, I'd better get on. I just thought I'd introduce myself.' He turned to leave, feeling flustered and embarrassed, and after the briefest of hesitations, he added, 'I hope you'll be happy here, Tara.'

Her muttered, 'I doubt it,' followed him outside.

–

Tara held herself rigid until Cal was out of sight, then she slumped against the counter and buried her face in her hands. She was shaking, her heart raced, and she badly needed a sit down and a shot of something alcoholic.

She hadn't expected to see Calan Fraser ever again. She hadn't wanted to. Yet here he was, slap bang in the middle of the new life she hoped to forge.

Pulling herself together, she hurried around the counter and locked the door, switching the lights off as she did so, before flipping the sign hanging in the window from 'Open' to 'Closed'. The craft centre didn't shut until five p.m., but no crafter was in their studio all day every day, she'd discovered, so she had no qualms about closing early.

She simply couldn't face seeing anyone, and neither was she in the right frame of mind to do any more work today. The frame of mind she was in involved a bottle of wine and time to think. She needed to get her head around seeing Calan again, so she returned to the boat-house.

The wine was nicely chilled, but as Tara took it out of the fridge she wouldn't have cared if it was as warm as a hot bath. She wasn't going to drink it for enjoyment. She was hoping the alcohol would stop her hands shaking.

She briefly considered curling up on the sofa with the wine and staring out of the window, but the boathouse felt claustrophobic, and honestly, what was the point of staring at the view through glass when she could go outside and stare at it without any barrier?

She would have liked to sit on the edge of the jetty but felt she would be too exposed (the last thing she wanted was for Cal to spot her there) so she took her wine and a glass further along the shoreline until she was out of sight of the lane, and hunkered down amongst the rocks, leaning against one.

It was warm on her back, and the sun was still high in the sky. She tilted her head back to stare at the expanse of blue over her head, tears prickling.

Angrily she brushed them away. She refused to cry over that man again. She'd shed too many for him already, and he hadn't deserved a single one. Shock vied with pain and anger. Tara didn't know what she felt or how to deal with seeing him again, and as she sat there the memories that she'd tried so hard to keep down resurfaced in all their technicolour misery.

Calan Fraser had broken her heart. He'd been her first love (maybe her *only* love), and he'd almost destroyed her. *He* was the reason she hadn't been able to complete the final year of her degree. It hadn't seemed important any more. Nothing had. She'd never felt more alive, more in tune with her art, the city and the universe, than during the year of loving Cal.

After he'd broken up with her, it was as though her world had lost all colour, and she no longer felt alive. How could she when she was dead inside?

But the world hadn't stopped turning and Tara'd had to do something. When she saw a 'Staff Wanted' notice in the window of a scruffy shop that was an Aladdin's cave of tiny houses and every conceivable thing to go in them, she'd walked in off the street with no CV and little hope of getting the job.

No one had been more surprised than Tara when she'd found herself starting work there the very next day. She'd been even more surprised to discover how much she enjoyed it and, fascinated by the tiny items of furniture, she'd wanted to have a go at making her own miniatures for the inside of her first house. So, she'd taught herself – with loads of help from online videos and lots of trial and error. Discovering she had a talent for it had sealed her fate. Tara had been bitten by the doll's house bug, but as a creator, not a collector.

Would she have found her calling – because that's what she believed it to be – if she'd gone on to do the final year of her Fine Art course?

Probably not. But the knowledge didn't change how she felt about Calan.

The love and adoration she'd felt for him had turned to bitterness and anger. If it hadn't been for a photograph, Tara might have understood, although not accepted, his reasons for breaking up with her. Yes, they had been young – at twenty she'd been so naive and unworldly, despite believing she knew it all. Yes, it would have been difficult to continue their relationship with her in Glasgow and him an assistant manager on some godforsaken private estate north of Inverness. But he hadn't even tried, despite her pleading with him to give it a go. He'd been adamant he wanted a clean break, and Tara hadn't been able to do or say anything to change his mind.

She'd soon discovered the reason why, after compulsively stalking his sister on social media and seeing some photos of him at a wedding a mere seven months after he'd told Tara they were over.

The wedding had been his own.

–

Mhairi was poring over her accounts when Cal found her, glasses perched on the end of her nose as she squinted at the computer screen, pen in hand to scribble numbers on a pad, a big-buttoned calculator sitting next to it.

She scowled when she saw him. 'Whoever invented spreadsheets deserves to burn in hell.'

He dropped into a chair, feeling drained.

'It's not been a good first day back for you, has it?' she observed.

'Eh?' How could she possibly know about him and Tara?

She asked, 'Is Bonnie feeling any better?'

Cal blew out a long breath as he realised she wasn't referring to Tara at all. 'I don't believe my daughter was as unwell as she made out.'

Mhairi gave him a knowing look. 'She told me about Yvaine and the move to Portree.'

'I'm sorry. When the school called, I didn't realise she was putting it on.'

'She probably wasn't. Emotional distress can cause physical distress, too.'

Wasn't that the truth, Cal thought. He remembered how ill his father had been. And Cal was feeling quite sick himself right now.

'She'll be OK,' Mhairi continued. 'She's young, she'll adapt. But you're thinking *you* might not.'

'Are you a mind reader?' He managed a small smile.

'No, I just know you. You're worried.'

He was, and not just about Bonnie. 'I didn't realise the empty studio's new tenant is living in the old boathouse. I hope you're charging her rent.'

The comment earned him a stern look. 'Tara McTaigh? Of course I am.'

'What do you know about her?'

'Not much.' Mhairi put her pen down. 'She's thirty or thereabouts, getting a divorce and selling her house in Edinburgh, and she makes the most exquisite doll's houses and will be a good addition to the craft centre. Did you go say hello?'

Divorce? His heart went out to her. 'I did,' he said grimly.

'Oh, Cal, I hope you didn't scare her. You can be rather dour, you know.'

Calan debated whether to keep it to himself that he knew Tara from years ago but decided against it. It would come out sooner or later, and if he didn't mention it now, Mhairi would wonder why he hadn't said anything.

'I didn't scare her,' he protested. 'Actually, I know her from uni.'

Mhairi's eyebrows rose. 'If that's true, why did you ask me what I know about her? Is there something I should be aware of? She is legitimate, isn't she?' The old lady's expression became worried.

'Nothing like that,' he hastened to assure her. 'We had a thing.'

'A thing?'

'Yeah, we dated.'

Mairi studied him silently.

'For a while,' he added.

'How long is a while?'

'A year. My last year in uni, her second.'

'Was it serious?'

'We were little more than kids.'

'That's not what I asked.'

'I thought it was.'

'Oh, Cal, I'm sorry. If I had known… Did she break your heart?'

'I broke it myself when I ended it.'

'Why, if you don't mind me asking?'

Cal gave her the sanitised version, the one he had given Tara at the time. 'She was too young and had another year in uni to go. I'd just been offered a good job and my parents thought I was too young to settle down.' He snorted at the irony. Just seven months later he was married to Yvaine and was about to become a father. And all because he'd stupidly wanted to ease the pain of losing Tara.

Mhairi knew all about his marriage and his subsequent divorce. She could also do the maths. 'You don't get over a broken heart that quickly.' Her expression and her voice were full of sympathy and understanding.

'No, you don't,' he agreed. The problem was, he didn't think ten years was long enough to get over a broken heart either, even if it was self-inflicted.

Calan had a suspicion he might never get over it.

And an even worse suspicion that he might still be in love with her.

Chapter 9

It had been a long and fraught week, so when Friday finally arrived Tara was more than ready for a visit to the pub later that evening. She prayed Cal wouldn't be there.

Hoping to find out, Tara popped along to the gift shop, ostensibly to check the stock levels on her stand, but in reality she wanted to ask Jinny who was going, and she was relieved when his name wasn't mentioned. Maybe he didn't fraternise with the staff.

However, she couldn't resist mentioning him herself, albeit in a roundabout way, her desire to know more about him as difficult to curb and as painful as the habit of probing at a sore tooth with a tongue.

'Calan's daughter is lovely,' she began, her face averted as she examined the packets of miniatures on the stand. 'How old is she?'

'Nine, the same age as my eldest, Katie.'

Tara felt sick. The child must have been born not long after Cal had got married. He hadn't wasted any time, had he?

'You don't have to do that,' Jinny reminded her as Tara continued to fiddle with the stand.

'I know, but I like to. It makes me feel good to see how well they're selling.' Her hands shook slightly and she hoped Jinny wouldn't notice. 'Bonnie wants to sign up for a doll's house workshop, but I haven't decided whether to run one yet.'

'Give yourself time to settle in, you've only just got here.'

'I know, but Bonnie wants me to hold one and…' She trailed off, not sure where she was going with this.

'And she's the boss's daughter?'

'Um, yeah.'

'Don't worry, Cal won't insist you run one.'

'What is he like to work for?'

'He's the best! He used to be an assistant manager at some big estate near Inverness but,' Jinny lowered her voice, 'he moved here to be near Bonnie. He's divorced. His ex – Yvaine – is from Skye originally and she came back to the island after they split up. Her mum and dad still live in the village.'

Something loosened in Tara's chest at the news that he was no longer married. Yvaine had haunted her ever since she'd seen the photos Cal's sister had posted online. Tara had scrutinised each and every one of them, over and over again, trying to read the expression in Calan's eyes, comparing herself to Yvaine, and hating the woman who had unknowingly driven another nail in the coffin of Tara and Cal's dead romance.

Tara wanted to ask more but didn't see how she could, so she scurried back to her studio hoping she wouldn't bump into him.

She'd managed to avoid him all week, although she'd caught the occasional glimpse that had sent her pulse soaring and tied her stomach into anxious knots. She couldn't go on like this, though. Something would have to give. Maybe if she became more used to seeing him around, she wouldn't have such an extreme reaction. What was it called…? Exposure therapy? Immersion therapy? Whatever, she had to learn to cope with his presence if she intended to remain at the craft centre.

It wouldn't be so bad when she had a home of her own, because that could be anywhere within a reasonable commute to the castle (a house in Duncoorie would be ideal), but until then, she'd have to get used to Calan living a mere stone's throw away. He was so close she could see his cottage from her bedroom window. Last night there'd been a light on at two thirty-five, and she'd lain there in the darkness knowing he was awake. It had taken her a long time to drift off to sleep.

Tara kept a keen eye out for Cal for the rest of the day, but if he'd ventured anywhere near her studio, she wasn't aware of it, and neither did she see him when she returned to the boathouse to get ready to go out. She was looking forward to getting to know some of the other crafters better, and apart from the dash to the supermarket in Portree the day after she'd arrived, she hadn't left the castle grounds.

The evening was warm, but Tara took a fleece with her in case the temperature dropped later. Although the loch was sheltered with hills rising steeply on either side, there was usually a breeze near the water, and with the village following the contours of the loch, she suspected the walk home might be fresh.

Duncoorie was only a fifteen-minute walk from the castle, and the pub was halfway along the main street, not far from the post office. It appeared to be busy, which wasn't surprising considering this was the beginning of summer and the tourist season was in full swing.

Tara approached it hesitantly, hoping she wasn't the first to arrive. Not recognising anyone sitting on the benches outside, she made her way indoors where she was met with delicious cooking smells, and her mouth watered as she realised how hungry she was. Her appetite hadn't been great these past few days and although she'd made a meal every evening, she'd done little more than pick at it. The wine had taken a hammering, though.

The pub was noisy and full of people, but she recognised Jinny, and a woman called Giselle who made the most glorious pictures out of sea glass, and Fergus, the glassblower who was sitting with his brother Shane, so she made her way across the room. Smiling self-consciously when she reached them, she realised they'd commandeered two tables which they'd pushed together and had placed a variety of personal items on the chairs to secure them.

When Fergus noticed her, it took him a second to register who she was, and when he did he removed a jumper from the seat next to him. 'Tara, isn't it? We have met, but in case you don't remember, I'm Fergus.'

When she told him she remembered and had admired his vases more than once, his face lit up. 'It's always nice to get some feedback,' he said. 'I love your wee houses, by the way.'

'Thanks.' She was about to ask what they were drinking and whether she could top up their glasses, when several others arrived, along with Gillian.

When Tara finally settled back into her chair with her drink, she was content to listen as the conversation ebbed and flowed around her, not feeling in the least bit left out as they chatted about people and events she had no knowledge of. But her ears pricked up when they talked

93

about sales and the number of visitors to the castle and craft centre. She also listened avidly for any mention of Cal.

His name did crop up, but only in a professional capacity. His private life wasn't discussed at all. Which was just as well, Tara decided, as her meal arrived and she tucked in with gusto. She'd ordered braised beef and it was absolutely delicious.

Conversation subsided while the meals were consumed, but gradually it resumed to its former level as the amount of food on the plates decreased. Another round of drinks also helped.

Replete and happier than she had been for most of this week, Tara's anxiety began to fade. Everything would work out, she was convinced of it. So what if her ex-boyfriend ran the place – she didn't have to have anything to do with him, did she? And if there was any contact between them, it would be to do with the studio. As long as she paid her rent on time, he didn't need to bother her. She could handle it. The shock at seeing him again, had been just that: shock. And maybe some left over emotion caused by how badly he'd treated her and how broken her heart had been.

But it wasn't broken now. She'd put herself back together by losing herself in her newfound love of doll's houses and everything associated with them. Tara was determined that what had happened a decade ago would have no bearing on the present. She was an adult, a different person from the naïve girl she had once been.

But the naïve girl was still there, Tara abruptly discovered, when a casual glance at the bar revealed a familiar face that made her heart stop and her mouth go dry.

She swallowed and looked away, paying her empty plate far more attention than it deserved.

'Are you all right?' Jinny asked.

'Pardon?'

'You were frowning. Was everything OK with your meal, because if it wasn't you should have said. They're very good here, they would have sorted it for you.'

'No, it was delicious. I just remembered something I have to do,' she lied, as her skin tingled. A sixth sense told her Cal was close.

He was so close that he was standing at her elbow, and she imagined she could feel the heat of his skin and smell the aftershave he wore, as memory and reality swirled together.

'Can I buy anyone a drink?' he asked, and his voice sent a shiver right through her.

There were murmurs of assent and 'Ta, hen,' or 'Nice one, Cal,' but Tara couldn't bring herself to speak.

Fergus got to his feet. 'You'll need a hand to carry that lot back.'

Cal spoke to her directly when she failed to say anything. 'Tara? Can I get you another drink?'

'No. Thanks. I'm fine.' Her voice was wooden, stilted.

'She won't admit it, but I think something was wrong with her meal,' Jinny said.

'My meal was fine,' Tara insisted. 'Lovely, in fact. I'm tired, that's all. It's been a long week.'

'Yes, it has,' Cal agreed, and she had the feeling the comment was aimed at her.

Maybe he was finding this as awkward as she? For the first time since she'd seen him in her studio, she wondered how he felt about her being here. Guilty, maybe? She hoped so. Ashamed? So he should be. He'd behaved like a complete shit.

When he walked away, Tara breathed out slowly. Could she make her excuses and leave now? She'd already laid the groundwork by saying she was tired. Then she remembered her resolution not to avoid him, but to get used to his presence so that she didn't act like a schoolgirl with a crush whenever she bumped into him.

No, that was the wrong analogy. A crush presumed she still had feelings for him, which couldn't be further from the truth. So she stayed put, her own personal endurance test of how long she could stand to be in his company before she did a runner.

Hopefully he would deliver the drinks to their table and bugger off.

However, Cal did no such thing. After distributing the fresh drinks, he took a chair from a nearby table and pulled it up to theirs, wedging himself between her and Jinny.

Tara shuffled her chair away as unobtrusively as she could.

'I know you said you didn't want a drink,' Cal told her, 'but I got you one anyway. Is vodka and cranberry juice OK?'

It used to be her favourite tipple and she was surprised he remembered. Her mouth dry, she took it from him and gulped at it.

'Thanks,' she muttered belatedly, then forced her lips into a semblance of a smile as she realised that both Cal and Jinny were staring at her.

'Are you sure you're all right?' Jinny's expression was concerned.

She finished her drink. 'I think I'll get off – my bed is calling.'

Out of the corner of her eye she saw Cal stiffen, and she could have slapped herself for mentioning the word 'bed'. They had spent a lot of time in bed, and the last thing she wanted was to remind him of that. Hell, she didn't want to remind *herself* of that. Now that she had, she was thoroughly disconcerted.

He got to his feet. 'I'll walk back with you.' His beer was untouched.

'No, no need. You stay and finish your pint. It isn't dark, so I'll be fine,' she gabbled.

'I was about to head off anyway. Early start in the morning. Fishing.' He shoved his hands in his pockets.

Tara glanced at his pint. 'Stay. I'll be fine walking back on my own.'

'I wanted to speak with you, actually.'

'Oh.' Left with little choice and feeling as though she'd been backed into a corner, Tara said goodbye to the others, studiously ignoring Calan.

Fergus said, 'I'll have that,' and moved Cal's pint closer. 'Shame to waste it.' He didn't seem in the least bit bothered by her or Cal's departure.

Jinny, however, had a speculative look in her eye.

Tara turned away from the table. 'Come on then, if you're coming.' She headed towards the door, not checking whether Calan was following. But as she stepped into the twilight, she was conscious of his nearness, and she lost her patience. 'What did you want to talk to me about? How you broke my heart?' And there she goes, sounding like bloody Rod Stewart.

'About commissioning a doll's house, actually.'

Dear God. Tara briefly closed her eyes, hoping he would have disappeared when she opened them again. No such luck. He was still there, gazing at her intently. The sight of him infuriated her. 'Why don't you go boil your head!' she snapped.

His blink of surprise gave her momentary satisfaction, until she realised how childish she sounded. What on earth had possessed her? *Professional, eh, Tara?* Good grief!

She marched off up the road, her movements stiff and jerky, her jaw clenched shut lest she said anything equally as stupid.

Cal quickly caught up with her. His voice was soft as he said, 'I'm sorry, I didn't mean to.'

'Whatever.'

'I thought I was doing the right thing.'

'*What?!* How can shagging me while you had a girl-friend back home be the right thing?'

'I wasn't! I didn't have a girlfriend.' He sounded shocked.

'Fiancée, then.'

'I didn't have one of those, either.'

'It sure didn't take you long to find one after you dumped me.'

They were at the edge of the village, the road ahead devoid of people, cars or buildings, and Cal grabbed her arm, bringing her to a halt.

'It wasn't like that. It was a mistake.'

Tara was incredulous. 'You got married by *mistake*?' She glared pointedly at his hand. His touch sent her heart rate skyrocketing.

His expression was apologetic as he let go of her arm, saying, 'Not the getting married part, although that was definitely a mistake. Yvaine, my wife – ex-wife – I never should have… She was a rebound date.'

'*Rebound?* What the hell were *you* rebounding from? *You* dumped *me*, remember?'

'For all the right reasons.'

Tara put her hands on her hips. Anger flared in her chest, quelling the rush of remembered desire she'd felt when he'd touched her. 'Which were?'

He looked away, staring over her shoulder and shrugged. 'We were very young, I'd just got a job in the middle of nowhere, you had your degree to finish…' He sounded as though he was ticking them off against a check list.

'I didn't finish it.' She dropped her hands, clasping them together in front of her, the anger dissipating, replaced by heavy regret and the sadness she'd carried with her for the last ten years. She'd thought she'd buried it nice and deep, but it had bubbled to the surface like spring water through rock.

'Why not?' She could tell he didn't want to ask the question but felt compelled to ask it anyway.

'Because of you.'

His exhaled breath was long and slow. 'Oh, Tara.'

'Yeah, *Oh, Tara.*' She was thankful for the scorn in her voice, because it was better than the hurt that might otherwise have been there. Reining in her emotions, she pretended indifference as she said, 'It doesn't matter. It's water under the bridge.'

'But you loved your course.' The sympathy in his eyes was unbearable.

'I did, but I love making doll's houses more.' It was the truth.

'You're good at it, too.'

'Thanks.' Her reply was sarcastic. She neither needed nor wanted his praise. What she wanted was for him to sod off.

He said, 'That's what I wanted to speak to you about. I'm sorry, I should have waited and come to the studio. This is your downtime.' He grimaced. 'I'm like one of those people who bump into their GP in the pub and want to talk to them about their piles.'

'Do you have piles?'

His lips twitched. 'No, I do not.'

'Shame.' Tara began walking again and Calan fell into step beside her. She said, 'I take it that the doll's house is for your daughter?'

'Yes. Yvaine and Bonnie are going to live with Yvaine's boyfriend, and she's putting the house on the market. Bonnie was really upset, which was why she wasn't in school on Monday. Bonnie thought that if she had a scale model, it might help her with the transition, make her miss it less. That's why she wanted to do a workshop, but I want to commission one instead.'

'It'll cost.' Tara didn't want the commission. She didn't want to spend any more time with Cal than necessary.

'How about you give me a quote and we take it from there?'

We? They hadn't been a 'we' for a very long time. 'I'll need measurements and photos. The cost depends on what you want. A shell is considerably less expensive than a fully furnished house with accurate details.'

'I see. Can you quote me for both?'

'I'll need loads of photos – every part of every room.'

'OK. I'll get them to you. How is the coffin coming along?'

She didn't want to make small talk, but he clearly did, and considering she had to work with the man she decided to play nice. Or as nice as she could manage. 'You heard that?'

He chuckled. 'You've got to admit it was funny.'

'It wasn't at the time. I honestly thought she wanted me to measure a corpse. I've never been asked to make a funeral parlour before.' Tara could see the boathouse in the deepening gloaming. Her relief was profound. 'This is me,' she said unnecessarily. 'Good night.'

She didn't wait for a reply, anxious to put some space between them, but she was aware of him watching her as she walked down the track.

She didn't look back as she unlocked the door and slipped through it, but as soon as she was inside, she hurried into the bedroom and peered through the window.

Calan had gone.

Moments later she saw a light come on in his cottage, and she let out a sigh. That had been both as bad as she'd feared, and easier. The fool she had made of herself was counterbalanced by the ice having been broken. She'd proved to herself that she could be civil, friendly even. It was the best she could expect, for the moment. Each time she saw him from now on, it should get easier. She wouldn't try to run away a second time.

Too strung up to even think about going to bed, Tara poured a glass of milk, picked up the novel she'd been reading and curled up on the sofa nearest the picture window.

As she watched the last of the silver light fade from the sky, the novel lying forgotten next to her, Tara lost herself in the memory of her first – and possibly her only – love.

Chapter 10

How to make an eejit of yourself in one easy lesson, Cal thought, disgusted with himself as he watched Tara flee to the boathouse.

He didn't blame her for scurrying off. In her eyes, he was a total bawbag, a ratbag, an utter shite. Even if she'd been too polite to say it outright, her dislike of him radiated off her like heat from a stove.

Until today he hadn't realised quite how badly he had hurt her. Yes, he knew she would have been upset, but he'd been certain she would soon get over it – that she would quickly find another boyfriend amongst the thousands on campus, someone else to cuddle up with on a dreary Sunday morning, someone else to shower with kisses, someone else's ear in which to whisper, 'I love you'. After all, she'd been so young and first love never lasts. They had existed in an artificial bubble of lectures and assignments, evenings at the student union, days spent being passionate about politics and good causes, and nights spent being passionate between the sheets. But bubbles don't last forever, and theirs had burst at the end of the academic year when he'd returned to Inverness, leaving her behind in Glasgow.

Whenever he'd thought about her since, he imagined her still there. It didn't occur to him that she would have left.

Edinburgh, Mhairi had said. Cal had confirmed it by reading the email that Tara had sent when she'd expressed an interest in renting the studio. He'd even looked up her address, feeling grubby as he street-viewed her house. It was a nice house, in a nice area.

He hadn't been able to imagine her living there. And he certainly hadn't been able to visualise the man she had lived there *with*, the man she was in the middle of divorcing.

After watching Tara hurry inside, he hurried off himself to the sanctuary of his cottage. What must the others in the pub have made of his strange behaviour? He hoped they'd thought he was being chivalrous in walking Tara home, but Jinny had had an odd look on her face, and he suspected she guessed there was more to it.

Was the gift shop manager aware that he and Tara had history? He didn't think so, but Coorie Castle was a small place and the news would leak out at some point. He'd already decided not to hide the fact that he knew Tara – as demonstrated by him telling Mhairi – but he wasn't about to blurt it out to all and sundry. If it came up in conversation, or the time seemed right to mention it, then he would.

How would Tara feel about that? Did she want to keep it quiet? Should he ask her, or would that be making a meal out of it?

Gah! Cal raked his fingers through his hair. Why had his life suddenly become that much more complicated? What with Tara turning up and Yvaine taking Bonnie to live in Portree…

A groan escaped him. Why had he insisted on speaking to Tara, especially since he hadn't had anything lined up to say to her? Telling her that he wanted to enquire about a commission had been the first and only thing that had sprung to mind. And now he was stuck with trying to get measurements and photos of the inside of his ex-wife's house.

It briefly occurred to him that he could simply tell Yvaine what he was planning, but knowing how defensive she was about this move and realising his reaction had been less than supportive, he had a feeling she might veto the idea. Yvaine might even believe that giving Bonnie a miniature version of the house they no longer lived in was a step in the wrong direction, encouraging her to look back and not forward. It was a catch-22 situation. He couldn't ask Yvaine for help, but neither could he get what was needed any other way.

Cal decided not to mention it again. If Tara brought the subject up, he would make an excuse. He had no idea what the excuse would be, but he was sure he'd think of something.

He got undressed in the dark, but before he slipped under the covers, he fetched a glass of water from the kitchen and noticed a soft light coming from the boat-house's bedroom window.

It was enough to keep him awake long after he should have fallen asleep.

Cal wasn't often completely off duty (the two weeks spent with Bonnie at his parents' house had been a rarity), but this morning he decided to leave his mobile at home. Until he'd made the excuse in the pub last night that he wanted to leave because he had an early start this morning, Cal hadn't had any intention of going fishing.

As he'd lain awake watching the hours tick by, he still hadn't had any intention of going out in the boat. But after finally drifting off, he'd woken up with a jolt to the unmistakable bugle calls of whooper swans overhead. Or maybe he'd dreamt it, because it would be unusual to find any here at this time of year. Most should be in their summer breeding grounds in Iceland, although a few birds had been known to nest in Scotland.

Wide awake and with little possibility of going back to sleep, he decided he might as well go fishing after all. He hadn't been out on the loch for a while and some time on the open water would do him good.

It was close to high tide, making the skiff easier to push into the water, so he grabbed his rod and bag of tackle from the lean-to out the back, and set off down the narrow track through the trees that led to the loch.

He wasn't the only one awake at four thirty in the morning – the birds were too, and their song accompanied him to the small crescent beach. A flock of gulls, startled by his presence, launched into the sky, their flapping wings sounding like a round of applause, their alarm calls filling the air.

Cal shot a quick look at the boathouse only a short distance away, and hoped the commotion hadn't woken Tara. He couldn't see any movement, so he assumed she must still be asleep.

A vision of her dark hair spread across a pillow forced itself into his mind, and a jolt went through him. How many times had he seen her like that? Too many to count. And yet, not enough.

Cal gave himself a mental shake. The past was the past. Regret was pointless. He could no more reverse it than he could hold back the tide.

Inhaling deeply, he let the salt air fill his lungs, the smell of brine and seaweed both comforting and invigorating.

Despite his lack of sleep, he felt more alive than he'd done for a while.

The surface of the loch was flat, a sheet of satin stretching to the opposite shore, the water a cerulean blue. Colours seemed more vivid this morning. The green of the grass near the shoreline would put an emerald ring to shame, and the damp rocks at the edge of the small shingle beach had an obsidian sheen where they weren't hidden by strands of seaweed.

Cal placed his rod and tackle bag in the skiff, then checked the oars. Although *Misty Lady* had an outboard motor, the damned thing was temperamental and had a tendency to cut out. Whenever that happened, he rowed back, hauled the boat out of the water and gave it a squirt of WD40 which normally got it going again. He really should get it seen to, but he never seemed to find the time.

The skiff entered the water with a splash, sending little wavelets over his wellies, but before the boots filled with water, he jumped in. Settling his backside on the seat nearest the bow, he inserted the oars into the locks and made sure they were secure, then he lowered the blades into the water and began to pull, quickly finding his rhythm.

The repetitive movement was soothing, and soon the boat was in the middle of the loch. His destination was a lump of rock near the far side, where he knew pollack could often be found. He would have to take care though. Despite the skiff being a shallow-bottomed boat and not drawing much water under its keel, many rocks lay just below the surface and could prove dangerous if he didn't keep his wits about him.

For most of the short trip he'd been facing the way he'd come, and it was only when he stowed the oars and moved to sit at the stern so he could start the motor, did he realise that his gaze had been on the old boathouse and his mind had been on the woman who was living there.

He couldn't think about her now, though. He needed to focus on navigating around the rocks, so with one hand on the tiller, he eased the skiff into what he hoped was a good position, then cut the engine.

The sudden cessation of noise made his ears ring, then gradually other sounds made themselves known – the gentle lap of the water against the hull and the rocks, the raucous call of a rook overhead, and the almost pig-like grunt of a cormorant, wings outstretched and beak lifted to the sky as it dried itself in the early morning sun.

A splash had him glancing around to find the sleek, speckled head of a common seal gazing at him, its dark, liquid eyes filled with curiosity. As he watched, it slowly slipped beneath the surface.

Moments like this filled his soul with joy, and he wished Bonnie was here to see it. She adored seals, and otters, although it was rare to spot one of those.

Yvaine wasn't keen on Cal taking Bonnie out in the boat though, so he didn't do it often. Despite Yvaine growing up on Skye and having all its amazing natural wonders on her doorstep, his ex-wife had never been an outdoorsy person. Ironic, considering that when he'd met her his job on a large estate north of Inverness meant he was outdoors most of the time. And even when he hadn't been at work, he'd loved being outside – hiking, kayaking, watching wildlife. He should have realised then that he and Yvaine were never going to work.

But by the time he did, it was far, far too late.

He'd tried his darndest to make it work, though. He'd had to, for the baby's sake.

Another splash caught his attention, this time a fish jumping, and aware of the time, he quickly set up his rod and attached the lure.

Cal spent the next hour happily dropping the line over the side of the boat then reeling it in at a steady rate. He performed this same action over and over until it was time to go back.

Three fish later (two pollack and one coalfish, all of whom he released back into the sea unharmed), he was done.

Feeling satisfied, he powered up the motor and puttered across the loch. He could have rowed back, but it was easier to use the outboard.

It also meant he was able to see the old boathouse directly ahead – but that hadn't been a factor at all.

–

Early morning found Tara on the sofa, her feet tucked under her and a soft, cosy throw across her knees. Her book lay open on her lap, cover side up. After spending most of the short night tossing and turning, she'd eventually given up trying to sleep and had made some tea.

The drink had long since been consumed, and the mug sat on the side table next to her as she stared out of the window.

She had been gazing out of it for quite some time, ever since movement on the little beach had caught her attention. She'd stiffened and shrunk back a little, even though she was fairly sure Cal couldn't see her. But he *was* looking, so she'd inched back even further.

A flock of birds flew noisily into the air, briefly obscuring her view of him, and when she could see him clearly again, he was no longer looking in the direction of the boathouse but was gazing out over the loch.

Free to study him without him being aware of her scrutiny, she drank in the sight.

The sun had just risen over the top of the mountains, highlighting the auburn of his hair, and casting a long shadow that reached to the water's edge. Cal had filled out over the years. With broad shoulders and muscled legs, he was chunkier than she remembered, and she was fascinated by the bunch and flex of his body as he put his weight into pushing the small brown boat into the water.

When she'd first seen it, she'd assumed it to be a wreck, abandoned on the beach to slowly rot, and as Calan waded into the water and jumped into it, she hoped it was seaworthy.

He appeared to think it was, because he picked up a pair of oars and rowed the little boat to the other side of the loch. And as he rowed, he stared so intently at the boathouse that she was convinced he could see her.

She continued to watch, even when the distance between them grew too great to make out his face and his boat was little more than a dark shadow on the water.

Tara didn't stop watching until Cal eventually returned to the sliver of shingle, dragged the boat out of the water, and disappeared into the path between the trees.

Only when she was certain he was gone did she move, and even then, she was careful to make sure he wasn't in the shadows of the trees before ending her vigil. The last thing she wanted was for him to guess she had been spying on him, because he might wonder why.

Chapter 11

'You look tired, my dear,' was Mhairi Gray's opening gambit as she entered Tara's studio four days later.

Tara was standing by the window, debating whether to change the display. If she did, she'd be doing it more for herself than anyone else, because the visitors to the centre were primarily tourists so they would visit once, then move on to the many other attractions that Skye had to offer.

'Are you not sleeping?' Mhairi asked.

'Had a bit of a restless night,' Tara admitted. Every night seemed to be restless lately.

'You have my sympathies. I don't sleep well myself, but that's because I'm old. What's your excuse?'

'I, er, don't know.'

'I thought I'd pop along and see how you are settling in.' Mhairi's eyes darted everywhere. 'And I wanted to have a proper look at your lovely doll's houses.' Her gaze came to rest on a selection of photographs pinned to the corkboard. 'Oh my, that looks remarkably like the inside of a funeral parlour.'

'It is.'

'You're not going to…?'

'I am, although I'm not sure I want to make all the little details.'

'Gosh. Is that something you do on a regular basis?' The old lady looked faintly alarmed.

Tara didn't blame her – she was faintly alarmed herself. 'It's a first for me,' she said, 'and if I'm honest, I hope it's the last. It has given me the idea of producing some Halloween miniatures, though. Just a few, to see how they go.'

'I know you said that all your sales are online, but I've noticed you are selling through the gift shop.'

Tara brightened. 'I am. I didn't think I'd do much – I mean, how many people come on holiday and go home with a doll's house? But the smaller items appear to be going quite well.'

'I knew they would, dear. They would sell even better if you gave them a Scottish twist. Tartan cushions and curtains, maybe? A tartan throw? Teeny weeny bottles of whisky?'

'That's genius! Why didn't I think of that?' Suddenly Tara was all fired up. 'How about I make a crofter's house to put centre stage in the gift shop? It'll be a display piece only, but it would give people a taste of Highland living.'

Mhairi gave her a satisfied smile. 'That sounds lovely. I'll look forward to seeing it when it's done.' She patted Tara on the arm. 'I won't keep you any longer, but you know where I am if you need me.' As she turned to the door she hesitated. 'By the way, I can't remember if I showed you around the castle?'

'No, you didn't, but I'd love to have a tour.'

'I'll ask Avril to arrange it. Seeing photos on the website isn't the same as seeing it in person.'

Tara wholeheartedly agreed. She often wished she could view the houses she'd been asked to commission, but it wasn't always possible due to the distances involved.

Tara accepted commissions from all over the UK, and from abroad once, so it wasn't feasible to take a look in person at the buildings she had been asked to model.

She glanced at the corkboard, feeling thankful in this instance. She had no desire to have a guided tour of a funeral home. Seeing it in miniature was bad enough.

Deciding to stop faffing about and leave the perfectly fine window display as it was, Tara perched on her stool and opened her laptop. It was time to work out exactly how the funeral parlour was going to fit together.

Eating lunch in the cafe was becoming a habit – an expensive and waistline thickening habit – but the food was so good there that Tara was finding it difficult to resist. Not only that, going to the cafe meant she was forced to take a break and stretch her legs, even if the walk was short. And there was the added attraction of having a chat with Gillian, if she wasn't too busy.

Today wasn't one of the 'not too busy' days. There was quite a queue waiting to be served, and all the tables inside were taken. After Tara finally gave her order over the counter, she wandered outside to sit on one of the picnic benches and enjoy the sun and the view of the loch.

It was four days since she'd watched Calan row to the other side of it, and she hadn't seen him since, making her wonder whether he was deliberately avoiding her. She wished he wouldn't. Expecting to bump into him at any moment was proving to be worse than actually bumping into him. So much for her theory that she'd get used to seeing him around.

A shadow fell over her and she jumped, expecting it to be Cal, but she calmed when she realised it was Jinny.

'Do you mind if I join you? I had to get out of the shop for a bit. Honestly, some people can be so rude! I've just had a woman ask if "this lot" is made in China. Doesn't she know what craft centre means? Even if she didn't, you would think she would have noticed all the crafters hard at work making stuff.' Jinny blew her fringe out of her eyes. 'Sorry, I just needed to vent. Sometimes people are just too peopley.'

'Peopley?'

'It's a word.'

'A made-up one?'

'It might be.'

'I've got the opposite problem – not enough people-ing.'

Jinny gave her a sympathetic smile. 'It can't be easy moving into a new area. Avril tells me you're from Edinburgh. Is that where your family are?'

'I'm originally from Glasgow but moved to Edinburgh when I got married.' Tara noticed Jenny looking at her left hand. 'We've just got divorced.' The decree absolute had come through this week.

'I'm sorry, hen. I didn't mean to pry.'

'You're not, it's fine.'

'Is that why you moved to Skye?'

'Partly for a fresh start, and all that, and because properties are cheaper here. But the main reason was that as soon as I saw the craft centre, I fell in love with it. I've always worked out of my attic, so having my very own studio is a dream come true. The castle is lovely too, and everyone is so friendly.'

'You didn't want to go back to Glasgow? Ah, here's your lunch and my coffee.'

Tara waited until she'd eaten her first mouthful before replying. 'There's nothing there for me now. My mum and stepdad moved to the Isle of Wight about five years ago – they run a caravan park – and I've drifted away from my friends.' Tara wiped her mouth with a serviette. 'Crumbs, that makes me sound sad and lonely, when I'm not.'

OK, she was *a bit* lonely, but looking back, she'd actually been lonelier when she and Dougie had still been living together. He'd worked long hours (yeah, right!), and Tara had been ensconced in her attic room like bloody Rapunzel, not seeing a soul from dusk 'til dawn, unless she had a delivery or orders to post. Being in Duncoorie and having loads of people around was a real treat. And if it became too much, she had the solitude of the boathouse to retreat to until her social battery recharged.

'Come to tea this evening,' Jinny suggested, and Tara immediately felt awful. She didn't want her to think she was so pitiful that she needed to be invited to tea.

Flustered, she gabbled, 'No, that's fine, honestly. No need to… I've got stuff to be getting on with, and there's a chicken breast that has to be used up.' Oh, dear. As the words poured out of her mouth she knew she was making it worse.

'It's nothing fancy,' Jinny continued, as though Tara hadn't spoken. 'Just pasta, sauce and garlic bread. The kids would love to meet you. Well, Katie would – I've told her all about your doll's houses – but I'm afraid Ted isn't as keen. Dolls and little houses aren't his thing. My husband, Carter, won't be in this evening, so I need a buffer between me and the kids and you're it.'

'Katie is nine, you said?' The same age as Bonnie, Tara recalled.

'That's right, and Ted is six.'

Tara would have liked to have had children, just not with Dougie. Even on her wedding day, the thought of having a baby with Dougie didn't even enter her head. What did that say about their relationship? About *her*?

An image of Calan's russet-haired daughter sprang into her mind. If she and Cal had made a baby, would their child have looked like Bonnie?

Flippin heck! What was she thinking? Her head was in the shed these days and she blamed it on the upheaval of this past month or so. No wonder she wasn't thinking straight.

Jinny picked up her cup and drained it. 'See you at five thirty. My place is the third on the left after the post office. You can't miss it.'

And with that she was gone, leaving Tara to finish her lunch.

—

Calan was walking towards the castle from the direction of the maze, when he decided to take a gander at the rear of the craft complex. One side of it faced the loch and got most of the weather, especially when a storm blew in from the sea, so he wanted to have a quick scan of the roof to check for loose slates. He highly doubted any had come loose since the last time he'd checked, but there was a cold front moving in overnight bringing rain and squally wind, breaking the run of nice weather Skye had enjoyed these past few weeks.

Although the dry, sunny weather was brilliant for tourism, Cal loved the wild stuff. In his opinion, little could beat a walk along the shoreline when it was howling a gale, or being tucked up snug and cosy in front of a roaring fire when it was lashing it down outside.

He'd just rounded the corner and was thinking with satisfaction that the cafe looked busy, when he spied Tara sitting at an outside table. She was side-on to him and staring across the loch, her chin resting on her hand.

He halted abruptly, then turned on his heel and went back the way he'd come.

'Forgotten something?' the castle's head gardener, Paul, called as Cal hurried past.

Cal didn't answer, giving the man a vague smile and a wave instead, feeling ridiculous. This couldn't go on. He tried to foster a reputation of being friendly and approachable, someone they could come to if they had a problem or wanted advice or a helping hand. He didn't so much regard himself as their boss, but more as a friend and a colleague. After all, they were in this together and they all wanted the castle and the craft centre to succeed. Mhairi kept insisting that they were one big, happy family and she was right. But if he kept avoiding Tara or not being himself around her, sooner or later someone would notice and the gossip would start. It occurred to him that Jinny already had, remembering her speculative expression at the pub the other evening. Maybe it would be better not to hide the fact that he and Tara had once had a relationship, but mention it casually so it didn't seem like a big deal. And he knew exactly who to mention it to.

'Looking good, as always,' he said, when he entered the gift shop, his eyes roving over the racks and shelves.

'Me or the shop?' Jinny joked.

'You, of course,' he replied gallantly. Jinny was an attractive woman who always looked lovely.

'Thought so,' she smirked, before becoming serious. 'It is, isn't it.'

His attention settled on the doll's houses and the accompanying display. 'Tara's work fits in well. Have you seen her recently? She's not in her studio.'

'She was having lunch at the cafe just now.'

'I won't interrupt her then. No doubt I'll catch up with her later,' he said, making no move to leave. 'How do you think she's settling in?'

'OK, I guess. I get the feeling she's lonely. She doesn't know a soul here and—'

'She does,' Cal interrupted, seizing his chance. 'She knows *me*.'

Jinny tilted her head to the side. 'What do you mean?'

'We were at Glasgow uni together.'

Her eyes widened. 'Did you know her well?'

'We dated for a while.' He was doing his best to sound nonchalant, as though it hadn't meant anything.

'Tara didn't say.'

What Cal had hoped was a self-deprecating laugh, came out rather strained. 'She probably doesn't remember.'

'Bull poop! Of course she remembers.' Jinny pursed her lips. 'I thought I could sense a bit of tension between the two of you in the pub on Friday.' With a stern look in her eye, she said, 'What aren't you telling me, Calan?'

'I don't know what you mean.'

'You're hiding something.'

'How can I be hiding anything, when I've just told you that we dated?'

'Hmm,' she said, not sounding convinced. 'I still don't get why she hasn't said anything.'

'Maybe she's worried because I run this place.'

Jinny snorted. 'You *think* you do. Mhairi's hand is still firmly on the tiller.'

'True, but I'm second in command.'

Jinny snapped to attention and saluted. 'Aye, aye, sir!'

Shaking his head in mock despair, Cal said, 'One day someone around here will take me seriously.'

'Don't hold your breath,' she teased.

Cal decided it was time to go. He'd done what he'd come here to do. But as he left, he hoped he hadn't put the cat amongst the pigeons, as he doubted Tara would thank him. But surely it was better to rip the plaster off than peel it away slowly and more painfully? There was bound to be an initial flurry of excitement when people heard the news, but it would soon die down – especially if there was no more fuel to add to the gossipy fire.

–

Jinny lived in a whitewashed cottage set back off the road, with planters on either side of the central doorway in full bloom and a neat lawn with pretty flower beds.

Tara didn't have to knock. The door opened as she was halfway up the path.

Jinny looked frazzled. 'Come in, come in. Excuse the mess. I've not long picked the kids up from the child-minder's and I haven't had a chance to tidy up after this morning's chaos.'

Tara didn't think it looked messy at all and said so as she was ushered into the house, adding, 'It's lovely, so bright and welcoming.'

The sitting room was painted a pale duck egg blue, with windows front and back, letting light flood in from both ends. Two children, a boy and a girl, were sprawled on the floor, an upended tub of Lego between them.

'Kids, say hi to Tara. Tara, this is Katie and Ted. Katie, remember me telling you that Tara makes doll's houses?'

The boy uttered a brief 'Hello', his attention on the little plastic bricks, but Jinny's daughter got to her feet. 'Mum says they're proper doll's houses, not kids' ones.'

'She's right. If you're ever up at the craft centre, perhaps you might like to pop in and see them?'

'Can I, Mum?'

'I expect so. Now, put this lot away, wash your hands and come lay the table.'

Katie's open expression turned into a pout. 'Do I have to? It's not fair, just because I'm the oldest.'

'Ted is going to hang your school bags up and put your shoes away. He's also going to put his stinky PE kit in the laundry basket. Or he could lay the table if you prefer, and you can sort out his PE kit.'

'Gross!' Katie brushed past her mother in her haste to avoid stinky PE kit duty, and Jinny and Tara followed her into the open-plan kitchen-dining area.

This was also dual aspect, with views over the loch from the dining table, and views of the mountain behind through the kitchen window. A saucepan was bubbling away on the hob, and a pan of red sauce simmered next to it. The smell of onions and garlic made Tara's mouth water.

'Would you like a glass of wine?' Jinny asked. 'Please say you would. It'll give me an excuse to have one.'

Tara laughed. 'In that case, I will, thanks.'

Jinny pointed out where the glasses were kept, and soon Tara was perched on a stool with a drink in her hand.

'Did Cal catch up with you?' Jinny asked. She was stirring the pan of spaghetti, but glanced at Tara as she asked the question.

Tara stiffened. She couldn't help it, and hoped her new friend hadn't noticed. 'No, I haven't seen him today,' she replied, pleased that her voice sounded normal. 'I must have missed him.' She wondered what he had wanted.

'I didn't realise you two already knew each other. He told me you used to date when you were at uni.' Underneath the curiosity lay a modicum of rebuke.

Tara froze, then willed herself to relax. So what if people knew? It was bound to come out sooner or later.

'We did.' She shrugged to show that it wasn't a big deal. Guilt plucked at her, and she caught Jinny's eye and pulled a face. 'I'm surprised he remembered me. It was a long time ago.'

'That's strange; Cal said the same thing. You are a dark horse.' Jinny turned her attention back to the stove. 'Almost ready. Could you give the kids a shout for me?'

Tara was more than happy to if it meant putting an end to the conversation, and she was relieved when the subject wasn't mentioned again. Hopefully she'd managed to persuade Jinny that her and Cal's past relationship was no big deal. Tara could cope with people knowing they used to be an item. What she couldn't cope with was people knowing he'd broken her heart.

Tara was cradling her second glass of wine and watching Jinny stack the dishwasher after her offer of help was refused, when Katie sauntered into the kitchen in search of a biscuit.

'When can I see Tara's doll's houses, Mum?' she asked as she rooted in a cupboard.

'Soon,' Jinny replied vaguely.

Tara, wanting to repay her new friend's hospitality – and still feeling guilty for not telling her about her and Cal – said, 'I'm probably going to run something soon. Mhairi mentioned that the craft centre puts on loads of activities for children during the summer holidays, so how about I put Katie down for it? She can be first on the list.'

Tara wasn't sure what that activity would be yet. She'd have to look into what would be feasible. She also wanted to run an adult workshop. All the other crafters did, and visitors often stayed at the castle itself and attended more than one workshop during their stay.

If Tara thought she'd been busy *before* she moved to Skye, she was positively run off her feet now, and was inundated with fresh ideas and new projects that she was itching to get started on.

'Yay!' Katie cried. 'I'm going to paint a picture of what I want it to look like.'

Her mother said, 'Not this evening, you're not. Tell Ted he can stay up until eight. You don't need to go to bed until nine.'

Katie pouted and Jinny sent her away. 'Scoot. Go find something to do and let the grown-ups talk. Nothing messy, mind.' She turned to Tara and explained, 'I can't face cleaning up paint just before bedtime.'

Tara kept an eye on the time and made sure she left before eight o'clock and Ted's bedtime. As the evening was still quite young, she thought she might do some work when she got back. She always started a new project with a sketch or two, using coloured pencils, and she was looking forward to sitting on the sofa in front of the picture window with the late evening sun streaming through it.

As she stood on Jinny's doorstep, thanking her for her hospitality and promising to return the favour soon, Tara spied Bonnie getting out of a car and walking up next door's path.

'Is that where Bonnie lives?' she asked, her mouth suddenly dry.

'Yes, but not for much longer. Yvaine, Bonnie's mum, is moving in with her partner Lenn, who lives in Portree. I'm expecting to see a "For Sale" sign go up any day now. Oh, look, there she is. Hi, Yvaine.'

Jinny waved to a woman who had just emerged from the car, and Tara's breath caught in her throat.

Yvaine was even more beautiful in real life. With her tall, slender figure and spiky platinum hair, the photos hadn't done her justice.

A pang of jealousy stabbed Tara in the gut, and she felt sick.

No wonder Cal had dumped her. How could she ever have competed with that?

Chapter 12

Cal seriously didn't want to go knocking on Tara's door this morning, but Mhairi had informed him that Tara was expecting a tour of the castle and that he was the person who would be showing her around because Avril, who was supposed to be doing it, was busy. Cal couldn't help wondering what Avril was so busy with that she couldn't spare an hour, but he didn't bother to argue – what Mhairi wanted, Mhairi got. The woman was a Rottweiler, despite her granny-like appearance and genteel demeanour.

As he made his way to the boathouse, Cal felt apprehensive. Tara was expecting Avril, and he guessed she mightn't be pleased to find that he had been roped in as a substitute.

As he suspected, when Tara saw who was at her door, she didn't look thrilled.

'I know you were expecting Avril, but she's otherwise engaged,' Cal leapt in before Tara could say anything. 'Mhairi asked me to step in. Is that OK?'

She was glaring at him, so he assumed not.

When she said, 'I suppose Mhairi knows about us, too? I had a rather embarrassing conversation with Jinny yesterday,' he knew that she most definitely wasn't.

Cal thought it best to front it out, and he put a confused expression on his face as he said, 'Was it supposed to be a secret?'

'Well, no, but...' Tara faltered, then she appeared to rally. 'I wouldn't have thought you'd want it to be common knowledge, considering.'

'Considering what?'

'What you did.'

'We broke up. People break up all the time. It's hardly anything to be ashamed of.'

That seemed to take the wind out of Tara's sails. 'Shall we get on? I haven't got all day.'

'Are you sure you want to do this today? You could wait for Avril to be free.' Even as he said it, Cal had a feeling Avril was never going to be free. He had a suspicion Mhairi was forcing him and Tara together so they could learn to play nice and get along. He also had the feeling that he and Tara might regret it if they didn't. Mhairi didn't like being thwarted, and if she felt that her happy family of a workforce was threatened, he had no doubt she would lay down the law.

'Let's get it over with,' Tara sighed. She seemed resigned.

'It's not root canal, you know.' He was trying not to smile at the sight of the two little lines dissecting her brow and the disgruntled jut of her chin. How many times had he seen her wearing the same expression and it had always made him smile.

'It may as well be,' she muttered as she went back inside, leaving him to hover on the doorstep.

Whilst he waited for her to return, he hoped Tara would be able to put aside her obvious dislike of him. If she didn't, it was going to make working together difficult. Admittedly, he didn't need to have a great deal of contact with her day-to-day but, damn it, he didn't want to have to slink around trying to avoid her either. He had enough going on right now with Yvaine's move to Portree, without the added pressure that Tara's presence was causing.

Why did she have to come to Coorie Castle? Surely there were other places she could have gone.

But if she had, a voice in his head pointed out, *she wouldn't be walking towards you now, looking more beautiful than you've ever seen her look, and making your heart do somersaults.*

He'd been trying to ignore the nagging inner voice, because it kept trying to tell him that the love he'd once had for her hadn't disappeared. It was still there, and burying it underneath a decade of life hadn't made it go away.

The realisation was akin to being hit with a wrecking ball.

Cal was still in love with her.

There, he'd admitted it. He had never stopped loving her.

Now all he had to do was hide it from everyone, and especially from Tara herself, who hadn't forgiven him for the way he had treated her, who was obvious in her dislike of him, and who didn't want anything to do with him. But, most importantly, he had to hide it from his daughter. He'd promised her he wouldn't have a girlfriend, and although the promise was easy to keep, Cal didn't want Bonnie to suspect he had feelings for anyone. It would be too unsettling for her, especially with the forthcoming move.

Cal said very little on the short walk to the castle and Tara seemed equally happy to remain silent. But once inside the impressive grand entrance, he had no choice.

'Coorie Castle dates from 1278 and possibly even before that,' he began. 'The first structure was built on the site of an earlier fortress. It was originally a series of four interconnected towers, encircled by a huge wall.' As he spoke, he wasn't concentrating on what he was saying, the words flowing effortlessly as he knew the castle's history by heart. His attention was on the woman by his side as he guided her through room after room.

After thoroughly exploring the ground floor, he led her up the sweeping staircase. Portraits hung on the walls, the people in them staring down with stern, forbidding expressions.

'Are all these Mhairi's ancestors?' she asked, pausing when she came to a painting of a gentleman with a particularly grim countenance.

'None of them are. Her grandfather bought the castle lock, stock and barrel in 1893 for a song, when Laird Meighan ran up huge gambling debts and was forced to sell the estate. Tandy Gray didn't do a lot with it, but his son, Mhairi's father, turned it around and made it profitable again. He was a wealthy shipping magnate and was able to throw money at it to restore the castle. However, by the time Mhairi inherited it, the money had all but dried up. Faced with handing it over to the National Trust or selling it, Mhairi used the last of the money to turn the sheds and outbuildings into a craft centre. The rest is history.' He paused by a door. 'Do you want to see one of the guest bedrooms?'

A hint of pink spread across her cheeks. 'Yes, please.'

'This one is unoccupied,' he said, taking an old-fashioned key out of his pocket. Unlocking the door, he pushed it open.

'It's lovely!' she exclaimed, as she entered the spacious room.

It had high ceilings and panelled walls painted a pale green, with light flooding in from the large window, and a view of the loch beyond. But it was the four-poster bed that caught Tara's eye, Cal noticed.

'Wow, fancy spending the night in this!' she cried, running a hand down one of the green and gold drapes which were tied to each post.

The image that leapt into his mind made his heart skip a beat, but thinking about Tara naked on the bed wasn't going to do either of them any favours, least of all him.

'Are all the bedrooms as lovely as this one?' she asked.

'Yes, they're all much of a muchness.'

'How can you be so blasé? Or are you so used to it, that you don't see it anymore?'

'I'm not used to it at all,' he said. 'I live in a humble cottage, remember?'

'Yet you are surrounded by this every day. If I were you, I wouldn't be able to stop admiring it. The castle is simply gorgeous.'

It was, but it wasn't as gorgeous as Tara. Her face shone and her eyes were alight with wonder. It was a far cry from the expression she usually wore whenever she saw him now.

She used to look at him with love and, once upon a time, it was the only thing he'd lived for...

Tara had taken several photos as she was being shown around the castle, and in the beginning he assumed she was doing what most visitors did, taking photos as a memento, but gradually it occurred to him that she was storing up material for future – or maybe even current – projects.

She confirmed his suspicion that her mind was on work when she asked, 'When are you going to get those photos and measurements to me?' It took him a second or two to realise she was talking about his request that she make a doll's house for Bonnie.

'I, um, I haven't managed to get around to it yet. There's a bit of a—' The ping of an incoming message interrupted him mid-sentence and he reached for his phone with relief. 'Excuse me, I'd better see who it is.'

It was Yvaine, and the message was short and to the point.

> FYI the house has gone on the market today. Bonnie knows.

Great, that's all he needed right now.

How is she? he replied.

> Not pleased. She'll get over it.

Yes, she would, Cal thought, but wouldn't it be better for their daughter not to have to 'get over it' in the first place? Sometimes he didn't understand Yvaine. He knew she loved their daughter more than anything, but now and again she came across as dismissive of Bonnie's feelings. Or did she take his concern as being judgemental of her parenting skills? She always had a tendency to go on the defensive.

'Bad news?' Tara was studying him.

'Put it this way, it's not the news I was hoping for.'

128

Properties in Duncoorie didn't come on the market often, and when they did they were quickly snapped up. He didn't anticipate Yvaine's house lingering for long. It was a pity that Tara's house in Edinburgh hadn't been sold yet, because she might have been interested.

Or maybe not. It would be more than weird to have his first love live in the house that had once belonged to his ex-wife. Or it might be beyond Tara's budget, or she mightn't like it when she saw it.

Cal paused, an idea beginning to form. 'A house in Duncoorie has just come on the market. Would you be interested in taking a look?'

–

'I've not had a chance to put it on the website yet,' the estate agent said, as Tara walked up the drive to meet him. 'Mrs Fraser was delighted to have a viewing so soon. Shall we go inside?'

'Please.' Tara plastered a smile on her face, feeling awkward.

It was true that she intended to buy a property, and she was aware that houses didn't come up for sale in Duncoorie very often, but it felt surreal to enter the house belonging to Cal's ex-wife. She wasn't convinced she wanted to buy it for that very reason.

However, she was curious, and teamed with Calan's stilted and reluctant explanation that it would be a good idea for her to get the feel of the place and take some measurements and photos whilst she was there, because Yvaine would be too busy to take them herself, she'd agreed to arrange a viewing with the agent who was handling the sale.

'You have a property in Edinburgh, is that right?' the man asked.

'Yes. It's already on the market. I've relocated to the island and am looking for a permanent home here.'

He pushed open the front door and gestured for her to go inside. 'This is the hall,' he said, unnecessarily. 'As you can see, it's a bright and welcoming first impression, and it benefits from storage space under the stairs and a radiator.'

'I'm going to take some photos, if that's OK.' She didn't wait for his consent, taking out her phone and snapping away. She also had one of those laser measurement thingies, so she got that out too.

The agent gave her a suspicious look.

Tara had an explanation prepared. 'I've got some quite large pieces of furniture – family heirlooms – that need to be accommodated,' she said. 'I need to make sure they'll fit into whatever property I buy.'

The man didn't look impressed, but neither did he make a comment, and Tara guessed he'd heard it all before. However, she didn't want to explain why she was being so precise, in case he didn't think she was a serious buyer and asked her to leave. She *was* a serious buyer – she just didn't think she could be serious about buying this particular property, even though it was exactly what she was looking for.

Structurally, Yvaine's house was a replica of Jinny's next door, but that was where the similarity started and stopped.

Jinny's house was a home.

Yvaine's house was a photo in a lifestyle magazine. It was immaculate and incredibly stylish, but as far as Tara was concerned, it lacked soul. The decor was tasteful, in various shades of white, linen and biscuit, the cushions were plumped to within an inch of their lives, there wasn't one personal item on display, and even the books on the coffee table were arranged in an artful stack. The ornaments dotted around the room looked as though they had been chosen purely to dress the house for sale.

The kitchen was equally as devoid of heart, and the master bedroom and guest bedroom were just as sterile. The only room with any character was Bonnie's. It looked as though an explosion had taken place, with clothes and toys scattered everywhere. Tara wondered whether Yvaine hadn't got around to tidying her daughter's room, or whether she'd asked Bonnie to do it and Bonnie had ignored her.

The agent seemed a little put out at the state of the room. 'The vendor has a young child,' he explained, 'but I'm sure you can see beyond the personal items and realise that this is a generously proportioned room. One could easily fit a double bed in here, or two singles. Along with the third bedroom, the property is an ideal size for a family.'

'It will just be me, I'm afraid.'

The estate agent rallied quickly. 'Plenty of room for entertaining, and the smaller bedroom could be turned into a lovely office.'

'I think I've seen enough,' Tara said.

'Is the property of interest? Or maybe I could arrange to show you around one of the others on our books?'

'No thanks, this is perfect.'

He beamed at her. 'You've got my number if you'd like to make an offer. I suggest you be quick though, as I don't anticipate it being on the market for long.'

'Neither do I,' she replied honestly. It was a lovely house and Tara could imagine how much nicer it could be with the addition of some personal touches. She added, 'However, I intend to wait for an offer on my own property before I put an offer in on this one.'

His beaming smile lost some wattage. 'I see.' He ushered her outside. 'As I said, you've got my number. Please call if you have any questions.'

'I will. Thank you for showing me around.'

Tara lingered for a few minutes more, taking photos of the outside, and when she was done, she made her way back to the castle.

As she walked, she decided she needed to speak to Calan before going any further with this commission, because she had a feeling that the house she had photographed today was a far cry from the house Bonnie called home.

Chapter 13

Cal wasn't wearing a shirt. That was the first thing Tara noticed when she knocked on the door of his cottage later that day. It was the *only* thing she noticed for several agonising heartbeats, until she managed to pull herself together and stamp on the unexpected and unwelcome spike of desire that stole her breath and made her mute.

It was the fine russet hairs trailing down his stomach and heading south into his jeans that did it. She knew how soft those hairs were, and she knew exactly where they led.

Tara swallowed, forcing down her lust in the same way she forced down her multivitamin tablet every morning.

'Tara.' His voice was little more than an exhaled breath, a whisper of the wind across the loch. He cleared his throat. 'Hi, won't you come in? I was just getting changed.'

Her gaze was drawn to his chest again, then upwards to his face. Was that amusement she could see in his eyes?

Annoyed at being wrong-footed (if a man had stared at her chest the way she'd just stared at Cal's torso, she would have been tempted to deck him), she said, 'I won't stay. I just wanted to tell you that I've taken the photos, but I'm not sure they'll be of any use.'

'Why not?'

Tara stabbed at her phone's screen, her movements jerky. She turned it to face him, scrolling through the many images, before coming to a halt.

'I don't understand. Why can't you use them?'

'Your— Bonnie's mother has dressed it for sale. It's like a show house, apart from Bonnie's room. It's been totally de-personalised. Do you have any photos of what it looked like before? I mean, Bonnie is going to want her doll's house to be how she remembers it, not as it is now.'

The puzzlement on Cal's face disappeared as his expression hardened. 'This is *exactly* how Bonnie will remember it.'

Oh, dear… 'Ah. Well, in that case, I'll do a quick calculation and get back to you.'

'I bet her mother doesn't know her bedroom is in such a state. Yvaine won't be happy.'

Judging by the pristine condition of the rest of the house, Tara didn't think Yvaine would be happy either. The poor kid. Where were the photos, the keepsakes, the paintings on the fridge held in place by silly magnets? Where were the wellies by the door, the shelves full of books and board games, the pink glitter bubble bath that smelt of strawberries? Where was the *soul*?

Cal turned away from the door and retreated into the cottage, leaving Tara staring after him and wondering whether she should follow him inside or leave.

Curiosity is going to be the death of me, she thought, as she stepped over the threshold against her better judgement. But wanting to see where he lived, wanting to see more of *him*, outweighed the voice in her head warning her of the risks of playing with fire. Cal had burned her once. He could so easily burn her again if she was stupid enough to let him get too close.

The porch was crammed with boots, coats, tweed caps and walking sticks, and led into a small hallway with a twisty staircase directly in front and doors to either side. Her head snapped back and forth as she wondered which room he was in, realising he was upstairs when his feet appeared on the stairs, followed by the rest of him as he trotted down them tugging a T-shirt over his head.

With his chest now covered, Tara noticed that his feet were bare.

A memory of tickling those very same feet until he was breathless with laughter as she'd leant all her body weight on his legs to stop him squirming, flashed into her head and she felt like crying.

He looked surprised to see her, as though he'd forgotten she was there. 'Fancy a wee dram?' he asked.

'I haven't had my tea yet.' Whisky on an empty stomach was never a good idea.

'Salmon steaks, then?'

'Pardon?'

'I was about to cook myself a salmon steak. There's one going spare, if you fancy it.'

Tara was taken aback. Was Cal seriously offering to cook for her? 'Why are you trying to be nice to me?' she demanded. 'Do you feel guilty about stringing me along and then dumping me? I thought we had something, Cal.'

'I need that drink,' he muttered and stalked off.

Tara followed him into the lounge. She wanted answers and she was damned well going to get them – they were long overdue.

He poured amber liquid into a couple of crystal tumblers and handed one to her. The whisky was smooth and mellow, with a heat that failed to thaw the ice in her chest. She couldn't believe she was confronting him. But she'd asked the question and there was no walking it back.

'I didn't string you along.'

'What else do you call it?'

'Love. I *loved* you.'

She noticed the past tense. 'You couldn't have loved me that much. You married Yvaine less than a year after you broke up with me.' Her tone was scathing and bitter.

'She was pregnant.'

Tara needed a second to process what he'd just said, so she sipped her whisky, stalling for time, her thoughts a jumbled mess. Eventually she asked, 'Are you telling me you only married her because she was pregnant?'

His sigh came from deep within. 'That's exactly what I'm saying.'

'Did you love her?'

Cal took a mouthful of his drink. 'I cared for her, but I didn't love her.'

'Oh, Cal… Why did you marry her?'

'I wanted to be a good father. I wanted to be there for my child.'

'You didn't have to *marry* Yvaine to be a good dad.'

'You don't understand.' His tone implied that she couldn't understand because she didn't have kids, and she flinched. She didn't have kids because she hadn't wanted any with *Dougie*.

She wished she'd realised that before she'd married him. It would have saved them both a lot of heartache. It was safe to say that both she and Cal had made mistakes.

'I wanted to be there for my son or daughter all day every day, not just every other weekend, or when Yvaine needed a babysitter.' He shook his head sadly. 'But that's exactly what I've ended up becoming.' The look he gave her made her want to weep for him.

The man was hurting. Whether he'd loved Yvaine or not when they'd got married wasn't the point now. His love for his daughter was.

'I would like to say I'm sorry that I broke up with you,' Cal continued, 'but I'd be lying. Because if we hadn't split up. I wouldn't have Bonnie.' He smiled, a sad little upturn at the sides of his mouth. 'I am sorry I hurt you, though.'

Tara perched her backside on the arm of a battered leather chair, her legs unsteady. 'I know you said we were too young, that long-distance relationships never work out, blah-di-blah, but if you loved me as much as you claim to, I don't understand how you managed to move on so soon.' It had taken Tara years to move on – if she ever had.

'I was trying to forget you.'

'Right there, see, that's the difference between you and me. I didn't want to forget *you*.'

His sigh drifted around the room. 'We can't do anything about the past. It's the future we need to think about now. I don't want any bad feeling between us, Tara.'

'There won't be.' She straightened, squaring her shoulders. 'We're adults, we can put it behind us.'

'Are you sure? Because when I spoke to you outside the pub—'

'It was the shock. I never expected to see you again, and when I did it brought everything back.'

His eyes searched her face, and it took an effort not to show how raw that heartbreak still was.

She must have hidden it well because he said, 'Salmon steak?'

'Go on then, it'll save me cooking.'

Seeing him in the kitchen, watching him dress the fish with garlic, lemon juice, chilli flakes and a teaspoon of honey, was bittersweet. She'd often watched him cook. He used to enjoy preparing food, and it seemed he still did.

'Oi, don't just stand there,' he instructed. 'There's a salad to prepare, and you can cut a couple of slices of that olive bread.' He pointed a spatula at a loaf-shaped paper bag next to a bowl of fruit. 'The salad stuff is in the fridge.'

As she washed, chopped and sliced, it was hard to believe that more than ten years had passed since the last time they'd made a meal together. It seemed like yesterday. And a lifetime ago.

Tara felt surreal, as though this was a dream and she would wake from it with his name on her lips and the ghostly feel of his body curled around hers. In the early days after the split, she'd woken from that same dream night after night, the brief moment of bliss shattered when she remembered he was no longer hers. That he had never truly been hers.

But it seemed he hadn't been Yvaine's either, despite what a marriage certificate said. And maybe Yvaine had sensed it. Or maybe Tara was reading too much into it, and she should get a grip.

'We'll eat on the deck,' Cal said, when he saw that the salad was done and the bread was cut.

The deck was a small wood-slatted area to the front of the cottage, the boards silvered by the elements. It housed a table, two chairs with bright cushions, and a lantern containing a stubby candle. After helping Cal carry their meal outside, Tara sat at the table and realised she could see the boathouse quite clearly from there. It shouldn't have been a surprise, considering she could see Cal's cottage from her bedroom window, but she nevertheless found it unsettling.

Movement caught her eye. A rope swing, not too high off the ground, swung idly as a breeze caught the branch above.

Cal followed the direction of her gaze. 'Bonnie loves that swing, but don't tell her mother. She reckons they're not safe.'

'Are they?'

'It's probably not as safe as a swing in a play area, but the excitement is in that little bit of danger.'

Tara felt he had described what she was doing right now. Cal was exciting and dangerous. However, the danger wasn't a scraped knee. It was a broken heart, but only if she let him get close again, if she dropped her guard a second time and let him in.

The salmon was delicious, the salad edible, and the bread reminiscent of her holiday to Corfu the summer before she'd met Cal. But she'd had to force the meal down, too tense to enjoy the food properly, too conscious of the man sitting at right angles to her with his knee almost touching hers.

'Cheese and biscuits? And a coffee?' he asked.

'Just coffee, please.'

He laughed. 'Thank goodness for that. I've just remembered that the only cheese I've got is the plastic slices that come in a plastic container, along with slices of plastic ham and those round salty crackers. The crackers are quite nice. Not too keen on the ham or the cheese, though.'

'Bonnie?'

'How did you guess? And those salmon steaks could easily have been fish fingers.'

'I quite like fish fingers.'

'In a sandwich,' he said. 'I remember.'

'Hey, I was a poor student. I couldn't afford salmon steaks.'

'That's because you preferred to spend your money on wine, not food.'

'True.'

'Do you remember that girl who used to work in the student union bar? The one who always won the yard of ale competition?'

'Gosh, yes. I'd forgotten about her. She must have spent a fortune on booze to get as good as that.'

'I saw her last year. She was visiting Skye with her wife and three kids. I didn't recognise her, but she recognised me.'

Tara wasn't surprised. Cal hadn't changed much. He was still a handsome guy.

Over coffee, they reminisced about the people they used to know, and Tara realised they were both being careful not to touch on anything that might bring their relationship to the fore. The conversation flowed easily, and a second cup of coffee was called for as the sun dipped below the mountains on the other side of the loch, the sky's palette painted in dove grey, with mauve ribbons of high cloud highlighting streaks of apricot and pink.

Tara tried not to think about how romantic this would be if the man she was experiencing this beauty with had been anyone other than Cal.

'I never tire of this,' he murmured, lifting his head to the sky. The sunset was reflected in his eyes, wonder on his face.

'It's stunningly beautiful,' she admitted, and she was suddenly glad to be sharing this breathtaking moment with someone.

The waters of the loch grew still and dark as the light faded from the sky, only the flame from the candle in the lantern keeping the night at bay. The air held its breath. Not a leaf stirred, not a wave lapped. The silence was so deep, she thought she could hear Cal's heart beating.

A fox's harsh bark broke it.

Tara said, 'I saw you on the loch the other day.' Her voice was low.

Cal turned to look at her, his eyes as dark and unfathomable as the water. 'You were up early.'

'Yes.'

'I was fishing.'

'I guessed as much. Did you catch anything?'

'Three, but I put them back.'

The ease of earlier was no longer there. This conversation was stilted and tense.

It was time to leave. Tara had enjoyed the evening – far too much, if she was honest. Best to go now, before it was ruined.

'Would you like to go out on the loch sometime?' His question took her by surprise. 'I could take you,' he added.

'Maybe.' She imagined the view from the other side, looking back at the boathouse and the castle. She imagined being alone with Cal in that boat, the muscles of his chest and arms rippling as he rowed. 'I'd like that.' She got to her feet. 'Thanks for a lovely evening.'

Cal also stood. 'You're welcome. Take care, Tara.'

For a moment, she thought he was about to kiss her, but then he shoved his hands into his pockets.

'Bye, Cal.'

She stepped off the deck and onto the path leading to the loch. It was just about light enough to enable her to pick her way along the shoreline to the boathouse. Only once did she look back. She couldn't see him, but the light from the candle flickered in the distance.

Was he still on the deck?

When she reached the boathouse, she turned to look again, but Cal's cottage was now in darkness.

It was a long time before Tara went to bed, and even longer before she fell asleep.

–

There was a lighter area in the sky above the village, the streetlights casting a glow into the heavens, but it was faint and not enough to drown out the myriad of stars overhead.

After Tara left, Cal blew out the candle and tracked her progress across the white sand to the boathouse. Only when he was satisfied she was home safe did he relax and sit back in his chair to enjoy the night and reflect.

He'd been shocked when he'd answered the door to find her standing there, as beautiful and as bewitching as ever, and had felt a jolt of longing so acute it had shaken him to his core. It had taken him a moment to understand that she wasn't here to see *him*, but to query whether he wanted her to go ahead with commissioning the doll's house for Bonnie, in light of the photos she'd taken earlier.

Until Tara had brought it to his attention, Cal hadn't considered how other people might view Yvaine's home. She'd always been intensely houseproud, wanting everything just so, and she used to study glossy magazines and follow various influencers online to try to emulate what she saw on their social media posts. On reflection, their home near Inverness had been just as sterile, but he hadn't noticed at the time.

He smirked as he thought of the photos Tara had shown him of Bonnie's bedroom. He would bet any amount of money that his daughter had waited until Yvaine was about to usher her out of the door for school to pretend she'd forgotten something so she could dash upstairs to trash her room. He wondered whether Bonnie had managed to tidy up the mess before her mother saw it, or whether she'd had a telling off. He hoped it was the former, both for his daughter's sake and because he derived childish satisfaction from someone getting one up on his ex-wife. He supposed he should be more mature, but he was finding it increasingly difficult to act like an adult since seeing Tara had catapulted him back a decade.

Chatting for hours about their uni days this evening hadn't helped, but he'd enjoyed it so much that for a while he'd felt like a student again, when he'd been young and in love.

Cal let his breath out in a huff. Thirty-three wasn't old, but he felt the weight of every one of those years. They pressed down on him, reminding him that he was a father, and he had responsibilities which went beyond himself and his own wants and desires. And that was why he should never have invited Tara to share his evening meal. He couldn't afford to let her slip into his heart again, not when she no longer thought of him that way.

Again? Ha! She'd never left it. And that was why he should keep his distance, and not suggest taking her out on the loch in his skiff. He wasn't sure what he'd been thinking, but whatever it was, he hadn't been using his head – he had been using his heart.

And that was a very dangerous thing to do.

Chapter 14

Tara rescued the piece of paper before the printer spat it onto the floor and examined it closely, turning it this way and that as she held it up to the light. The pattern had come out quite well she decided, as she compared it to the photo that had been emailed to her by the sister of the woman who owned the funeral parlour. With the construction of the building itself complete, Tara was now turning her attention to the part she liked the best, the interior decorating. She always began with the ceilings, then the walls and finally the floor covering, before installing any furniture, fixtures or fittings.

Today she was wallpapering. Using the photograph of the white and gold paper on the walls of the reception area, Tara had reproduced the image on the computer, shrunk it down, and printed it out. She was about to cut it to the right size when the studio door opened and Bonnie bounded in.

'What are you doing?' the girl asked.

'I'm in the middle of decorating this, um, house.' Tara wasn't sure what to call it.

'Can I watch?'

'Sure. Come through.'

Bonnie lifted up a section of the counter so the door underneath it opened and scurried through it. She came to stand by Tara's elbow.

'I've never seen a doll's house being decorated before,' she said. 'Can you really change it whenever you want, like a real house?'

Tara remembered telling her the same thing the first time they'd met. 'Yes, you can. Many people buy just the shell with no paint on it whatsoever, because they like doing it themselves.' Tara pointed to a cardboard box on the floor under one of the shelves. 'Take a look in there.'

Bonnie peered inside, and Tara smiled to see that the girl was careful not to touch anything.

'You can take them out and have a look at them,' she said. In the box were various rolls of paper, from brick-effect to slate, tiles to cobbles.

'Wow!' Bonnie picked up each one in turn. 'They look real.'

Tara smiled. 'That's the idea.'

Bonnie returned to stand next to her as Tara explained how careful she had to be when measuring and cutting, and as she spoke, Tara kept glancing at her. The child had Cal's eyes – the same colour and shape. She had his hair too, and his smile.

Tara wondered where he was right now. What was he doing? She hadn't spoken to him since the night on his deck, although she'd glimpsed him in the distance, and if he'd gone out in his boat again, she hadn't noticed. She wondered whether he was avoiding her because he was regretting his offer. Maybe he was regretting the evening itself.

She didn't regret it at all. To be told that he'd only married Yvaine because she'd been pregnant had flipped a switch in Tara's head. She was no longer bitter. Instead, she felt sad and regretful. If only he hadn't been so sure back then that he knew what was best for her, she might have talked him around and persuaded him that they could have made their relationship work.

Instead he'd had rebound sex and a whole lot of grief had been the result. But, as he'd pointed out, if he and Tara had stayed together, the beautiful child standing by her side wouldn't exist, and that was unimaginable.

Bonnie was gorgeous, and Tara's heart went out to her. Tara mightn't be able to ease the girl's sadness at having to leave Duncoorie, but the doll's house she was going to build for her might smooth the transition a little. She would start work on it as soon as she'd completed the funeral parlour.

An hour later – by this time Bonnie had borrowed a chair from one of the other studios and was perched next to Tara, 'helping' her – the door opened again.

Tara's heart lurched when she saw it was Cal.

'I thought I'd find you here,' he said to his daughter, then he turned his gaze to Tara and said, 'I hope she hasn't been a nuisance?'

'I've loved having her here,' she answered truthfully. Bonnie was good company. She was enthusiastic, inquisitive, bright and chatty. She was a quick learner too, picking things up faster than Tara had when she'd first started making doll's houses and all things tiny.

'If she gets on your nerves, just kick her out. She won't take offence, will you, Bon-Bon?'

'Dad, stop calling me Bon-Bon.'

'OK, Bon-Bon.'

'*Dad!*'

He chuckled, and it warmed Tara's heart to see what a lovely relationship he had with his daughter.

'Mack has a couple of spaces in the boat for this afternoon's trip,' Cal said, his attention reverting to Bonnie. 'Would you like to go?'

'Me and you?'

'Yes, me and you. Who did you think I meant?'

'Me, you and Tara.'

Cal's eyes widened a fraction. 'I'm not sure Tara would want to come.'

'Can you ask her?' But before Cal could open his mouth, Bonnie said, 'Mack does whale and dolphin watching trips. Have you ever seen a whale?'

'Actually, I haven't.' Tara replied.

'A dolphin?'

Tara shook her head.

'Would you like to?'

'I would, but perhaps not today.'

'Please come. It'll be fun.'

'Yes, come,' Cal chimed in. 'You'll enjoy it, although there's no guarantee that any whales or dolphins will put in an appearance.'

Tara wasn't sure. She didn't want Cal to feel obliged to back up Bonnie's impromptu invitation. 'I've got to finish this,' she said, indicating the partly decorated funeral parlour.

'If I promise to help, will you come?' Bonnie stared at her hopefully. 'Dad says that all work and no play makes Jack stupid.'

'Dull,' Cal laughed. 'It makes him a dull boy, meaning he's boring because he works all the time and doesn't enjoy himself.'

'You don't want to be boring, Tara,' Bonnie told her solemnly.

'No, you don't.' Cal twinkled at her, and Tara blushed.

'If you're sure,' she hedged. 'I don't want to impinge on your time with Bonnie.'

'You won't,' he assured her. 'Pick you up in half an hour? Wear something warm. It can get blustery out there.'

–

Cal was pleased to see that Tara had heeded his advice. She was wearing a padded jacket, and also had a knitted hat in her hand and a sturdy pair of boots on her feet. She smiled uncertainly, and he hoped she hadn't felt railroaded into accompanying them, despite saying she would be happy to go out on the loch in the skiff.

Bonnie kept up a steady stream of chatter from the back seat on the short drive along the loch to Mack's place, leaving Cal free to wonder what the hell he was doing. Cooking a meal for Tara the other evening was a step beyond having a professional and friendly working relationship with her. It had bordered on being intimate. And now he was taking her on a boat trip? Thank goodness for Bonnie. She would hopefully act as a buffer between them. However, if it wasn't for Bonnie, Tara wouldn't have been accompanying them in the first place.

Cal spied Mack as soon as he pulled into the parking area. He was on the boat, dressed in his customary shorts and T-shirt. He rarely wore anything different. The man didn't seem to feel the cold and was impervious to rain.

'Cal.' Mack grinned as Cal approached and held out his hand. He chucked Bonnie under the chin, then turned his curious gaze on Tara. 'Who's this?'

'Tara Sh— McTaigh. She's just moved to Skye.'

Mack offered her his hand to shake, speculation in his eyes as he glanced at Cal, then back to Tara. Cal also saw something else in his friend's eyes – appreciation and interest.

It ruffled Cal's feathers.

No doubt Mack would ask him about her as soon as he managed to get him on his own. What should he tell him? *Back off, because I loved her once and I'm pretty sure I still do*? Or should he tell Mack to go for it, because there was next to no chance of him and Tara picking up where they left off? But the thought of her being with someone else, especially a mate, was unimaginable. Then it struck him that he might have to get used to it. Although Tara hadn't long come out of a marriage, she was young, incredibly attractive and a lovely person, and sooner or later she would want to start dating again.

A knife twisted in his gut, sending a dart of pain right through him. If only he had told her about his father and the promise he'd made, things might have been so very different. They might have got married, and Bonnie might have been *their* daughter—

'Dad, why are you frowning?' Bonnie was wearing a frown herself as she stared at him.

'I didn't realise I was.'

'Are you cross?'

'Not at all. Shall we go onboard and sit down?'

Bonnie wanted to sit as near to the prow as she could get without being in the cabin, and Cal placed himself immediately behind her, so he could grab her if he needed to. Tara sat on his other side.

Tara was forced to shuffle closer as the boat filled up with passengers, and he became conscious of her thigh touching his and her arm pressing against his shoulder. It seemed only natural to drape his arm along the gunwale to allow her more room. His hand itched to curl around her shoulder and pull her close, but he resisted the urge. Touching her more than this would be too much to cope with, and being this close to her was already sending his pulse into overdrive.

After Mack and his crew cast off and the boat had chugged away from its mooring, Mack launched into his usual spiel, informing people of the area's geology and history and what wildlife they might see.

Cal tuned out. He'd heard it several times before and was well aware of the wildlife that inhabited the waters around Skye.

He was more interested in trying to watch Tara's expression out of the corner of his eye. She was scanning the sea, her eyes narrowed in concentration, and he hoped today would be lucky for her and she would get to see a whale or a dolphin, because they didn't always show up. However, the loch was sheltered from the open sea and was a good hunting ground for fish, so maybe they'd get lucky.

Seals were a common sight though, and as the boat skirted around the coast and the small islands just offshore, Mack pointed out the harbour seals that were hauled out on the rocks. Bonnie was excited to see them, but not nearly as excited as Tara.

'Haven't you seen a seal before?' Bonnie asked her.

'I have, but not often. You are so lucky living here and having them on your doorstep.'

'You live here, too,' Bonnie pointed out. 'Dad says you live in the boathouse.'

'I do, but not for much longer. The boathouse belongs to Miss Gray, and I'm hoping to buy a house of my own soon.'

'But you'll still live on Skye?'

'Yes, I will.'

Bonnie gave her a satisfied grin. 'You'll be lucky, like me. All this,' she threw her arms wide, nearly smacking Cal in the face, 'will be on your doorstep, too.'

'By the end of the summer, Tara will be sick to death of seals,' Cal joked.

'I won't.' Tara shook her head. 'How can anyone be sick to death of seals? Look at those cute faces.'

'I like seals, don't I, Dad?'

'You do.'

'And rabbits and deer. Sometimes I see foxes, and once I saw an otter.'

'Otters are quite elusive,' Cal said.

'That means they hide a lot,' Bonnie explained seriously.

Cal caught Tara's eye, and he could see she was trying not to smile.

'One time, Dad took me to this place in his boat, and we got out and had to walk for ages, then we hid in the grass and waited and waited. It was a long time, wasn't it, Dad? And we had to keep really quiet and still, and that was hard. But we saw a mummy and a baby otter. They were *so* cute, but I sneezed because the grass tickled my nose and it scared them away.' She looked sad, but not for long. 'Then we had a picnic, didn't we, Dad? Did you bring anything to eat?'

Cal laughed. 'No, I didn't. You're worse than a gannet, always hungry.'

'Gannets eat a lot,' Bonnie told Tara before turning back to him. 'What's for tea?'

'How about a chippie supper? But don't tell your mother.'

'Yay! And Tara can have some too, can't she?'

He met Tara's eyes again. 'If she wants,' he replied steadily.

'Dad has got beer in his fridge,' Bonnie announced. 'He drinks it after I've gone to bed.'

Tara pressed her lips together, her eyes crinkling at the corners as he said, 'Bonnie, you can't go telling people that.'

'Why not? It's true, you *have* got beer in your fridge. Mummy has wine in hers. Do you like wine, Tara? I don't. It's nasty.'

Cal was appalled. 'How do you know what wine tastes like?'

Bonnie's expression became sly. 'I had a sip once when Mummy went to the loo.' She pulled a face. 'I didn't like it.'

'Good! I hope you continue not to like it for years and years.'

'I don't like coffee either, or tea, but—'

Whatever Bonnie was going to say was lost as a cry went up and passengers leapt to their feet as the boat came about. Whales had been spotted off the starboard bow, and Bonnie who was in an ideal position, turned towards the water.

'Look, Tara. Whales!'

There were at least three, Cal counted, as they expelled puffs of air out of their blowholes. Their bodies were sleek and black, breaking the surface before sinking below again.

'Minke,' Cal said, just as Mack announced it. 'Quite common in these waters.' Then he shut up to allow Tara to listen to Mack's commentary.

He also wanted to be free to gaze at her face, which was alight with wonder, her eyes shining as he stepped back a pace to allow her to move in front of him for a better view. The sight of her stole his breath, as a memory of seeing that very same expression when she'd opened his Christmas present to her flashed into his head. They'd made love on the floor, to the soft strains of 'Away in a Manger' and the crinkle of wrapping paper. He wondered whether she still had the pendant.

The boat kept pace with the whales whilst maintaining a respectful distance, then after the magnificent creatures had sunk below the waves for a final time, Mack turned the boat around and they headed back to shore.

Mother Nature hadn't finished with them yet, though. She had another treat in store by way of a pod of bottlenose dolphins which surrounded the boat, to the delight of everyone aboard. Leaping from the water or riding the bow wave, they produced squeals of excitement from the younger passengers, and Bonnie had difficulty containing herself.

Tara didn't say a word. She didn't need to. Her face said everything. She was transfixed, and when the playful creatures had enough and darted away, she dropped back onto the seat, her face glowing.

'That was one of the best experiences of my life,' she said. 'Thank you so much for persuading me to come.'

'I knew you'd like it!' Bonnie cried. 'Uncle Mack is the best! He always knows where to find them, doesn't he, Dad? If you ask him, he might show you a basking shark. They're awesome.'

Cal muttered an unintelligible reply. It might be selfish, but he didn't want Tara asking Mack for anything.

Mack's interest in Duncoorie's newest resident became apparent after the boat docked and Cal thanked him for taking them out. Mack's gaze lingered on Tara for far too long, and when he caught hold of Cal's arm and drew him briefly aside, Cal bristled at being asked whether anything was going on between them.

'She's an old friend,' Cal said, reluctantly. 'From uni.' And then he added, because Mack would undoubtedly find out, 'We used to date.'

Mack studied him intently, then held up his hands. 'Message received.'

'What message?' He glanced around to see that Bonnie and Tara had reached the car and were waiting for him to unlock it.

'You still fancy her.'

'I don't.'

'Yeah, right.' Mack followed his gaze. 'Bonnie likes her.'

'She does.'

'And Tara fancies the pants off you.'

Cal shook his head. 'I told you, she's an old friend. It's not like that.'

Mack clapped him on the back. 'You keep telling yourself that. I think you'll find I'm right.'

Mack might have given Cal food for thought, but it was fish and chips that Bonnie was interested in. 'Dad!' she yelled. 'I'm hungry. Hurry up!'

Cal hurried, despite his appetite having deserted him. It soon reappeared when he was unwrapping the steaming bundles in the kitchen back at the cottage, as Bonnie got the plates out and Tara poured the drinks.

The three of them sat at the table to eat their supper, and as he devoured his, Cal put his rediscovered appetite down to the hope that he and Tara had proved they could put the past behind them and be friends and colleagues going forward.

It had absolutely nothing to do with Mack's ridiculous comment.

What Mack had said about Tara fancying the pants off him continued to prey on Cal's mind well into the evening. If only Mack knew the true extent of what had passed between them. Cal and Tara had been inseparable. The hot, intense love they'd shared had gone way beyond fancying each other.

And deep down he knew they weren't done. He sensed they had unfinished business. That he still loved her was a given, but did she still have feelings for him?

Mack seemed to think so.

Cal hated that Tara thought he'd thrown away what they had because he'd told her that long-distance relationships didn't work. He hated even more that she thought she'd meant so little to him that he'd leapt into bed with the first woman who'd batted her eyelashes at him.

Tara deserved to know the truth.

His phone rang, cutting into his thoughts.

'Hi, Mum.'

'Hello, my lovely boy. How was your weekend with Bonnie?'

'Exhausting.'

'I bet! Did you do anything nice?'

'We went out with Mack. He had a couple of cancellations.'

'I bet she enjoyed that. I wouldn't be surprised if she goes into something to do with wildlife when she's older.'

'Or doll's houses.' Cal chuckled. 'One of the studios has been let out to a woman who makes doll's houses, and Bonnie is fascinated. In fact, Tara came with us on the trip.'

'Did she now?' His mum's tone was full of hope. 'What's she like?'

Cal hesitated. How could he describe the woman who held his heart in her hands and didn't even realise it? There weren't enough words to do her justice.

'Cal?'

'I used to date her. At university.'

Something in his voice must have pinged on his mother's radar. 'What aren't you telling me?'

'I…' God, this was hard. 'I love her. I always have.'

'I see. That explains why Yvaine is the way she is.'

Did it? Cal couldn't see how. 'Yvaine knew I'd dated someone called Tara when I was at uni, but she didn't know I was in love with her.'

'Trust me, sweetheart, she knew. If you don't mind me asking, why did you and Tara break up?'

'Because of Dad.'

There was a sharp intake of breath, then silence. Finally, she spoke. 'Who broke up with who?'

'I broke up with her. She was in Glasgow and I had just landed that job in Inverness, and…'

'And you weren't able to tell her why you couldn't go to Glasgow to see her every weekend, or why she couldn't visit you,' his mum finished.

She understood immediately, without him having to explain.

He heard her sigh. 'I knew something was wrong, but I put it down to all the worry over your father. Why didn't you tell me?'

'You had enough to be getting on with.'

She snorted. 'Liar. It was because you didn't want me to feel guilty about asking you to keep your dad's condition quiet.'

'Yes.'

'That bloody job of his had a lot to answer for.' The anger in her voice made him flinch.

It was true, though. His poor dad had been under so much pressure at work that one day he'd snapped. A proud man, he hadn't wanted his family, friends or colleagues to know the full extent of it. So he'd kept it quiet as much as he had been able to, taking early retirement. Slowly, with his doctor's help, he'd recovered, but it had been too late for Calan – He was already married to Yvaine.

His mum said, 'I take it Tara doesn't know?'

'No.'

'Tell her.'

'Are you sure?'

'Does she still care for you?'

He blew out a breath. 'I don't know. I hope so.'

'Has she forgiven you?'

'Probably not.'

'Do you think she will if you tell her the real reason you ended it?'

'Maybe.'

'Then you must tell her.'

'Will Dad mind?'

'If it means you have a second chance at love, then no, he won't mind. Anyway, ten years is a long time and people's attitude towards mental health has moved on.'

Cal let out a sigh, releasing some of the tension he'd been carrying. 'Thanks, Mum.'

'I'm sorry. If I'd known, I never—' Her voice broke, but she managed to say one last thing before ending the call. 'I hope she makes your heart sing.'

Chapter 15

Tara's keys were in her hand and she was about to unlock the studio door when she heard her name being called. Jinny was hurrying towards her, clutching her hood to keep it on her head as the wind whipped around the side of the building.

Tara held the door open for her and Jinny dashed inside, brushing the raindrops from her fringe. 'Welcome to Skye,' she laughed. 'You've been spoilt with all the lovely weather we've been having. This is more typical.'

Flicking the lights on, Tara said, 'I did hear a rumour that it rains a lot.'

'Aye, that's what gives it its character.' Jinny gave her a sideways look. 'You had good weather for your boat trip yesterday.'

Tara didn't bother to ask how Jinny knew. She was quickly beginning to realise that everyone knew everyone else's business in Duncoorie, especially in the castle.

Jinny told her anyway. 'Mack is my brother-in-law. He's thirty-five, single, solvent and sober – most of the time. He does like a dram or two.'

'That's, um, good to know.'

'He's bonnie, too.'

Tara had noticed. Mack was an attractive bloke. Tall, well-built, muscular – probably from hauling all those ropes and leaping in and out of his boat. She'd also noticed the speculative and appraising look he'd given her. She'd got the impression he'd liked what he'd seen. Had he asked about her, she wondered. He'd chatted to Cal briefly after they'd got off the boat. It could have been about anything, but as Mack had been talking, he'd cast a glance in her direction. Call it female intuition, but she thought he might be interested in her.

The possibility made her pause. She wasn't ready to start dating again, even though her feelings for Dougie had withered and died a long time ago, but at some point she would be, and Mack was a good-looking guy. She intended to make a new life for herself on Skye, and that included romance.

Unbidden, Cal's face popped into her mind, and she shook her head to rid herself of it.

'Don't you think so?' Jinny asked, and Tara realised that her friend had assumed she was replying to her comment about Mack being attractive.

'Sorry, I was thinking about something else. Yes, Mack is good looking.'

'But you don't fancy him?'

'Are you trying to set me up?'

'There's not much point, considering you've still got the hots for Cal.'

'I have not!' Tara blushed furiously, but her denial was met with the scepticism it deserved as Jinny raised her eyebrows and gave her an arched look.

Jinny said, 'He's single, solvent and sober, too.'

'He's also my ex, my landlord and a single parent.'

'So? Ever heard of second chance romance?'

'In books.'

'It happens in real life as well.'

Tara let that pass. 'Landlord,' she reminded her.

'Irrelevant. It's not like he's your line manager. You rent a studio from the estate, that's all.'

'Single parent?'

'I was under the impression you get on well with Bonnie.'

'I do.'

'Well then, what's the problem?'

'I'm pretty sure he's not interested in me.'

'Girl, have you seen the way he looks at you? *Of course* he's interested. Even Mack says so.'

Tara had enough of the conversation. 'Did you want me for anything?' She didn't care that the change of subject was blatant.

Jinny frowned, then her face cleared. 'I did. I came to tell you that we sold the smaller of the doll's houses and loads of furniture and stuff to go in it. Have you got another we can put in its place?'

Delighted, Tara let out a whoop. 'I certainly have! As soon as the rain eases, I'll bring it over. That's great news! Thank you.'

'I didn't do anything,' Jinny protested. 'Like everything else in the shop, it sold itself.'

Tara didn't believe her for one second. She'd seen Jinny in action and knew what a brilliant saleswoman she was. Once again, Tara thanked her lucky stars for bringing her to Coorie Castle.

It was yet to be seen whether she was equally as thankful for them throwing her and Cal together again.

–

Three days later Cal stuck his head around the door to Tara's studio, seemingly to congratulate her on the brilliant sale she'd had earlier in the week, but mainly because it was killing him to keep away. Since the boat trip, he hadn't been able to stop thinking about her. Although, if he was honest, he hadn't been able to stop thinking about her for weeks. She'd been lurking in his mind ever since he'd discovered she'd leased the studio.

'I hear you had a nice sale the other day,' he said.

Tara beamed. 'I did. It was such a lovely surprise. Talking about surprises, thank you again for persuading me to join you on the boat trip. It was amazing.'

'You're welcome, but it was Bonnie's suggestion. Not that I didn't want you to come with us, of course. You've certainly made an impression on her.'

'She's a nice kid. I've planned out her doll's house if you'd like to take a look.' She got up from her stool and walked over to her laptop on the opposite workbench.

Cal tried not to notice how well her jeans fitted, but it was hard not to. He remembered all too vividly what she looked like underneath. Heat crept into his face, and he swallowed hard as he forced himself to concentrate on the image on the screen and not on how wonderful she smelt or how dearly he would like to kiss her.

She was busily explaining that because of its internal layout, Bonnie's doll's house would have dual openings, one at the front and one at the back, allowing full access to all the rooms, which wasn't the case with most doll's houses because they usually had a fixed back and sides.

Cal was only half-listening; he was too distracted by her nearness. His arms itched to envelope her, and his mouth tingled with a longing to taste her lips.

'If you're happy, shall I go ahead?' she asked.

'Er, yeah, great. Please do.'

'Can you do me a favour and let me know whenever Bonnie is at the castle? I don't want her coming in and finding me working on it.'

'Of course.'

'I've got plenty of other things on the go that she can help with – if you don't mind.'

'I don't mind, as long as you don't. Feel free to send her packing when you've had enough of her. She won't take offence.'

'I will,' Tara smiled.

There was a pause, and Cal wondered if she wanted to send *him* packing but was too polite to say. 'I'm going into Portree later, if you need anything picking up,' he said, moving towards the door.

She caught her bottom lip between her teeth as she thought. 'Um, there are a few bits and pieces I could do with. Actually, never mind, I'll pop in myself at some point, then I can't tell you off for fetching the wrong thing.'

A memory bubbled to the surface. She'd done that very thing when she'd asked him to pick up a book on contemporary art, but he'd bought the wrong one. He'd apologised, and Tara had shown him she'd forgiven him by taking him to bed.

'Why don't you come with me?' he suggested, and he got the impression she was going to refuse, when her phone rang.

'Excuse me a sec. Oh, it's the estate agent,' she said with a frown.

Cal automatically assumed it was the same agent who was selling Yvaine's cottage, but Tara cried, 'That's great news. Thanks. Tell him I accept.'

When she came off the phone, she was grinning widely. 'I've just accepted an offer on my house. Or should I say *we* have. Dougie is happy with it, so with any luck contracts will be exchanged in a couple of months. It shouldn't be long, because the people who put the offer in are cash buyers with no chain! Woo hoo!' Her eyes sparkled. 'You know what that means? I can start looking at houses, so I will come to Portree with you, if that's OK? I've got an estate agent to visit.'

–

Cal parked the Range Rover in a square with a war memorial in the middle, not far from Portree's main street. Tara noticed a selection of shops, restaurants and other businesses, as well as a post office, but she didn't see any estate agents.

'There's one just there,' he said after she'd asked, guiding her around the corner. 'And a couple further along the street. Shall we meet back at the car in about an hour? Will that give you enough time?'

Tara hedged, not knowing whether it would or wouldn't. Besides, since she was here, she wouldn't mind taking a quick look around the town.

'Or,' he said, 'I could wait for you in The Isles Inn, and we could have a bite to eat once you're done. They do great bar snacks.'

'Sounds good,' she replied, and after Cal had told her where to find the pub, Tara went off to explore.

Her first stop was the estate agent he'd pointed out. It wasn't the same company that had shown her around Bonnie's house, but even if it had been, Tara no longer felt like a fraud. She was legitimately looking for a property, and with an offer accepted on the house in Edinburgh, she was in a good position to put an offer in on a property herself – assuming she found something suitable within her price range.

Yvaine's cottage was eminently suitable and within her budget, but Tara couldn't bring herself to consider it. It would be too weird. And what would Bonnie make of it? And Cal?

Tara came away from the first estate agent armed with the details of several properties, only one of which was in Duncoorie, and by the time she'd visited the other two estate agents, she was feeling a bit overwhelmed. There were so many variables that she didn't know where to start with putting them in any kind of order.

After a quick scoot around the shops to purchase a few essentials and a trot down to the waterfront with its colourful houses and view of Loch Portree, it was time to make her way back to the square and the pub where Cal was waiting.

Tara's heart leapt when she saw him. He was perched on a stool chatting to a woman behind the bar, and both of them seemed to be enjoying the other's company.

Jealousy jabbed at her with bony fingers, and she flinched.

Plastering a smile on her face, she strolled casually up to the bar and was gratified when Cal noticed her and broke into a grin.

'Can I get you a drink?' he offered.

'Soda and lime, please.'

He nodded to the barmaid, who didn't look anywhere near as pleased to see Tara as Cal did. 'And can we have a couple of menus?' he asked, after she'd poured their drinks.

Taking them over to a table near a window, they sat down and Cal handed Tara a menu. It was only after they'd ordered did he ask whether she'd had any joy with her property search.

'Yes and no,' she replied, cryptically. 'There're quite a few houses within my price range, but hardly any in Duncoorie.'

'I didn't think there would be. And those that come on the market are snapped up pretty sharpish.' He stared into the unlit fireplace. 'There's always Yvaine's house.'

Tara shuddered. 'I did think about it, but it would be too weird.'

Cal must have been thinking the same thing because after hearing she wasn't interested in it, he brightened. 'Show me what you've got?'

Tara took them out of her bag and for the next half hour, whilst eating cheese toasties and soup, they hashed over the various properties until Tara felt she had a better understanding of what was out there and what she wanted. The most important consideration was the distance from Duncoorie. Although Portree was only a thirty-minute drive away and there were many more properties for sale in the town, she wanted to be as near as possible to her studio.

That she would be nearer to Cal wasn't a factor. Or so she told herself.

'Did Mhairi give you a time limit on how long you can stay in the boathouse?' he asked.

'She didn't, but I'm guessing she doesn't want me there indefinitely. I've got some leeway to find the right property, but I don't want to outstay my welcome.'

'What about this one?' Cal picked the topmost sheet off the little pile they had created. 'It's only a mile out of the village. I'll grant you it's a bit old-fashioned, but it's perfectly habitable.'

It was, and the price was reasonable, too. It was a detached, substantial three-bedroom house, with quite a bit of land. The whitewashed walls and grey slate roof were typical of the area, and there were lawns to the front and back. It needed some updating inside, but she could live with it as it was for the time being.

So what was stopping her from going to view it?

She told herself it would be better to wait until her share of the Edinburgh house was safely in her bank account, and that setting her heart on a property now might lead to disappointment should it fall through. But deep down Tara knew the real reason – she wanted to stay at the boathouse for as long as possible. Knowing that Cal lived just a short walk away anchored something in her soul that she hadn't realised was adrift.

What if Jinny and Mack were right, and Cal still had feelings for her? Could she trust him not to break her heart again?

Quietly Tara snorted to herself. *Again?* It hadn't healed from the last time. It was still broken, and she strongly suspected only Cal could mend it. However, she'd reached a state of equilibrium and if she allowed Cal back in, she was in danger of losing that.

But did she want to spend the rest of her life wondering what might have happened if she'd had the courage to give it another go? And if she didn't and he began a relationship with someone else, could she live with that?

Feeling courageous and more than a little reckless, she said, 'Where would *you* like me to live? Duncoorie or somewhere further away?'

'Duncoorie.' His reply was immediate. Then he looked her in the eye and said, 'If it was up to me, you could live in the boathouse forever.'

She swallowed. 'I thought that after everything that had happened between us, you wouldn't want me here.'

'Tara…' His voice was a low rumble. 'Believe me when I say I *do* want you here.' The intensity of his gaze made her drop her own for fear he might guess she still loved him, despite what he'd done and everything that had happened throughout the intervening years.

For so long she'd told herself she hated him, but it couldn't be further from the truth.

Suddenly she felt incredibly sorry for Dougie. He hadn't stood a chance, had he? No wonder he'd sought solace elsewhere. She hadn't been able to give him her heart because it had already belonged to someone else.

Neither she nor Cal spoke on the way back.

When they reached the castle, Tara expected him to drop her off at the top of the track leading to the boathouse, but instead he drove down it and pulled up outside.

'I meant it,' he said, as she reached for the handle. 'I do want you to stay. Very much. But there's something I've been wanting to tell you. Something I should have told you years ago. And if I'd told you back then, we mightn't have split up.'

'What?' She searched his face for a clue, but he wasn't giving anything away. He looked serious though, and her heart gave an uncomfortable lurch. Whatever it was, she had a feeling she wouldn't like it.

'I lied to you. I didn't split up with you because we were too young, or because you lived in Glasgow and I lived in Inverness, or any of the other reasons I gave. I ended it because my dad had a breakdown and my parents made me promise not to tell anyone. I might have broken my promise and told you, but they needed me there and I didn't know how long it would be until he was better. I didn't know if he ever *would* get better, that he'd ever be well enough for my mum not to worry that he'd do something unspeakable if he was left on his own.' Cal's eyes filled with tears.

Tara wanted to reach across and brush them away, but she sensed he needed to get it off his chest first.

'We thought he might have to be sectioned at one point, but he begged and begged, and Mum—' He swallowed and took a deep breath. 'It took him a while to improve, baby steps, but he got there in the end. But it was too late for me and you.'

'Oh, Cal…' Tara's heart was breaking all over again. 'I would have waited for you, if I'd known.'

'It could have been a very long time. A very long time indeed. I didn't want to do that to you.'

All those wasted years, all that heartache. 'How is he now?'

'Better. He still has his down days, but that's all they are – days.'

She had to ask. 'Yvaine?'

Shame flared in his eyes. 'After I broke up with you, I went off the rails a bit. It wasn't serious, until it became very serious.' He pulled a face. 'But I wouldn't be without Bonnie. She means everything to me.'

The honesty in his eyes made her heart melt, and the last remaining brick in the wall she'd built around it to keep all those broken pieces together, tumbled.

And that was when Tara kissed him.

It was only a brief flutter of her lips against his and she didn't linger long enough for him to react before she was out of the car and running towards the boathouse. But when she opened the door and slipped inside, she couldn't help glancing back.

Cal had a smile on his face.

Chapter 16

And so it began… Maybe Tara should have paused to consider what she was doing, but as it had been pointed out, both she and Cal were young (early thirties *was* still young, wasn't it?) and single. The connection they'd once had was still there. It was love on her part, and although she wasn't sure he still loved her, he'd told her he wished he'd never let her go, so she clung to that, even though it might be foolish.

Tara also thought she must be mellowing as she grew older. What had once been black and white, now had more shades of grey than the waters of the loch on a rainy day.

And hadn't she made enough mistakes of her own? Poor Dougie, he hadn't deserved to have her for a wife. But the past was the past, and the future was there to be moulded into something bright and new, if only she dared.

Tara had found the courage to kiss Cal, however fleeting the kiss had been, and Cal appeared to have found the courage to ask her out.

It wasn't a date, as such. More of an 'I fancy taking a hike to The Old Man of Storr, would you like to join me?' type of date.

Cal told her it was the most famous and busiest moun-tain on the island. Although they wouldn't be going right to the top, because that would involve crampons, helmets and proper climbing equipment, the average walker could get to the base of it relatively easily and still enjoy fantastic views.

That had been Cal's sales pitch.

However, if Tara had realised beforehand quite how high it was and quite how unfit *she* was, she mightn't have agreed to go with him.

The day had started easily enough, although getting up at four a.m. to be on the road by four thirty hadn't been *that* easy.

'Remind me, why the ungodly hour?' she'd asked when she climbed into the passenger seat of his car, her eyes heavy with sleep and her limbs having not yet woken up properly.

'Because it gets really busy. It'll be better to get there early for the parking.'

Tara yawned. 'I need a coffee.'

'I've brought a flask. And some BLTs.'

'What time did you get up?' Tara was impressed, even if she did think Cal was off his rocker.

'I couldn't sleep,' he said, his eyes on the road.

'Too excited?' she teased.

'Something like that.'

There wasn't much more talk for the next half an hour or so, until Cal indicated left and drove onto the car parking area, and even then, Tara didn't have a great deal to say. She was too busy just enjoying being with him.

They'd fallen back into the easy way they used to have with one another, an ease she'd once taken for granted, and hope flared inside her. Maybe they did have a future together after all.

But there wasn't time to think about that now, because when they exited the car and began walking up a gravel track, Tara got her first proper look at where they were headed and groaned.

'Are we going up *there*?' 'Up there' was a huge lump of bare rock turrets towering above them.

'Not right to the top, but almost. Isn't it magnificent!'

'Hmm.' It *was*, but Tara wasn't sure she'd make it. They hadn't gone far and she was already breathing heavily. The track was easy underfoot, but steep, and they were already a few hundred feet above sea level. The view behind, of Rona, Raasay and beyond, would have been enough for her. She didn't need to see it from the top.

But neither did she want Cal to think she was a light-weight, so she kept plodding ever upwards. When the gradient ramped up so did Tara's determination not to stop for a rest, despite her aching thighs and burning lungs.

'We've picked a good day for it,' Cal said, stopping and turning around.

Tara halted, grateful for the respite. The sky was cloud-less, and the sea was painted navy, sapphire and corn-flower. The horizon was grey and purple, the distant peaks reaching for the heavens. But the sunlight didn't make the bare rocks above the path any more appealing, and she wondered how much further it would be.

'What's that down there?' Tara asked, hoping to keep Cal talking for a few minutes more to enable her to catch her breath.

'Loch Leathan. See that island in the middle? Legend has it that there was a castle on it in the mid-1600s, but there's no evidence of it now.'

He began walking again and Tara reluctantly followed. As though sensing she was struggling, he held out a hand

and she took it gratefully. After that, the hike didn't seem quite as strenuous.

At least, not until the gravel path turned into a muddy, uneven, rocky scramble.

'Take your time,' Cal advised. 'There's no rush. We don't want to risk a twisted ankle.'

It was like climbing up a staircase made out of large boulders set into the mountain, and Cal had to help her over more than a few. By now it wasn't only her thighs that ached. Her ankles, calves, knees and the muscles in her behind were all shouting out for her to stop. Still Tara pushed on. Or should she say *dragged*, because Cal was more or less hauling her up the steep slope.

But at some point, it wasn't the gradient that was stealing her breath, it was the sight of the vast basalt columns above them. They were so close she was convinced they were going to topple on her. And then she was amongst them, those rocky fingers reaching heavenwards, framing the stunning view.

She drank it in for a long time, awestruck and humbled, until the need for the promised coffee became too great.

Leading her a short distance from the path, Cal found a flattish rock for them to sit on and dished out their breakfast. Never had a BLT tasted so good, and she sighed with contentment as she washed the sandwich down with rich, strong coffee. What a place to eat it!

'This even beats the view of the loch from my living room window,' she declared, sipping the last of her coffee. 'Thank you for bringing me.'

'You did brilliantly.'

'For someone who only walks to the pub and back?'

'Exactly!'

'I need to do more of this kind of thing. It makes you feel alive.'

'I call it soul food. Being in nature, in the mountains, and with views like this, feeds your soul. I always feel calm and at peace afterwards.'

'I can see why. I could stay up here all day.'

'Me, too, but unfortunately I have to get to work.'

'Work?' Tara had forgotten about the studio. She'd forgotten she had commissions to fulfil and a workshop to plan. All that mattered right now was the mountain, the view, and the man she was with.

So she kissed him again.

This time it started slow and light, a mere meeting of the lips, the warmth of his mouth, the lingering but not unpleasant taste of coffee, then his arms came around her, crushing her to him and the kiss deepened.

Instantly Tara was transported back in time and place. She was twenty again, madly in love and the future held so much promise.

It could again, her inner voice whispered as his tongue found hers, and she thought she would like that very much.

It seemed to be a day for being breathless, because when the kiss finally ended, she was breathing almost as hard as she had on the hike up. Her heart pounded just as much and her legs felt equally as weak, she discovered, when she tried to stand. Cal had to steady her, which resulted in another kiss. It was lucky it was still early, and few people were on the mountain to witness it.

'We'd better start making our way down,' Cal said, ending the kiss far too soon for Tara's liking. 'We should be back at Duncoorie by nine thirty at the latest – just in time for you to open up. If that's what you're planning on doing today.'

Tara hadn't planned on doing anything in particular after the hike, even though Cal had advised her that they would only be out for part of the morning. The thought of sitting at her bench making tiny sofas didn't appeal when all she could think about was Cal.

'I don't want to go back either,' he said, as though reading her mind. 'I would love nothing better than to spend the rest of the day with you.'

'Doing what?'

His russet eyes darkened. 'Whatever you like.'

Tara licked her lips. Her pulse pounded and her tummy fluttered. She knew exactly what she'd like to do, but kissing was one thing, making love was another thing entirely. A glorious, wonderful thing, that used to make her heart sing and her soul cry out with joy.

One day, she hoped to feel that again. And from the look in Cal's eyes, Tara thought he might, too.

Cal was still feeling invigorated from his walk when he called in to see Mhairi later that morning. She was in her parlour, which also doubled as an office, and when she saw him, she informed him that she would like to do a walk-through of the estate. Not all the castle's grounds, obviously, because Mhairi, although fit and active for her age, was nevertheless an eighty-something lady who would probably struggle on the more rugged areas. For others, such as the maze and the woodland trail, she would use the golf buggy, which Cal drove.

Driving it was fun, although he didn't do it often. 'Where do you want to start?' he asked.

Mhairi was dressed in a tweed hat, a Barbour jacket, corduroy trousers and a pair of smart Wellington boots without the slightest hint of mud on them. Her outfit was appropriate for a misty, drab day. However, the morning was bright and warm, and Cal hoped she wouldn't bake.

He handed her into the golf buggy as she said, 'The duck pond first, then the children's play area. I don't think we need to go through the maze, do you?'

Cal shook his head. Paul had trimmed all the hedges last week, so he knew the maze was in good condition.

'Then I'd like to see how the rewilding is going,' she added.

One of the first things Mhairi's father did when he bought the estate was to plant native trees, and the woodland was now fairly well established. However, it would take many generations to restore it to its former state, before Skye's trees had been felled for wood, fuel and timber and to create open land for cattle and sheep to graze.

The castle's wooded area wasn't particularly large, but Cal adhered to Mhairi's planting programme, and the area was carefully managed.

By the time Cal had driven Mhairi around the more accessible parts of her property, they were ready for some refreshment.

'I think we'll stop at the cafe,' Mhairi announced. 'I haven't seen Gillian for a while. Then I want to visit the gift shop and the studios.'

After the drinks were ordered – coffee for Cal, Earl Grey for Mhairi – Cal took out his tablet and made a note that one of the lights in the kitchen area needed replacing. The note joined all the others that Cal had jotted down this morning. Maintenance and repairs were an ongoing fact of life for an estate manager, and the job list never seemed to shrink.

Mhairi blew on her tea, saying, 'How is Tara settling in? I see she sold a doll's house recently.'

It never ceased to amaze Cal how well-informed Mhairi was. Nothing escaped her notice, and she had all eight fingers and both thumbs firmly on the castle's pulse.

'She's very skilled,' Cal said. 'Her work is top-notch.'

'That's not what I asked.' Mhairi peered over the rim of her bone china cup.

'I think she's finding her feet.'

'With your help?'

'Of course; that's my job.'

'It's not your job to kiss her.'

Cal was mortified. 'I assure you my relationship with Tara won't affect my work.'

'I didn't think it would for one minute. I'm pleased to see that you've reconnected. Bonnie likes her. She can't stop talking about her. When is Yvaine moving?'

Relieved that Mhairi was no longer focusing on him, Cal said, 'Sometime before the start of next term. She's having Lenn's house remodelled over the summer.'

'Like a cat marking its territory,' Mhairi said. 'I'm not surprised that she wants to make some changes. Didn't Lenn used to live there with his ex-wife?'

'I believe so.'

'It's not easy being second,' Mhairi observed, her gaze keen, and Cal winced.

It probably wouldn't have mattered so much that Yvaine had also been *Cal's* second if he'd been honest with her from the start, but Cal's mum telling him that Yvaine probably knew he hadn't loved her the way a man should love his wife – with all his heart – had made him re-evaluate their relationship.

And now here she was, second again, Lenn's ex-wife having taken the number one slot.

But Lenn was in his mid-thirties, so it was inevitable there would have been other women before Yvaine.

His inner voice piped up, *There wasn't another woman before Tara.*

Then it occurred to him that Mhairi asking him about Yvaine's move to Portree wasn't changing the subject at all. The conversation was still about him and Tara.

He had a feeling that the conversation, for him at least, would *always* be about him and Tara, because it always had been.

Chapter 17

When Cal arrived to pick up his daughter the following Friday, Bonnie gave him a quick hug, then scampered down the path and into the car. Cal made to follow her, but his ex-wife held him back.

'You're going to have to step up to the mark and look after Bonnie for a while,' Yvaine announced.

'Excuse me?' It wasn't a question as such, more of an expression of disbelief. 'Are you accusing me of *not* stepping up to the mark?' He checked that Bonnie was in the car and not within earshot.

'Of course not.'

'Good, because you're the one who decided what "the mark" would be. Every other weekend and anytime between when you fancy a break from her.'

Yvaine flushed. 'It's not like that. You make it sound as though I dump her on you whenever the mood takes me.'

Cal glowered before dropping his eyes to the ground. Maybe he was being unfair, but she made it sound like he didn't pull his weight where Bonnie was concerned. Which was totally untrue, of course, as he would have Bonnie all day, every day, if he could.

Yvaine's stony expression softened a little. 'She breaks up from school at the end of next week and my parents have to go to Aunty Jacqueline's tomorrow because she's

180

not been well. They could be there a while,' she explained, somewhat more reasonably.

Jacqueline was older than Yvaine's mum by several years and had lost her husband recently, Cal recalled. Yvaine's parents usually looked after Bonnie during the school holidays while Yvaine was at work, and although Cal helped with his daughter whenever possible, he knew how difficult she sometimes found it to juggle work and childcare.

'Do you want me to have her every day?' he asked. He hoped it wouldn't be a problem, but even if it was, Cal would find a way around it because Yvaine and Bonnie would be moving into Lenn's house in Portree soon, and Cal wanted to spend as much time as possible with his daughter before that happened.

He knew how upset she would be, and he intended to be there for her for as long as she needed him. With so many imminent changes to her life, he vowed to be the one constant she could rely on.

Yvaine said, 'Not every day, because I've arranged to work part-time for the duration, but I want to supervise the renovations. Lenn has given me free rein to do what I like with the house.'

This last was announced with satisfaction, and Cal gritted his teeth. He knew he shouldn't take it as a dig, but he couldn't help it. When they were married, they'd lived in rented accommodation on the estate (hell, he still lived in rented accommodation on an estate, albeit a different one), and she'd always resented it. As long as he'd had a roof over his head and enough food on the table, where he lived hadn't bothered him unduly. It had bothered Yvaine, though. She thought she deserved more, and perhaps she did.

'So, you want me to look after Bonnie, not because you have to work, but because you want to choose whatever shade of white you're going to paint the living room?' He couldn't resist biting back.

'It's a bit more involved than that.' Yvaine pursed her lips. 'We're having an extension built on the back – a sunroom, if you must know – and we're opening up the kitchen, dining and living room, so it will be one large family space.'

Cal bet Lenn wasn't thrilled with that idea. Lenn didn't strike him as a 'family space' kind of guy. He never appeared to be entirely at ease around Bonnie, which got Cal's back up. Didn't the man realise that Yvaine and Bonnie came as a package? Or was Lenn hoping that Cal would be willing to 'step up to the mark' more often so he could have Yvaine all to himself?

Even as he had those thoughts, Cal recognised that he might be reading more into the situation and Lenn's feelings towards Bonnie than was warranted. He suspected he might feel this way about any chap Yvaine took up with.

As he returned to the car and an impatient Bonnie, he wondered how Yvaine would feel if he became romantically involved with someone. Would her nose be put out of joint at the thought of Bonnie spending time with another woman whilst she was being looked after by Cal?

Wait up… *If* he became romantically involved? He already was. There was no doubt about it. Not after those kisses at the top of The Old Man of Storr. Or the kisses he and Tara had shared several times since. They'd been to the pub together for a drink and had taken another walk, this one along the shores of the loch, so not nearly as strenuous. And on both occasions, kissing had been involved.

Remembering them made Cal burn. Each time, he'd been forced to hold himself in check, scared to give in to his desire. If they made love, there would be no going back. And the reason he was scared was twofold. One, he didn't want to risk his heart being broken again, although admittedly, the first time he'd had no one else to blame but himself; and two, he'd promised Bonnie that he wouldn't have a girlfriend. A promise he feared he'd already broken. Which was why he needed to speak to Tara and warn her before she inadvertently mentioned anything to his daughter.

He'd have to take things nice and slow when it came to Bonnie and Tara. It was great that Bonnie liked her, so that was a good starting point. If he built on that, his daughter mightn't object when he told her he and Tara were an item. All he had to do was to ensure Bonnie didn't find out until then.

–

Tara laid out some white polymer clay and a selection of circular cutters ranging from 0.75 to 1.5 cm in diameter. She'd also laid out a thin acrylic block to use as a thickness guide, and a variety of tools to form the edges around the tiny plates she was about to make. Then she put out paints and fine-tipped brushes. All she needed now was for Bonnie to 'give her a hand'.

What she got was Cal.

Tara wasn't complaining, but she'd been expecting his daughter. He was supposed to fetch her after school because she was staying with him for the weekend.

'Where's Bonnie?' she asked, looking past him into the courtyard.

'Plaguing Cook for some cake,' Cal said. He glanced over his shoulder. 'I haven't got long, but I wanted to ask whether you'd mind not mentioning anything to Bonnie about us. Me and you.' He looked shifty, and Tara immediately suspected something fishy was going on.

She didn't say anything, waiting for him to elaborate.

'She's not taking the move to Portree well and I don't want to give her anything more to worry about. Can she get to know you better, before we tell her that we are…?'

'What?'

'Dating.'

'Is that what we're doing?'

'If you want. We've not talked about it and I completely understand if you don't want a relationship with me, after what I did. If I could turn the clock back, I would.'

Tara placed a hand on his arm and smiled into his eyes. 'No, you wouldn't – because you wouldn't have Bonnie. You told me that yourself.'

'But all those wasted years…'

She shrugged and dropped her hand. 'Who says we would have stayed together?'

'True,' he conceded.

'Let's take this one step at a time, shall we? And of course I won't say anything to Bonnie.'

'Thank you. Ah, talk of the devil. Here she is!'

Bonnie bounced into the studio, all pigtails and knobbly knees. 'Dad, you said I can help Tara. Did you mean it?' She turned to Tara. 'Can I?'

'Absolutely! I'm going to show you how to make incy wincy plates. And if we've got time, cups and saucers.'

Bonnie squealed and leapt up and down. 'I want to be a doll's house maker when I grow up,' she declared.

Cal laughed. 'I thought you wanted to be a felt picture maker?'

'I can do both, can't I?'

'You can do whatever you want to do, be whatever you want to be,' her father said, and the love in Cal's eyes brought tears to Tara's.

'Come on, you,' she said to the little girl. 'I've got to make a whole load of these before teatime.'

'Is Tara having tea with us?' Bonnie asked Cal.

'If she'd like.'

Bonnie pleaded with her, 'Please say yes. Dad can be so boring.'

'Thanks!' Cal pulled a face.

'Sometimes he falls asleep in the chair. And he snores.'

'Does he now?' Tara smirked.

'I do not.'

She smiled at him over Bonnie's head and mouthed. 'You do.'

Cal narrowed his eyes. 'I'm sure Tara doesn't want to spend time with someone so boring that he falls asleep in the chair and snores.'

Tara said, 'Oh, I think I can put up with it. I'd love to have tea with you and your dad, Bonnie. Thank you for asking me.'

Bonnie did a little jig. 'Yay! You can go now, Dad. Me and Tara have work to do.'

Tara watched him go for a moment, then gave herself a mental shake and joined his daughter at the workbench.

Bonnie was such a sweetie. Hopefully it wouldn't be long before the two of them were the best of friends, and she and Cal wouldn't have to keep their budding relationship from her.

The glass studio was run by two brothers, Fergus and Shane. Fergus was the glassblower, and Shane's speciality was stained glass – windows mostly, but he also made beautifully intricate glass paintings and gorgeously colourful suncatchers. Today Tara was going to have a go. Nothing too difficult, but it would give her a taste of the craft.

She'd joined a workshop on Sunday morning to make a leaf-shaped suncatcher, and was currently in the process of choosing the colour of glass she wanted to use. It would have to be an autumn leaf, she decided, picking out a piece of glass that was a wonderful shade of deep orange, almost an amber colour. It was only a few shades lighter than Cal's glorious eyes.

Shane had already printed off a paper pattern for his students to use as a template, and her first task was to cut the pattern into its component shapes. They were numbered, so it should be easy to put them together again.

Tara had always wanted to try stained glass making and this was a real treat. But, like anything beautiful, it required skill, and Tara only fully appreciated how talented Shane and his brother were when she studied her finished creation with critical eyes. It looked vaguely like a leaf – if she squinted a bit and the lights were dimmed. Still, it wasn't too bad for a first attempt, although it may well be her last. Glass cutting was harder than it looked, and little slivers of glass from using the nippers to achieve the correct shape tended to get everywhere unless you were careful. Those bits were sharp!

Tara was having a lovely weekend, despite not being able to grab more than a minute or two alone with Cal. However, she was worried that she was intruding on Bonnie's time with her father, despite Bonnie insisting on involving her.

Yesterday afternoon Tara had been forced to tell the child that she needed to concentrate on work in the studio (which was true) and therefore wouldn't be able to let her help for a while, because she thought Bonnie needed to spend time with other people, not just with her. But Bonnie had been waiting for her when Tara had locked up, had grabbed hold of her hand and dragged her to Cal's cottage to join them for a pizza.

They'd played board games until a huge yawn and drooping eyes had indicated that it was time for Bonnie to go to bed.

Conscious of the little girl asleep upstairs, Tara had resisted the temptation to sit on Cal's lap, wrap her arms around his neck and kiss him senseless. Instead, they'd taken a glass of wine onto the deck and watched bats swoop and dive for insects, as they quietly chatted about the castle and the people who worked in it.

The conversation touched on the past occasionally, but they were careful not to discuss anything too deep or serious. Tara was just enjoying being with him. She felt like she was getting to know Cal all over again.

And now here she was, trotting down the lane with a poorly made suncatcher in her hand, about to eat Sunday lunch with him and his daughter. Roast chicken, she guessed, sniffing the air when Bonnie answered the door and dragged her inside.

'I helped Dad make the batter for the Yorkshire puddings!' Bonnie cried. 'We've made a lot, so Dad said we can have pancakes with the leftovers if we're not too full.'

'My, your dad is a real whizz in the kitchen.' He always had been, she remembered.

Lunch was a jolly affair, and a walk along the shore afterwards was fun and light-hearted as Cal challenged everyone to a 'find the roundest pebble' competition. But as the time grew nearer for Bonnie to go home, Tara sensed a change in the child as she became quieter and more introspective.

Guessing that Cal might appreciate some alone time with his daughter before he had to drop her back at her mum's, Tara said her goodbyes and returned to the boathouse.

Maybe she would see him afterwards…

Chapter 18

The following Saturday evening, Jinny breezed into the boathouse clutching a bottle of wine in each hand and grinning from ear to ear. 'Freedom, freedom, freedom,' she sang to the tune of George Michael's hit single.

Tara chuckled at her friend's obvious delight that school had finally broken up for the summer, and her children were spending a week with their grandparents, who were taking them on holiday.

'You realise that you're putting me off having kids, if this is your reaction to them not being around for a few days,' Tara told her.

'*A few days?* It's a whole week. A *week*, I tell you! No having to yell at them to brush their teeth and remember their PE kit. No having to cut a leisurely hot bath short because someone needs something they can quite easily wait for but don't want to. No having to double-check that both kids are fast asleep before Carter and I have a bit of nookie. And if they are asleep – miracles of miracles – we have to be quieter than a nun on Sunday. Hell, with the sex-police away, Carter and I can shag on the living room rug like rabbits if we want to, and if I scream the place down, no one will bat an eyelid. Here, open this.' She shoved a bottle of Co-op's finest white wine at her.

'So why are you having supper at mine and not doing the dirty deed on your rug?' Tara asked with a giggle.

189

'Shagging on the rug is OK in theory, but not too comfy in practice. And I'd better not make too much noise in case next door hears. Anyway, Carter is out tonight. Darts. So I may as well get blotto with you. And I'm looking forward to a girly chat.'

With Cal going for a drink this evening with Mack, Tara was also looking forward to it. She opened the wine and poured it into a couple of glasses, then gave one to Jinny, who had shrugged off her jacket and was now standing by the picture window.

'Thanks. This view is fab.'

Tara stood next to her. 'It sure is. I would happily live here permanently, for the view alone.'

'Nothing to do with Cal living just up the way?'

Tara could feel her cheeks growing warm. 'No...'

'Liar. Come on, spill. I want all the deets. By the way, you've made a big impression on Bonnie – she can't stop talking about you. Whenever I see her, it's Tara this and Tara that. I think you've got a fan. That's got to bode well for you and lover boy. Half the battle is getting the step-kids to like you, or so I've been told.'

'Bonnie doesn't know that Cal and I are an item. He wants her to get used to me being around first.'

'I can't blame him,' Jinny said. 'That's what I would do if I were in his shoes. But I don't think you've got anything to worry about on that score. She thinks you're wonderful.'

'And I think she's wonderful, too.'

'Aw, get you, that's so sweet. So, now we've established that you and Bonnie are firm friends, how goes it with the delectable Cal? Have you *fully rekindled* your relationship yet?' Jinny waggled her eyebrows.

Tara blinked. The question was rather personal.

'You can tell me to mind my own business,' Jinny carried on cheerfully. 'I won't be offended.'

'It's not that. It's just that it's early days yet,' Tara explained.

'I think it's lovely how you two have found each other again.' Jinny's expression was dreamy. 'I love a good romance. Fill me up.' She held out her empty glass.

Tara also loved a good romance, but there hadn't been a happy ever after with Cal the first time. Would it happen the second time? Could she trust him to put the pieces of her heart back together? Whatever happened, it was too late to back away now. She hadn't put just a toe in the water, she was immersed up to her neck and with every kiss, every look, every touch, she was in danger of being swept away.

The shrill sound of an incoming call woke Tara, and she groaned. Her head was thumping, her tongue was sticking to the roof of her mouth and she felt sick. She never should have drunk so much last night. It was Jinny's fault.

She groaned again when she saw the time.

It was her mother on the phone. 'Tara? Are you OK? I haven't heard from you in ages. I was beginning to worry. Sorry to ring so early, but I thought I might catch you in.'

'Yes, Mum, I'm fine. No, honestly, I'm good. Really good.' Damn it, she knew she shouldn't have left it so long since her last phone call, but she'd been so busy.

She'd sent her mum loads of photos and they messaged each other often, but she hadn't actually spoken to her for nearly three weeks. She didn't want to speak to her now, but only because she had a raging hangover, and the thought of talking to anyone made her feel queasy. Tara hoped Jinny was suffering equally as badly, since it was all her fault for bringing the bottles of wine.

'Toby and I will have to come and visit,' her mum said. 'But I honestly don't know when that will be; after Christmas probably.'

Christmas was half a year away, but with Mum and Toby owning a caravan park and this being the height of summer, Tara knew they would be hard-pressed to get away any time soon. The site was open ten months of the year, only being closed for January and February, so if she wanted to see her mum before then, she'd have to be the one who did the travelling. But not just yet. She had too much going on.

'I'll try to visit you before then,' Tara promised. The number of tourists to Skye dwindled as the days shortened and the weather turned stormier, so autumn would be an ideal time to fly south, like the swallows.

'It looks beautiful,' her mum was saying. 'But then, Skye is. Did I tell you that your father and I spent a weekend there before you were born?'

'Yes, Mum, you did.'

'We didn't climb The Old Man of Storr though, or go out in a boat to see whales. Maybe we could do something like that when we visit?'

'Maybe.' By then she would have told Mum about Cal, so perhaps they could all go together, including Bonnie. Tara knew that her mum would simply adore Bonnie. The one thing Mum lamented was the lack of grandchildren, and with the end of Tara and Dougie's marriage, the idea of grandchildren had been put on ice.

Would Cal want any more children, Tara wondered. He'd had Bonnie so young, that nearly all of his twenties had been taken up with a child. Maybe he felt he was done at one, because in another few years his nest would be empty and he could begin to do all those things he'd probably missed out on when he had a small child to consider.

How did Tara feel about the possibility of not being a mother? If she had to decide between being with Cal and having a child of her own, which would she choose? She would be Bonnie's stepmum, obviously, but would that be enough?

Tara thought it might…

With a sigh, she realised she was getting ahead of herself. She and Cal hadn't even slept together yet (or they *had*, but not for many years), and any future they might have hadn't been hinted at. Tara knew one thing, though – her mother wouldn't be happy when she found out that Cal was back in her life. Mum had witnessed first-hand the devastation he'd wrought.

Oh, well, that was a conversation for another day. Even if Tara didn't have a hangover from hell, there was no way she could face telling her mother about Cal right now. Their relationship would have to be on a much firmer footing before she put that particular cat amongst the pigeons.

A loud, persistent knocking woke Tara with a start. It took her a second to remember where she was and what day it was. She was in the boathouse and it was Sunday.

The knock came again, and she heaved her stiff body off the sofa and staggered to the door.

'Oh, dear,' were Cal's first words when he saw her.

'If that's all you can say, go away.' She pretended to shut the door on him.

'Heavy night?'

'You could say that.' She poured a glass of water from the tap and drank it down. 'What's the time?'

'Eleven thirty. Have you just got up?'

'I've been up since nine.' After her mum's phone call, she'd taken two paracetamols, made a cup of tea and curled up on the sofa, her head resting on the cushions as she stared vacantly at the loch. At some point, she must have fallen asleep.

'Are you working today?' he asked.

'I don't think I can.' Thankfully her headache had gone, but she wasn't in the mood for making anything more than a piece of toast. The thought of making fiddly little doors and windows for Bonnie's doll's house made her feel ill. Besides, a day off would do her good.

He said, 'What if I cook you a fried breakfast? Have you got any bacon?'

She did, though she wasn't sure a full English was the way forward. But her tummy had settled since earlier, and it was telling her it was hungry. When it rumbled loudly, she gave in. 'I like my bacon crispy,' she told him.

'I haven't forgotten.' His gaze caught hers and held it.

She wondered what else he remembered. She hadn't forgotten a single thing. The smallest detail was imprinted on her memory.

'Do you mind if I have a quick shower while you make breakfast?' she asked.

When he said he didn't, she hurried into the bathroom, grimacing when she saw herself in the mirror. Pale face, scarecrow hair, no bra.

The shower took care of the hair, make-up helped with the pale face and getting dressed helped with the droopy boobs.

Feeling more presentable, she emerged from the bedroom to the enticing smell of grilled bacon and hot coffee. The radio was on, and Cal was shaking his backside to an old Motown number as he fried a couple of eggs.

'Nearly ready,' he yelled over his shoulder, then yelped when he saw her watching him. Putting the spatula-free hand to his chest, he said, 'You scared me to death. I thought you were in the bedroom.'

'So I noticed.'

'You caught the dancing, did you?' He wiggled his hips. 'I've still got the moves.'

'You never had any moves to start with. You dance like a monkey who has eaten too many E numbers.'

'That's harsh. I'm insulted.'

'You know it's true.'

'OK, maybe it is, but at least I can fry an egg.'

'So can I.'

'You never used to be able to. You always managed to break them.'

'I've been practising.'

He slid an egg onto a plate where bacon, mushrooms, a grilled tomato and some baked beans were already sitting and passed it to her.

Her mouth watering, Tara sat at the table, noticing that Cal had already laid it. He'd even poured her a glass of orange juice and had remembered the salt and pepper. She began to eat, hesitantly at first, as she wondered whether her delicate stomach was ready to receive it.

It seemed it was, and she and Cal scoffed their food in contented silence, the only sounds being the muted music from the radio and the scrape of cutlery on plates.

Eventually replete, Tara mopped up the last of the bean sauce with the rest of her toast and popped it in her mouth.

'That was delicious,' she said. 'Exactly what I needed.'

'I know what else you need: fresh air.'

'I don't think I can face a walk,' she admitted with a shudder.

'How about if you don't have to walk anywhere, and can just sit and watch the world go by?'

'That sounds better.' She didn't mind going for a drive. She'd thoroughly enjoyed the scenery to and from their hike the other day.

Tara stacked the dishwasher whilst Cal went to get ready, but when she'd finished she was surprised to see him waiting for her and the car nowhere in sight.

'We're going out on the boat, aren't we?' she guessed, horrified. A boat bobbing on the waves and a hangover didn't make good bedfellows.

'Yep. I promised I'd take you out on the loch, and today is perfect.'

She had to admit that the conditions were at their optimum. There wasn't a breath of wind, and the surface of the loch was as smooth as the mirror in her bathroom.

'Do you promise it won't be too wavy?' she asked.

He crossed his heart. 'I promise.'

'Do I have to wear anything in particular? Like a wetsuit?'

She could see him trying not to laugh. 'Not unless you want to go for a swim, and even then, I wouldn't bother with a wetsuit. The water isn't that cold.'

Tara didn't intend to find out. She wouldn't even go as far as dipping her toe in. However, she was happy enough to sit in a boat where it was nice and dry, and she was even happier when Cal informed her there was a cushion for her to sit on and a throw if she got cold. He'd clearly thought about her comfort, because when she'd watched him row out to the opposite shore the other week, she was pretty certain he hadn't bothered with a cushion.

After making sure she had her phone – this would be a photo opportunity, if ever she saw one – Tara was ready, and they set off. Cal had already hauled the boat to the water's edge, and it only took a couple of shoves to push it all the way in.

He held her hand as she clambered into it whilst trying not to get her feet wet, and she was rather alarmed when it wobbled and bobbed in the water, although as soon as she sat down and Cal got in and took up the oars, it stopped rocking.

Soon he was rowing strongly, and the boat was gliding through the water. He sat directly opposite her, and she tried to focus on where they were going, rather than on the muscles of the man getting them there. But it was no good. His shoulders, chest, arms and thighs rippled and bunched as he powered the oars through the water in a steady, fluid rhythm.

It was mesmerising, and each time she managed to tear her gaze away from his body to his face, she found him watching her. It both excited and unsettled her.

Self-consciously she looked at the scenery over his shoulder, and noticed the far shore was getting steadily closer.

She wondered when he would stop rowing, put down those oars and take her in his arms, because the promise in his eyes told her that's what he was going to do. Sooner or later, he would gather her to him and kiss her. It wasn't as though he hadn't kissed her before. He had, and recently. But out here, on the flat mirrored water, its meaning would be deeper, more significant, because this was his special place.

'You don't go out in the boat just to fish, do you?' she asked with sudden insight.

'I come out here to think. If I catch a fish, it's a bonus.' His gaze roamed over the surrounding mountains. 'Look at it, it's magnificent and humbling, and it feeds my soul. I always feel more grounded when I've been out on the water.' His eyes were glistening. 'I love this place, the wildness, the freedom…'

The passion in his voice made her shiver and her heart race. He was so at home in this landscape, and his love for it was as clear as the water beneath them.

Bringing the boat in close to the rocks, he glanced behind him, turning his head from side to side as he checked they weren't about to be shipwrecked on those rough teeth of seaweed-draped stone.

She watched the skill with which he manoeuvred the fragile boat through the channels, and glanced over the side to see the hull glide over their submerged shapes as she held her breath.

With small sculling motions, Cal eased the boat closer to the shore and Tara heard the bottom scrape on the pebbly beach. Then he got to his feet in one fluid motion and leapt over the side, splashing into the shallows. Drawing the craft closer to the shore, he dragged it until the front was clear of the water whilst Tara gripped the sides, fearful of toppling in.

She took his hand when he offered it, and she expected him to help her jump to dry land. Instead, he scooped her effortlessly into his arms, holding her tight against his chest, and carried her beyond the high tide mark before depositing her gently on the grass.

'Kiss me,' she commanded, melting into him as he did as he was told.

With his mouth on hers, he lowered her onto the springy grass. She lay back, relishing the taste of him, the well-remembered feel of his body covering hers, the strangeness of new contours as her hands roamed over the less familiar landscape of his back and shoulders, and marvelled at the subtle changes that those lost years had wrought.

His tongue sought hers as she slid her hands under his T-shirt, and she gave in to the desire thrumming through her veins. And as she made love to Cal on the far shore of the placid loch, with the sounds of the gently lapping waves and the wild cries of sea birds overhead, Tara felt as though she was home. This is where she should have been all along, in the arms of the man she had never stopped loving.

The grass underneath her tickled and scratched, but Tara barely felt it. She was far too content to move, with one leg over Cal's, her body curled into his, her head resting in the dip between his chest and his shoulder while she stroked the fine chestnut hairs on his stomach.

Cal had fetched the throw from the boat and it was draped over them, covering their nakedness, although the only witnesses were the seabirds and the occasional curious seal. One had hauled itself out onto a rock not far from the boat and Tara's languid gaze rested on it as it sunned itself, a flipper raised to the sky.

Neither she nor Cal had spoken much since leaving the boat, except when she'd whispered his name and he'd moaned hers. The sound had made her shiver with ecstasy.

He lay there with one arm around her, the other under his head. His eyes were open as he stared at the sky, and she wondered what he was thinking but she was too scared to ask.

A quick, furtive, sleek movement near the water's edge caught her attention, but Cal's grip tightened and he held her still.

Tara subsided as he murmured, 'Shh, otter,' out of the side of his mouth.

She risked a glance at him. His eyes were on the otter and there was wonderment on his face.

She tracked the creature's slinky progress along the shoreline as it dipped in and out of the water and winnowed over the rocks until it eventually disappeared. Then she slowly sat up.

Cal's attention was on her, yet the wonder remained on his face, and she realised it wasn't for the otter, but for her and what they'd just done.

Lying down again, she pushed the throw to one side, her invitation clear, and with a groan on his lips and hunger in his eyes, Cal made love to her once more.

-

There was no going back from this, Cal realised, as the boat chugged across the loch, back to the jetty and the little beach, and reality.

Did he regret it?

Not one glorious second of it. Making love with Tara had been the most natural thing in the world, and he'd relished every kiss, every touch, every sigh of pleasure. It was as good as he remembered. Better, because now he knew how awful life was without her. How incomplete he'd felt, and once again he kicked himself for letting her go.

Letting her go wasn't accurate – he had pushed her away.

But what else could he have done?

They'd been out on the loch for hours and the day was edging towards evening, the shadows lengthening imperceptibly until soon they would be indistinguishable from the encroaching night. Sunset was still some way off, and he was glad because it meant there was more of this day to spend with Tara, and he didn't want it to end.

'Hungry?' he asked, after she'd helped him drag *Misty Lady* out of the water. 'I've got a couple of steaks at the cottage and some beers.'

'I can supply salad and focaccia. And me.' Her voice was light and teasing, but her eyes told a different story. He couldn't blame her for being a little fearful. After all, he had hurt her badly, and he suspected she was scared he might do so again.

'Food first. Then I want to take you to bed.' In his clumsy way, he was trying to tell her that what had happened on the loch wasn't a one-off.

They walked to the cottage together, her carrying the cushion, him carrying the throw, then they made their way to the boathouse, she with the steaks in her hand, he with four bottles of Speckled Hen clinking in their cardboard container.

Tara cooked this time, the meal quickly prepared, although eating it was a slower affair. As they lingered at the table, hands stretched across its surface to touch fingers, Cal marvelled at the difference between the meal earlier today and this one. Both had been eaten at the same table, but the emotional distance between the two was vast. Tara occupied his mind and his heart, filling up the empty spaces he hadn't realised were there until now.

With his stomach full, his heart even fuller, Cal suggested they take the two remaining beers and sit on the jetty. He needed to be outside, to breathe freely, because when he was indoors, Tara stole the very air from the room and the breath from his lungs.

Sitting on the edge of the jetty, the evening was serene and silent, in that magical time poised between day and night before the last rays of the dying sun tipped the world over the edge and into darkness.

When night finally descended and the beers had been drunk, Tara scrambled to her feet, slipped her sandals back on, held out her hand and led him back to the boat-house. And after they had made love once again and were snuggled under the duvet, limbs entwined, only one thing would make this wonderful, enchanted day even more perfect. Cal knew he was taking a risk that she mightn't want to hear it, or mightn't feel the same way, but it had to be said.

'I love you, Tara. I always have.'

She stiffened in his arms, and his heart lurched as he thought he'd lost her, that he'd ruined this perfect day, but when she drew in a deep breath, let it out slowly and said, 'I love you, too,' Cal didn't believe he could be any happier than he was right now.

Chapter 19

Tara glowed. She knew she did, because she could see it whenever she caught her reflection in the mirror. She could even spot the glow in the door of her portable oven (an essential piece of kit to dry polymer clay models) and in the window of her studio. Which meant that other people could see it too.

When he'd kissed her before sneaking back to his cottage, the grin on Cal's face had been brighter than the sun that had just peeped over the hillside behind the castle. Tara hoped he'd managed to dim the wattage down a bit before people started talking. She, for one, wasn't prepared for anyone to know just yet. Their relationship was too new, and she wanted to keep it to herself and savour it for a while, to get used to it.

She still couldn't believe yesterday had actually happened. And for Cal to tell her that he loved her... She hugged herself with joy. Never in a million years did she imagine that moving to Skye would rekindle a love she'd thought was lost forever.

Tara had never felt so happy.

The only midges in the ointment were her mother and Bonnie. Tara was fairly confident Bonnie wouldn't be a problem because they got on so well, and she was hopeful her mum would come around to the idea of Cal being in her daughter's life once more when she saw how happy he made her. Tara suspected she'd get a fair bit of flak before her mother accepted the situation though, which was a perfectly good reason not to tell her just yet. She would wait a while before she mentioned anything, so Mum wouldn't think it was a flash in the pan. Cal also didn't want to make their relationship public just now because Bonnie had enough going on in her young life without adding another thing for her to deal with, and Tara had to respect that. They had all the time in the world for his daughter to become used to having Tara around. There was no point in rushing things.

Cal had suggested the three of them get out, as he was looking after Bonnie this week and next now that school had broken up, so Tara was taking tomorrow off to visit somewhere called the Fairy Pools. It sounded magical and she was looking forward to it, apart from one thing: the words 'bathing costume' and 'wild swimming' had been mentioned in the same sentence.

Tara was no expert, but even she was aware that the rivers and streams on Skye were flipping freezing, and a quick search on the internet had confirmed her fears. Those pools were going to be cold. There was no way Cal would persuade her to dip her toe in, let alone immerse herself fully. Anyway, there was rain forecast for tomorrow, so the only part of her that would be exposed to the elements would be her nose.

Tara came up for air, her scalp aching from the near-freezing temperature of the crystal clear water, and let out a gasp. Cal was bobbing beside her, looking utterly unaffected by the icy pool. Bonnie, who was doggy-paddling beside him, didn't appear to be overly affected either, and Tara concluded that they must be made of sterner stuff.

Despite the crushing cold that invaded her bones, she felt remarkably alive and invigorated. But maybe it was the onset of hypothermia. Hadn't she read somewhere that victims of hypothermia could begin to feel warm?

'Swim through the arch with me, Tara,' Bonnie demanded, before disappearing beneath the surface like a seal and heading towards an underwater rock formation.

'I'm getting out,' Tara stammered, her teeth chattering so hard she was scared she would shatter a tooth.

Cal called, 'There are towels in my rucksack,' as she scrambled awkwardly out of the water.

Her skin was almost as blue as the pool and was dotted with goosebumps. Why, oh why, had she agreed to this? She would have been quite content to watch from the relative warmth of the bank, fully clothed and possibly with a cup of hot tea in her hands. But she'd had to rise to the challenge, hadn't she?

As she struggled to strip off her sodden swimming costume with one hand whilst holding the towel around her with the other, she had to admit that wild swimming in one of Skye's most famous locations had been an experience, and one she would never forget. Or repeat. Once was enough, but at least she could boast that she'd done it.

Still clutching the towel in a death-like grip, Tara managed to drag on her clothes, finally starting to feel a tad warmer, so she was on hand to help Bonnie get dressed when the girl emerged from the pool. Cal, the daft so-and-so, was big enough to take care of himself.

With all three of them finally dry and the wet costumes and towels stashed back in Cal's rucksack, he took out the large flask she'd been eyeing up. When he unscrewed the lid, an enticing aroma of hot chocolate wafted up her nose.

She would enjoy that – if she was able to stop shivering for long enough to hold the cup.

'Did you see me swim through the arch, Tara?' Bonnie asked, a film of chocolate-coloured liquid coating her upper lip. She licked it away as Cal plonked a knitted hat on her head.

'I did,' Tara said. 'I can't believe the pool was deep enough to swim in.'

She hadn't been able to touch the bottom with her toes, although she'd been able to see it. The water was as clear as glass and an unbelievable shade of turquoise blue. The Fairy Pools had been carved out by a burn flowing through the glen and cutting into the rock. The water itself came from the semicircle of mountains at the head of a wide glacial valley formed during the last ice age – so Cal had informed her on the relatively gentle walk up the hill from the car park.

The water gushed down the hillside in fast-flowing icy torrents, creating a series of waterfalls and pools in the rock. It was certainly a land of magic and fairies, and Cal had kept Bonnie and Tara entertained by recounting an old legend of selkies who were supposed to be people who'd been lost at sea. When the moon was full, they would transform back into human form, becoming mortal for just one night, and would walk from the sea to the pools to swim.

Tara thought that if she was a selkie and could be human for one night, she'd be buggered if she'd want to do any more swimming. But she supposed that toasting one's toes beside a roaring fire and scoffing a nice bowl of pasta wouldn't make such a good story.

'Shall we head off to Glenbrittle beach, or have the pair of you had enough of water?' Cal asked.

Bonnie, unsurprisingly, was all for the beach.

Tara had a condition. 'Only if you promise not to make me go in the sea.'

'I didn't make you go in the pool,' Cal pointed out.

'You *did*. You called me chicken. That's as good as pushing someone in.'

'I thought Tara was very brave,' Bonnie said loyally. 'It was really cold, Dad.' She finished her hot chocolate and gave him the plastic mug back.

As they'd been sitting there, the noise of the waterfall filling their ears, several people had stopped to take selfies with the pool in the background, and one or two intrepid souls had also taken a dip. All of them had emerged triumphant and more than a little shell-shocked.

Tara began to feel rather smug. She also felt recharged, as though every cell in her body had absorbed the energy of that wild, tumbling burn. Every inch of her felt alive and tingling, and when Cal slipped his hand briefly into hers as Bonnie scampered ahead of them on the trail back to the car, she said, 'Thank you for bringing me here. I've loved every minute.'

'And I love you!' His lips brushed fleetingly across her mouth, and then he moved away, jogging to catch up with his exuberant daughter.

'I love you, too,' she whispered back, knowing he was unable to hear but wanting to say the words anyway. She would tell him again tonight when Bonnie had gone back to her mother, and Tara had Cal all to herself again.

-

The beach at Glenbrittle wasn't what one usually thought of when the word 'beach' was mentioned, as it was a grey colour due to its volcanic sand.

Cal had brought Bonnie and Tara here because this was where the River Brittle discharged into the sea, and the burn they'd swum in was one of its tributaries. The beach also had a great cafe, and they could all do with some food.

He was starving. The water had been damned cold, although he hadn't admitted to Tara how chilled he'd been. He must have used a thousand calories just to stop his limbs from seizing up. To say he was impressed with Tara was an understatement. He didn't think he would persuade her to go in, but she'd surprised him.

Bonnie had been impressed by Tara, too. Yvaine would never have made it as far as the Fairy Pools, let alone go for a swim in them, and Cal knew it grated on his ex-wife's nerves that Bonnie was an outdoorsy child, and not the pretty dresses and pink bows daughter that Yvaine wanted her to be.

By the time the car reached the beach, the mountains and waterfalls had given way to fields and a more sedate river.

Cal had expected the car park to be busy – the whole of Skye was busy at this time of year – but he managed to find a parking space, and they slipped through the kissing gate to make their way along the lane running parallel to the beach and to the cafe beyond. He'd been here once before, in the early days of trying to get a feel for the island he'd found himself living on, and he remembered the food being excellent.

Faced with a choice of soup, goat cheese, tomato and basil torte, spicy Mexican bean rolls, or a cauliflower and roasted chickpea pastie, Tara couldn't decide. Neither could Bonnie, so Cal suggested they all have the soup (lentil, carrot and coriander), which came with a roll, and also order one of everything else, so they could each have a taste.

After they'd eaten, Bonnie wanted another hot chocolate – apparently the one the cafe served was much better than his – while he and Tara settled for coffee.

'Can we go play on the beach, Dad?' Bonnie asked as soon as her tummy was full.

Cal smiled indulgently. He'd brought a ball, a bucket and a net for that very purpose, although he couldn't remember whether there were any rock pools at the end of the horseshoe beach to dabble in.

Tara proved to be rather good at kicking a ball about and was brilliant in goal, deflecting enough of Bonnie's shots that the child didn't think Tara was deliberately letting her score a goal.

Two hours later, with the beach and the mouth of the river thoroughly explored, Cal called it a day. Yvaine would be expecting him to drop Bonnie off soon, as his fatherly duties didn't include having his daughter overnight this week, so it was time they made a move.

Bless her, Bonnie fell asleep on the journey back, her head lolling, allowing Cal and Tara to exchange steamy glances. He was careful not to say anything though, in case his daughter wasn't as deeply asleep as he thought.

'Do you mind if we drop Bonnie off on the way?' he asked when they were a mile or so outside the village. It seemed silly to drive back to the castle to drop Tara off, then have to turn around and go back into the village again.

'Of course not.' She sat up straighter, and he wondered whether it was because she might see Yvaine. Not for the first time, Cal wondered how she felt about his ex-wife living in the same village. One day he would ask, but not today.

Cal pulled up a short distance beyond the house, so Yvaine wouldn't have a clear view of the person in the passenger seat. Knowing Yvaine, she probably wouldn't notice, so uninterested was she in anything to do with his life. Unless it involved her directly (him not being able to have Bonnie when she wanted him to, for instance) Yvaine couldn't care less.

It used to rankle, but today he was glad of it. He didn't need her asking awkward questions with Bonnie in earshot.

Bonnie reached forward to give Tara a hug, and then she was out of the car and running towards the house. Cal followed quickly, his daughter's backpack dangling from his hand.

She barrelled through the door, yelling for her mother, and Yvaine appeared, looking preoccupied.

'Mum, we've been to the Fairy Pools and then we went to the beach, and we had soup and pasties, and I swam through the arch, and Tara—'

'Calm down, Bonnie. You can tell me all about your day in a minute. Take your bag upstairs and get changed.'

Cal handed the bag to Bonnie, who threw herself at him. 'Thank you for a lovely day!' she cried. 'Will I see you tomorrow?'

Yvaine met his eyes. 'If that's OK? Can you fetch her, instead of me dropping her off? I've got to be in Portree by nine. I need to have a word with the builders. You won't believe the day I've had.' She rubbed the back of her hand across her brow.

'I'll pick her up at seven-thirty,' he said. 'Make sure she wears old clothes as she's signed up for the junior pottery workshop.'

Yvaine rolled her eyes.

Cal didn't react. Yvaine was jealous that Bonnie loved spending time at the castle. If it had been one of her Portree friends who was offering to help Bonnie make a pot, Yvaine would have been much more enthusiastic.

'If you don't want her to take part, I suggest you tell her,' he said, knowing full well that she wouldn't.

He didn't bother saying goodbye, hearing the door close firmly behind him as he walked away. By the time he reached the car, he'd forgotten his ex-wife. His mind was wholly on Tara. They had a full evening ahead of them, and all he wanted to do was to take her to bed and make love to her until dawn.

Chapter 20

By the end of the week, Tara was getting used to rising early to share coffee and toast with Cal before he went back to his own place to have a shower and prepare to have Bonnie for the day.

After he kissed her goodbye this morning, Tara made another coffee and took it outside to drink. Skye was living up to its non-official name of the Misty Isle today, as low clouds obscured the mountains and a mist shimmered over the loch. The air was damp, and Tara's hair and clothes were soon coated in tiny droplets. She didn't mind. She'd be showering shortly and changing into her paint-daubed jeans and an old T-shirt. However careful she was, she always managed to get some splodges on her.

Since she was up early, she'd do what she had done all this week – go to the studio and work on Bonnie's doll's house. A few days ago, another commission had come in, so she needed to start on that, as well as make some more of the bread-and-butter houses she sold online.

Tara was busier than she could ever remember being, and she adored every minute of it. Her days were full of doing what she loved, and her nights were full of being with the man she loved. Two months ago, when she'd been faced with selling the house in Edinburgh and finding somewhere to live, she could never have imagined how brilliant her life could be.

A short while later, Tara was opening up the studio when she saw Gillian waving to her.

'I've got some scones fresh out of the oven,' the cafe manager announced. 'In case you fancy one. Mark my words, they'll be all gone by lunchtime.'

'Ooh, yes please. If you don't mind, I'll take it back to the studio and eat it later.'

As Gillian packed up a scone, adding a small pot of jam and a ramekin of thick cream, she asked, 'Are you all set for your workshop next week?'

'More or less. I still can't believe I'm running one. What if people don't like it?'

'Of course they'll like it. How many have you got booked in?'

'Eight.'

'A nice number. Any more, and you won't be able to give them the attention they deserve. Believe me, you'll take to it like a duck to water. You're a natural teacher.' She handed the stone to Tara. 'Bonnie showed me the tea set she made. Are you going to run any workshops for children?'

'Probably. Everyone else is.' Several events were planned for over the summer, and Cal was pleased with the sign-up numbers. Two of these were taking place in the next few weeks, as well as the adult-based residential workshops that Coorie Castle was becoming famous for. Tara was incredibly excited to be part of it, even if she was nervous about delivering a workshop of her own.

Thanking Gillian for the scone, she hurried back to the studio, anxious to begin work. She had such a lot to do, and now that she was spending her evenings (and some days as well, she thought, smiling as she remembered the amazing visit to the Fairy Pools) with Cal, she had less time to focus on her business. However, with this being Cal's turn to have Bonnie for the weekend, Tara would be able to catch up tonight and tomorrow – unless Bonnie insisted on her joining them for supper and board games.

It was hard hiding her feelings for Cal from Bonnie, and even harder not being able to kiss him, but she would survive. Absence – or abstinence – was supposed to make the heart grow fonder, and she was looking forward to Sunday night after Bonnie had gone back to her mum. Tara was already tingling at the thought.

A few minutes later, seated on the stool at the work-bench, the tingling had disappeared as she concentrated on laying the flooring in Bonnie's little house. The construction, although not the traditional single front opening, hadn't taken long, and neither had the exterior details, and Tara was now busy working her magic on the rooms themselves.

This was the fiddly bit, and where her attention to detail came into its own.

She had her head down and was concentrating hard when the studio door opened. People often came in for a gander, wanting to watch the crafters at work, so she didn't look up immediately, calling out a quick 'Hello' instead, before having the awful thought that it might be Bonnie. She'd been so careful to hide the doll's house from her that she'd feel dreadful if she spoiled the surprise now.

A glance told her that it wasn't Cal's daughter who had entered her studio.

It was his ex-wife. And the woman didn't look happy.

'I guessed as much,' Yvaine declared, scanning her up and down with disdain.

Tara was equally as unhappy. It had never occurred to her that Yvaine would walk into her studio, despite being aware that Bonnie's mum sometimes dropped her off at the castle.

If Tara was honest, she'd been hoping she wouldn't encounter Yvaine at all for some time yet. To see her standing in her studio, glaring at her, was rather a shock.

Tara didn't know how to respond to Yvaine's comment, so she said nothing.

'I had to see for myself,' Yvaine continued. 'Prince Cal and Princess Tara, indeed!'

Tara found her voice. 'Excuse me?'

'I would say he's all yours, but he's *always* been all yours, hasn't he? I was always second best.' Yvaine spat out the words, and Tara flinched. 'I bet you're pleased with yourself,' she added.

The power of speech deserted Tara once more as she stared at the bitter expression on the woman's face.

Yvaine said, 'I hope you'll both be very happy, but don't count on it. He dumped you once, he could dump you again.' And with that, she turned smartly on her three-inch heels and marched out the door.

Open-mouthed and shaking, Tara tracked the woman's progress towards the car park. When she could no longer see her, she got slowly to her feet and pushed the door closed, locking it for good measure.

Yvaine's visit might have been unexpected and unpleasant, but it confirmed something: Cal had been telling the truth when he'd said that he'd never stopped loving Tara. However, she gained no satisfaction from the knowledge. Instead, all she felt was pity for Cal's ex-wife. She also felt guilty. Poor Dougie... In hindsight, it must have been obvious to him that she hadn't loved him as deeply as she should have.

Between them, she and Cal had made a right hash of their respective marriages, and she just hoped Dougie and Yvaine would find happiness with their new partners.

–

Cal hadn't expected to see Yvaine quite so soon. She'd just dropped Bonnie off for the weekend, and he'd been supervising his daughter's unpacking of her overnight bag when Yvaine phoned him and demanded he come to the car park.

Assuming Bonnie had forgotten something and Yvaine couldn't be bothered to drive back down the lane, he left Bonnie to put everything away. Goodness knows what she might have brought with her. One time she had sneaked her mum's make-up into her case, and needless to say, Yvaine hadn't been pleased.

She didn't look pleased now either, Cal thought when he spotted her leaning against her car. Her arms were folded and she had a face like thunder.

'When were you going to tell me that the Tara Bonnie has been wittering on about for weeks is the same Tara you dated in university?' she demanded as soon as he was within earshot.

Damn, he was hoping she wouldn't join the dots for a while. 'I didn't think it relevant,' he said.

'I'll be the judge of that,' Yvaine snapped.

'What difference does it make?'

She shook her head, her eyes narrowed. 'You've always held a torch for her, and here she is, living in the boat-house and working at the craft centre. How convenient. I suppose you arranged it?'

'You suppose wrong. I didn't know she was here until Bonnie and I came back from visiting my parents. Mhairi sorted it out when I was in Inverness.'

'I don't believe you.'

'I'm sorry you don't, but it's the truth. Can we not have this discussion here?' He saw Jinny get out of her car and he smiled stiffly when she gave them a curious look.

'Scared your girlfriend will overhear?'

'She's not my girlfriend.'

'You could have fooled me.'

'It looks like I did.' Cal hated lying, but if he told Yvaine the truth she would mention it to Bonnie, and he didn't want his daughter to know about him and Tara yet. Anyway, *he* wanted to be the one to tell her, not Yvaine, and that wouldn't happen until Bonnie was settled in her new house and her new school. If that took a few months, then so be it. Tara understood why he didn't want details of their relationship bandied about, so not telling Yvaine was a necessary evil.

He stepped away as Yvaine got into her car, and it was with sadness and regret that he watched her drive away. He felt guilty for having hurt her so badly, and knew he never should have married her, despite the pregnancy. Trying to do the right thing hadn't been the right thing at all, for either of them – or for Bonnie. But he'd been determined to make it work, and God knows he'd tried his best.

It had proved impossible to force love though, and Yvaine must have sensed she didn't have his heart. His mum was right – Yvaine *had* suspected all along who did.

His heart went out to his ex-wife. He hadn't meant to hurt her, but he had anyway by not loving her the way he should have loved her. He hoped Lenn was that man, and she could find the happiness she deserved.

All morning Tara kept a weather eye out for Calan, but she didn't catch sight of him. She guessed he wasn't aware that she'd had a visitor this morning, and as it wasn't something she wanted to tell him via a message, she decided to wait until she saw him before she told him about her encounter with his ex-wife. So it was a surprise when Jinny messaged her to ask if Cal was OK.

He's fine. Why? was her puzzled response.

> He and Yvaine were having a barney in the car park earlier.

Was that before or after Yvaine had been to see her, Tara wondered. She didn't bother replying, locking up and hurrying to the gift shop instead.

'What were they arguing about?' she asked Jinny, as soon as she'd made certain their conversation couldn't be overheard. Thankfully, the only people in the shop were customers, as Fiona, who was the other staff member onsite today, had gone on her lunch. As long as Tara and Jinny kept their voices down, no one would take any notice.

'You,' Jinny replied.

Tara stiffened. 'What did they say?' she asked cautiously.

'I didn't hear all of it, you understand. But I did hear Yvaine accusing Cal of arranging for you to be here, and him saying that he didn't know anything about you being at the castle until he came back to work after his holiday.' Jinny was eyeing her speculatively. 'I know that's true, but even if it wasn't, what would it matter? Several of the studios have been rented out because one of the crafters knew someone who might fit the bill.'

'Did she say anything else?'

'She seems to think you're his girlfriend, but Cal said not. He is, though, isn't he? Or is he just a friend with benefits?'

'No! It's not like that. We're kind of seeing each other. How do you know anyway?'

Jinny gave her a disbelieving look. 'Bonnie says you've had dinner with them and have been on days out together. And I've got eyes in my head, as does everyone else at the castle.'

Tara knew when she was beaten. 'OK, we *are* seeing each other, but Cal doesn't want it made public because Bonnie doesn't know yet.'

'Why ever not? You get on all right, don't you?'

'We do, but she isn't happy about moving to Portree and leaving her school and her friends, so he wants to wait until she's settled before he tells her. And it gives her more time to get used to me being around.'

'Sensible,' Jinny said. 'She's told me she doesn't want to go. And Katie is upset, too. They're like a couple of bookends, lost without the other. Katie is going to miss her.'

'I'm certain Cal will make sure they get together on the weekends he has Bonnie.'

'But that's not fair on him. That's his time to spend with her.'

'He'll put his feelings to one side,' Tara said confidently. 'I know Cal. He'll do anything to make Bonnie happy.'

Unfortunately, Tara didn't realise how prophetic those words would be.

Cal let out a tired sigh. Looking after Bonnie was knackering. The child rarely stopped chattering long enough to draw breath, so the peace that had descended on the cottage now she was tucked up in bed and fast asleep was very welcome.

He took a beer out of the fridge and cracked it open. Carrying it outside, he sat on the deck and swigged a mouthful, automatically glancing at the boathouse as he did so.

A faint light showed through the window, and he wondered what Tara was doing and whether she had eaten. He'd sent her a message earlier, telling her that he and Bonnie were going out in the skiff this afternoon, but he hadn't invited Tara to come along even though he would dearly have loved her to.

Bonnie hadn't suggested it either, which made him think she may have been glad to have him all to herself for a change. That was also why he hadn't asked Tara to have dinner with them this evening. Although, whilst he and Bonnie had been out on the loch, he'd sensed Tara watching, and at one point he'd stared directly at the boathouse when Bonnie was facing the other way and had mouthed, 'I love you.'

He hoped Tara had seen.

The light in the boathouse went out and Cal took another mouthful of beer, imagining her getting ready for bed, her skin shadowed in the darkness. She slept naked when they spent the night together, but was she naked now, alone in that double bed? How he wished he was in it with her, but he would never leave his sleeping daughter unattended. And Tara couldn't come here, for obvious reasons.

Movement near the boathouse caught his eye, and he stiffened. One of the shadows was moving purposefully towards him, and he realised Tara was coming here after all.

He rose, walking quietly to meet her before she reached the deck, and when he was within touching distance, he drew her into the trees. Gathering her into his arms, he kissed her soundly, desire surging through him as he pushed her against a sturdy trunk.

'I had to see you,' she murmured after the kiss ended.

She kept her voice low, and he was grateful for that. Sound travelled far at night, and although he was fairly sure Bonnie was asleep, there was always the chance she mightn't be.

'Yvaine?' he guessed.

'She paid me a visit this morning.'

'So I gathered. I'm sorry.'

'It's not your fault.' Tara was generous in her absolution, but Cal knew he was to blame. He should have told Yvaine who the doll's house maker was. Although, how he would have gone about it without it becoming more of a thing than it already was, he hadn't been able to figure out.

He said, 'I told her you're not my girlfriend, but only because I didn't want her saying anything to Bonnie yet.'

He debated whether or not to mention the promise he'd made to Bonnie that he wouldn't have a girlfriend until she had a boyfriend (which was probably never in Bonnie's eyes, although she would soon change her mind when she became a teenager), but he decided against it. There was no point, since he was sure Bonnie would be OK with it when she realised his girlfriend was Tara – someone she knew, liked and looked up to. And by the time Cal told her, Bonnie would have gotten to know Tara even better.

'I understand.' Tara pulled him closer, and he pressed his mouth to hers.

It was a long time before they came up for air, and by then he was breathing hard and his pulse was racing.

Tara didn't appear to be in any better shape as she breathlessly said, 'I'd better go back before we do something we'll regret.'

'I won't regret it,' It came out as a hoarse growl, and Tara giggled.

'I refuse to make love with my back against a tree,' she told him.

'We could go down to the beach.'

'And what if Bonnie wakes up?'

Cal knew she was right, and his ardour cooled. 'I can't wait for Sunday night,' he said.

'You're going to have to.' And with that, she planted a kiss on his lips then danced out of reach.

Cal waited until a light came on in the boathouse before he went inside. Sunday couldn't come fast enough.

Chapter 21

'I'd better get a move on, and so had you,' Tara said in alarm after glancing at the digital clock on Cal's oven. She shoved a piece of toast in her mouth before stuffing her feet into her trainers.

Cal was leaning against the sink, watching her, his expression one of amusement as he watched her fumble as she made a hash of tying the laces in her haste.

She glowered at him. 'You won't think it funny if Paul comes looking for you. Aren't you supposed to be checking the deer fences this morning?'

She watched his amusement fade as he realised that she was right. Tara knew Paul wouldn't hang about waiting for him. He would come looking, and she thought it might have been more prudent for Cal to have stayed at the boathouse last night, which is what he usually did. But he'd cooked a meal for her in the cottage, and one thing had led to another...

She gave him a quick kiss, then left him to get ready while she went home for a shower. As she dried her hair, Tara realised she did think of the boathouse as home. It would be a wrench when she came to leave it, as she must do at some point, and probably sooner rather than later. Very shortly, half of the money from the sale of the Edinburgh house would be in her bank account, and then she'd have no excuse not to do some serious house searching.

Since that wonderful day when Cal had rowed her to the other side of the loch, she hadn't been thinking about house hunting at all. She was far too happy where she was. With Cal living just up the lane, it was so easy for them to sneak into each other's houses. That would change when she moved.

She supposed she'd better see if the house on the outskirts of the village was still on the market. If it was, she should go view it, because apart from Yvaine's cottage, that property was the only other house for sale anywhere near Duncoorie.

She didn't have time to check the estate agent's website now, but she vowed to take a look after she'd finished for the day.

Skipping along the lane to the craft centre, Tara mentally ran through what she had to do today, the main thing being to run the first of the children's model-making workshops. She'd collected loads of sturdy card-board boxes, which would form the houses themselves, and had stacks of miniature wallpaper designs, paints, brushes and glue. It was going to be messy, but fun. Hopefully.

It was Bonnie's idea. Tara had been considering providing pre-cut MDF boards, the same stuff she used to make her houses, but Bonnie reckoned the kids would have more fun designing their own from scratch. Bonnie and Katie were taking part in this session, so Tara hoped it went well.

It had been Cal's turn to have Bonnie this weekend, so Tara had hardly seen him. However, with the start of a new week Cal was back to having Bonnie during the day only, so Tara and Cal were able to spend the nights together. And next week, Yvaine's parents would take over, so things should get back to normal.

Sometimes, Tara felt like she was living a double life, but if that's what she must do to be with Cal, so be it. Anyway, as he kept telling her, it wouldn't be forever.

The barn was where the workshops took place. It was an enormous space with a high vaulted ceiling, the supporting beams exposed in large arcs overhead. The floor space had been sectioned into several areas to keep the individual crafts separate, with a pottery section at the back complete with a drying room, an artist's studio, and four other rooms containing workstations and stools.

There was also a small refreshment area to the front, supplied by the cafe when workshops were taking place, although lunch would be eaten in the cafe itself.

Today, there were several activities in the barn, ranging from pot throwing to silk painting, so it promised to be a fun day. And an exhausting one, as Tara was running a session in the morning and another in the afternoon.

Tara set everything out, dashing back and forth from her studio to the barn, making sure she had everything she needed despite double and triple checks yesterday. She couldn't believe she was so nervous, but considering this was her first time, she supposed it was only to be expected.

Bonnie walked confidently into the barn with Katie, who also looked quite at home. Tara hoped their attitude would help put the other children at ease, most of whom had never visited the craft centre before. Parents were welcome – and encouraged – to stay, and many of them chose to do so, using the time to explore the castle and the grounds, only popping back to the barn now and again to check on their offspring.

Those parents who had decided to stay could join the children for lunch in the cafe, but Tara doubted whether she'd get a chance to grab anything to eat, as she suspected her lunchtime would be spent clearing away the debris from the morning session and preparing for the afternoon one.

Cal, bless him, had promised to cook this evening, and had even offered to give her a massage, saying she could probably do with some destressing after a day of supervising all those children. She guessed he might be speaking from experience, and an image of him trying to keep a birthday party full of kids entertained popped into her head.

To Tara's surprise, after she'd stuttered and stammered through an explanation of what her young crafters would be doing this morning and had shown them several cardboard box houses she'd made earlier, she found she was enjoying herself. The children definitely seemed to be, and she noticed Bonnie helping Katie with her design when she was stuck for ideas.

Two and a half hours wasn't long to produce a doll's house, even if it was a cardboard one, but Tara was pleased with what the children had managed to achieve by the end of the session. And their parents were complimentary, too. Although the cardboard doll's houses wouldn't last, it gave the children a taste of what it was like to design a building, transfer that design from paper into 3D, and then assemble it.

She was stowing the last of the houses on the shelves which were dotted around the refreshment area and ensuring each house had its creator's name on it so they could collect them at the end of the day, when Cal popped his head around the door.

'Have you got a few minutes?'

Tara thought of the clearing up still to be done. 'Not really.'

He stepped inside. 'That's a pity. I'll just have to eat your lunch as well.' He held aloft a couple of covered plates.

Tara's eyes widened and her tummy rumbled at the sight of what was on them.

'Roast vegetable, tomato and lentil bake,' he said, 'with new potatoes and caramelised onion sauce. No? Shall I take it away?'

'Don't you dare!' she cried, and when he produced two cans of chilled ginger beer from his jacket pocket, she could have kissed him. She would have if they'd had the barn to themselves, but the other crafters were in and out like fiddler's elbows, so she settled for devouring her food instead.

Cal pulled some cutlery from another pocket, and Tara dived in. Teaching kids to make cardboard houses was hungry work.

After they'd eaten, Cal even helped her tidy the work-room, but he left her to set up the afternoon session on her own because they were beginning to attract curious glances, especially from Giselle, the woman who made sea glass pictures.

By the end of the second session, Tara was exhausted, and she had a newfound respect for teachers. It had given her confidence though, and she felt more assured that she would be able to deliver the adult workshops when the time came.

Wearily, she packed up the tools and unused materials, made sure she left the workshop as pristine as she had found it, dumped everything in the studio, and headed home for a shower and a relaxing evening with the man she loved.

The following week was somewhat quieter, much to Tara's relief. With the junior craft sessions out of the way, she was able to turn her attention to fulfilling her online orders, making new stock for the gift shop, getting to grips with a new commission and finishing Bonnie's doll's house. It was almost done, but it wasn't quite there yet. All the furniture was in place, but there were lots of little details yet to be added, and Tara was quietly thankful that Yvaine's house was so minimalist, because it was this attention to detail that took the time.

Along with a return to normality in her professional life, Tara's private life had also settled down in that Bonnie's grandparents had returned and were looking after her during the day once more. Tara missed seeing the little girl around the place, but it meant she could crack on with completing her house without fear of discovery. To top it all off, Jinny had emailed Tara last week's sales figures, and they were the best yet. Mhairi and Cal were also privy to those figures, so when Cal popped into the studio to congratulate her, Tara was on top of the world.

'I feel we should celebrate,' Calan said. 'Would you like to go out for a meal?'

Tara thought for a moment, then grinned. 'I'd prefer a picnic.' The weather, fickle as usual, was lovely today, sunny and warm.

'Where do you want to go?'

'Out in the boat.' She gave him a mischievous look, and Cal's lips twitched.

'I think I can arrange that. I know a nice little spot on the opposite side, where we won't be disturbed.'

'I did just mean a picnic,' she warned.

'Spoilsport. I was hoping for a repeat of some outdoor loving.'

'I prefer your nice comfy bed.'

'In that case, are you sure you want to bother going all the way to the other side? We could tie the skiff to the jetty and have our picnic there instead. It'll save me having to do all that rowing.'

'Watching you row is the best bit,' she said cheekily.

'Oh, well, in that case I won't deny you the chance to ogle my rippling muscles, my firm thighs, my—' Tara poked out her tongue, and Cal chuckled. 'If you want to have a picnic on the other side of the loch, then that's what we'll do,' he promised.

'There's also something else I want to do,' she said, smirking when his face lit up, knowing what he was thinking and that she was about to burst his bubble. 'Will you teach me to fish?'

As she predicted, his face fell. 'You want to learn to fish *this evening*?'

'I do. We can't spend all our time in bed.'

'Why not?' Cal seemed genuinely puzzled.

'Because we'll get bored of that eventually.'

'I promise you I won't,' he replied earnestly, making her giggle.

'We need to have some interests beyond the bedroom,' Tara insisted.

She was serious. Cal was a man who loved the great outdoors. Tara, by way of necessity, spent most of her time indoors. She wanted to experience more of his world, to join him in it wherever possible. Besides, the exercise would do her good, and Skye was such a stunningly dramatic island it was a shame not to enjoy its natural beauty. A nice pootle across the loch, a spot of fishing, an open-air supper, and another pootle back sounded idyllic, especially if it was followed by some additional exercise under the covers. A perfect end to a perfect day.

'You do it like this,' Cal said, and Tara watched carefully as he showed her how to attach the lure to the line. He passed a rod to her. 'Your turn.'

Tara was used to fiddly things and she'd always been good with her hands. Nevertheless, she was pleased when she managed to tie it correctly the first time.

'Brilliant. Now we have to cast the line.' He showed her the proper technique, and she followed suit. 'We let the lure sink, then retrieve it slowly, reeling it in steadily,' he explained.

'How do you know whether there are any fish down there?' she asked, getting into the rhythm of cast, reel in, and cast again. It was surprisingly hard work.

Cal laughed. 'You don't. Not until you catch one. But this has always been a good place for me, although late summer and early autumn are the best time of year for pollack.'

'Why do you bother, if you don't keep your catch?' She knew why he spent time on the water, but the fishing part was beyond her.

'I enjoy the challenge.'

'Outwitting a fish?'

'You'd be surprised. They can be canny creatures.'

They fished in silence for a while, the peace of the late afternoon settling over them. There wasn't a breath of air, and it was so warm Tara didn't need the fleece she'd brought.

'It truly is lovely and peaceful out here,' she said after a while.

'Make the most of it. It won't last. It never does. You rarely get two days the same on Skye.'

Tara grinned. 'I've noticed. No wonder you're all obsessed by the weather.'

'Summer in the morning and winter in the afternoon,' he agreed. 'I love the unpredictability. It makes life more interesting.'

Tara reeled her line in slowly and steadily, the way Cal had shown her. 'How long do we give it, before calling it a day?'

'Bored already?'

'No, but I am hungry.'

'Ten more minutes?'

'OK.'

It turned out to be fifteen in the end because, on what was supposed to be her very last cast, Tara felt a tug on the line. Amidst her squeals of excitement, Cal helped her reel it in. The pollack wasn't a particularly large specimen, but Tara was proud anyway, and held it whilst Cal took a photo. Then she gently released it over the side of the boat and watched it disappear into the depths.

'That was brilliant!' she cried. '*Now* I get it. I want to do this again.'

'We will, I promise. But not today. Do you, or do you not, want a slice of quiche?'

'I do,' she said, and when Cal laid out their picnic, Tara was impressed.

It was quite a spread. As well as the quiche, there were cherry tomatoes, a potato salad, crispy chicken and smashed avocado sandwiches, a couple of herb and feta pastry parcels, plus scones and flapjacks to finish.

'Did you make all this yourself?' she asked, as he poured bubbly Prosecco into plastic champagne flutes.

'I would like to say I did, but I can't lie. I asked Gillian to put a picnic together.'

'She's done a fantastic job. This is delicious.' The flavours of the pastry parcel exploded in her mouth, and Tara closed her eyes in bliss as she chewed.

When she opened them, it was to find Cal gazing at her. 'I love you, Tara. I always have.'

His words made her heart melt. 'I love you, too.'

She thought he was going to kiss her as he leant forward, but it was to brush a crumb from the corner of her mouth.

'Eat up,' he urged. 'I want to get you back home and make love to you.'

Tara ate, but she didn't rush her food. She wanted the moment to last, to savour it the way she was savouring this delicious picnic. After all, they had all night in which to make love.

After they'd finished eating, Tara helped Cal pack the remains of their meal into the wicker basket and stow it on the boat, then she got in, taking her customary perch on the middle bench.

Cal was about to push off when he said, 'Would you like to steer?'

'No, thanks! Rowing looks hard work.'

'I wasn't planning on rowing back. I want to save my strength.' He lowered the outboard motor into the water and leered at her. 'It'll get us back quicker, too.'

Tara rolled her eyes. 'Go on, then. I'll give it a try, but don't blame me if we hit something.'

'We won't.'

Tara wished she had his confidence, but hers grew the nearer they came to the jetty, although she did insist on Cal taking charge of the steering before they reached the beach because she was worried the boat might run aground.

'There's no chance of that,' he explained, cutting the motor and lifting it out of the water to let the boat drift gently to the shore.

She even jumped into the shallows to help him drag it up the beach and was surprised at how light the vessel was.

Despite only having been on the loch for about three hours, Tara felt as though she'd had a full day out. She was tired, covered in a fine coating of salt from the spray, and deliriously happy.

'I need a shower,' she declared, tasting the salt on her lips. Her hair was also sticky with it.

'Have one at mine,' Cal suggested when she made to walk towards the boathouse. 'My shower is big enough for two.'

'So it is.' And as she strolled hand in hand with Cal towards his cottage, she couldn't help feeling blessed and incredibly thankful. Not many people had a second chance at first love.

–

What was that noise? Cal opened one eye and felt around for his phone. It wasn't in its customary spot on the night-stand, so he had no way of telling the time. However, he knew it was morning because light streamed in around the bedroom curtains.

The noise came again, and he realised there was someone at the door.

Tara stirred next to him, and he eased his arm out from underneath her, wincing as it began to tingle.

'Whassa time?' she murmured.

'No idea.' He sat up.

'Whossat?'

'Don't know, but I'd better answer it before they break the door down.'

Grabbing a pair of shorts, he drew them on and reached for a T-shirt, pulling it over his head as he hurried downstairs.

'About time!' Yvaine exclaimed as he opened the door, and Cal stepped back in surprise. 'I was about to go to the castle and ask if anyone knew where you were.'

Bonnie was standing next to her, clutching her rucksack to her chest.

Confused, he asked, 'Am I supposed to have her today?'

Yvaine tutted. 'If you'd bothered to answer your phone or check your messages, you would know that Dad's got sickness and diarrhoea, so they can't have her. Mum blames it on the prawns he ate yesterday. Luckily, she had the monkfish. Anyway, I'm sorry to dump Bonnie on you. I know it's early, but I've got a work meeting this morning, so I've got no choice. You don't mind, do you?' She said it as though she knew he wouldn't, and he didn't, but—

Oh, God, *Tara* was upstairs, asleep in his bed.

'Gotta run,' Yvaine was saying. She gave Bonnie a kiss on the head, then pushed her towards Cal. 'I'll pick her up later, but I'm not sure of the time. I'll let you—' She stopped and her mouth dropped open.

Cal turned around slowly, guessing what she had seen.

Tara, her hair tousled, yawning widely and wearing one of Cal's shirts with her bare legs on show, was slowly descending the stairs.

Cal realised she was still half asleep. But she didn't remain that way for long. Blinking as the light from the open door reached her eyes, Tara faltered. Then a hand shot to her mouth and she turned, dashing back up the stairs.

Yvaine's shocked silence lasted a full ten seconds, until Bonnie broke it. 'Is Tara here for breakfast?'

Yvaine snapped, 'I think Tara is here for more than breakfast.' Her tone was accusing, her expression hard. 'I thought you said there was nothing between you. I don't call *that* nothing, so excuse me if I don't believe you. You couldn't stay away from your old girlfriend, could you? Although from where I'm standing, she doesn't look like an *old* girlfriend. More like a *current* girlfriend, I'd say.'

'Dad?' Bonnie was staring up at him, her little face pinched and drained of colour. 'Is it true? Is Tara your girlfriend?'

'Of course she is,' Yvaine barked. 'Although he denied it when I asked him.' She shot him a furious look. 'I don't know why, when he's—' She stopped mid-sentence, probably because she remembered that she was speaking to her nine-year-old daughter.

Bonnie looked stricken. 'But Dad, you promised. You said you'd never have a girlfriend.'

Cal leant towards her, but she took a step back. 'I'm sorry, Bon-Bon. I didn't want you to find out like this. I

235

was going to tell you, but I wanted you to get to know Tara better first. You like her, don't you?'

Bonnie backed away another step. '*You promised*,' she repeated, her eyes brimming with tears.

'I didn't mean to—' he began, but she cut him off, her little face furious.

'I *hate* you and I never want to see you again. I wish you were dead!' She glared at him, then at her mother. 'I hate you, too! And Lenn. I'm not going to live in his house and I'm not going to go to a new school and I'm not leaving Duncoorie and you can't make me!'

With that, Bonnie whirled on her heel and stomped off.

'Now look what you've done,' Yvaine hissed. 'She was just coming around to the idea, but now we're back to square one, thanks to you.'

'I'm sorry, I—'

'I don't want to hear it. Go back to your girlfriend. I've changed my mind about you having Bonnie today. In fact, I'm going to have a good think whether I should allow you to see her at all.'

'Yvaine, you can't do that! She's my daughter, you can't stop me seeing her. I have rights, parental responsibility—'

He knew she could. She'd tried it before. Going through legal channels to force Yvaine to comply could take months!

Yvaine's parting shot floored him. 'Anyway, Bonnie has made it perfectly clear she doesn't want to see you ever again, and I'm not prepared to go against her wishes.'

Cal hurried after her as she headed to her car. 'She's nine! She's had a shock. She doesn't mean it.' Bonnie *couldn't* mean it. If she did, it would destroy him.

Yvaine shot him a disgusted look and waved her hand in the air. For her, the subject was closed. But not for Cal.

He cried, 'You're happy enough to go against her wishes when it suits you. She told you she doesn't want to move to Portree or have Lenn for a stepfather.'

'As you quite rightly pointed out, Bonnie is nine. She has no concept of what's best for her. I'm thinking about her future. Lenn treats her like a princess and can give her opportunities you can't.'

As if money could buy their daughter happiness! Cal gritted his teeth as the dig that he didn't even own a house of his own hit it's mark. As if he needed reminding that if he lost his job, he would also lose his home.

'But I'm her father!' he protested. 'You can't stop me seeing her. You can't!'

'We'll leave that up to Bonnie, shall we? I believe I recall you saying she has enough to cope with at the moment getting used to Lenn, so I don't want her to have to get used to your girlfriend as well.'

Cal's heart sank as his ex-wife used his own words against him. She was right, Bonnie did have enough to cope with. Too many changes at once were bound to unsettle her, and he'd vowed that he would be the one constant thing she could rely on in the sea of her uncertain world.

And he'd let her down.

He'd broken a promise to his daughter. He had betrayed her trust, and now she hated him. He didn't blame her. He hated himself. He never should have put his feelings before hers. Bonnie's happiness was his priority. He had to make it up to her, one way or another, and get her to change her mind. If he didn't, Yvaine would use Bonnie's refusal to see him as a punishment for being in love with someone else, when he should have been in love with her. Otherwise it might be a very long time before she allowed him access to his daughter, and that would break his heart.

Chapter 22

When Tara hesitantly went downstairs, fully awake now and having thrown her clothes on, it was to find Cal in the kitchen, his face ashen.

'Cal, I'm so sorry. I was half asleep and I thought I was late.' She gulped, mortified that Yvaine had caught them in a compromising position. 'I heard what Bonnie said. I'm sure she'll be OK with the situation when she's calmed down and has had a chance to think about it. After all, it's not as though it changes anything. You're not the one who is whisking her off to Portree when she doesn't want to go. She'll still see you every other weekend. She'll still visit you here. And if she doesn't want me around, I can always make myself scarce.'

'She told me she hates me.' Cal's voice was strangled.

'She doesn't mean it. I used to say that to my mum all the time, and I definitely didn't mean it.'

He slumped against a worktop. 'Yvaine threatened to stop me from seeing her.'

'She can't do that,' Tara replied with more conviction than she felt. She had no experience of custody or parental rights, but she'd heard enough horror stories. But surely Yvaine wouldn't be so vindictive. She was just annoyed, that was all. She didn't want Cal herself, but neither did she want anyone else to have him.

Cal's expression was troubled. 'Tara, I—'

239

'Why don't you speak to Bonnie after work? I've got to go, I didn't realise it was so late and I need to pop to the post office before I open up this morning. That'll teach us to drink the best part of two bottles of wine when we've got work the next day.'

She walked over to him, wrapped her arms around his waist and laid her head on his shoulder. After a brief hesitation, he put his arms around her.

'Look at it this way,' she said. 'At least we don't have to sneak around any more. Although to be honest, I think everyone except Bonnie and Yvaine knew about us anyway. You said it's impossible to keep anything secret in Duncoorie.'

She lifted her head to give him a kiss, but he was staring out of the window, lost in thought, so Tara gave him a squeeze instead. 'I'll see you later. I'll cook this evening, so what do you fancy?'

'Anything.' He didn't look at her, and she suspected he was still reeling from his encounter.

She didn't want to leave him, knowing that he was hurting, but he had to go to work and so did she. She had so much to do that she didn't know where to begin, and the wine, combined with a rather late night and being woken so abruptly, wasn't helping.

Hoping Cal wouldn't brood too much and he would kiss and make up with Bonnie, Tara returned to the boathouse to get ready for the day. But later, as she worked on those all-important details on the interior of Bonnie's doll's house, checking them against the series of photographs she'd taken when she'd viewed Yvaine's cottage, her thoughts kept returning to Bonnie.

Her heart went out to the child as she imagined Bonnie at home, feeling betrayed that her father had broken his promise to her. Tara wished Cal had told her about it, although she wasn't sure what difference it would have made. She wanted to tell him he was silly to have made such a promise in the first place, but he had, and the damage was done. Tara hoped it wasn't permanent and that Cal's relationship with his daughter could be repaired.

It would be, she was certain. Bonnie's reaction this morning had surely only been shock. She'd come around, of course she would. She and Bonnie were friends, weren't they? They got on well together. This was just a little blip, and they'd soon get over it.

But even as she told herself this, Tara felt unsettled. She couldn't shake the feeling of dread that had shrouded her ever since she'd realised who had been knocking on Calan's door.

–

Tara was right, Cal thought. He did need to speak to Bonnie and explain. Bonnie liked Tara and they got on well, so he hoped that once his daughter had calmed down, she would be more amenable to the idea of him having Tara as his girlfriend. Tara wasn't some random woman who Bonnie had never met until today, and if that had been the case he could fully appreciate her reaction. As it was, he thought Bonnie had been overly dramatic and would soon get over it.

As he set about ticking things off his job list for today, he came to the conclusion that Bonnie's major gripe wasn't because Tara was his girlfriend, but because Cal had broken his promise to her. He wasn't entirely sure how he was going to remedy that. After all, a broken promise was a broken promise. It couldn't be *un*broken. However, he was fairly confident that if he apologised and explained what had happened, Bonnie would forgive him.

Yvaine's car wasn't on the drive when Calan came to a halt outside her cottage, so he decided to wait.

Wondering whether Yvaine had taken Bonnie to her meeting, or whether she'd found someone else to look after her, Cal cursed himself yet again for failing to take his mobile phone up to bed with him. He'd been too eager to dive into the shower with Tara to think about his phone and had left it on the worktop next to his keys and the picnic basket. When he'd looked at it after Tara left this morning, he'd discovered two missed calls and a message, and wanted to kick himself. Although Cal couldn't have known Yvaine's father would be taken ill overnight, he was the one who was insisting on keeping his and Tara's relationship low-key and that he didn't want Bonnie to find out just yet, so it had been up to him to ensure she didn't.

As he waited for Yvaine and Bonnie to show up, he went over and over the events of this morning in his mind, and the overriding image was of Bonnie's accusing face as Yvaine drove off. He had a feeling it would stay with him for some considerable time.

Calan's heart lurched when he caught sight of Yvaine's car in the distance. Emerging from his own vehicle, he stood nervously on the pavement as she swung onto the drive. Her expression was set, but it wasn't his ex-wife who claimed his attention. It was his daughter, who was refusing to look at him. Her little chin jutted out and she stared straight ahead, but he knew she had seen him.

It didn't bode well for the chat he wanted to have with her.

Should he give her more time and try again tomorrow, or would Bonnie perceive his departure as him not caring? And why was being a parent so hard? He'd always thought he had a good relationship with his daughter, but right now he felt he was walking on eggshells.

Yvaine got out of the car, Bonnie immediately afterwards. His daughter continued to avoid looking at him, but Yvaine had no such qualms and she glared as he approached.

She unlocked the front door and pushed it open. 'Go inside, Bonnie. I'm just going to have a word with your father.'

Bonnie stomped indoors, her back rigid, her movements jerky.

Cal's heart clenched at the sight of her obvious distress. 'Can I speak to her?' he asked Yvaine. 'Please?' He hated having to plead.

'You are an arse, Cal.'

'I know.'

'How could you make a promise like that when you were already sleeping with Tara? Then you had the brass-faced cheek to lie to my face.'

'I can explain.'

'I don't want to hear it. I'm over you, Cal. You can't hurt me any more.'

'I never meant to hurt you at all.'

'But you did anyway.' Her eyes flashed fury. 'Go away, Cal. I'll let you know if Bonnie changes her mind, but don't hold your breath. She follows me – I don't forgive people who break their promises either. You promised to love, honour and cherish *me*. Remember?'

Cal didn't have the words. What Yvaine said was true. He had made those promises on their wedding day.

And when she slammed the door in his face, he realised there was only one way to win Yvaine over. He had to sacrifice his own happiness for his daughter's.

When Tara returned to the boathouse and saw Cal's car parked outside his cottage, her heart fluttered uneasily. She'd been on edge all day, hoping he would be able to make up with Bonnie, and she'd been tempted to ring him once or twice, but she hadn't. He wouldn't have had anything to report until he'd spoken to his daughter anyway, and this morning she'd sensed he needed a bit of time to get his head around Yvaine and Bonnie catching them together.

Thankfully, Bonnie didn't have a key to Cal's house, otherwise Tara dreaded to think what might have happened.

She was about to head over to his place when she spied him on the jetty. He was sitting on the end of it, his feet dangling over the edge. His shoulders were hunched, and Tara felt another twinge of unease. Clearly things hadn't gone well with Bonnie.

Her heart went out to him. Cal could probably do with some TLC this evening – *if* he didn't prefer to be left alone.

Tara was prepared for either eventuality.

She consoled herself with the thought that Bonnie would unlikely sulk for long. The child would soon get used to the idea of having Tara in her life, and they could start to build a family unit of the three of them, albeit a part-time one. She would continue to be circumspect regarding any outward displays of affection towards Cal when Bonnie was around though, because she was conscious that Bonnie might feel a little possessive and not want to share her father.

Tara walked down the beach and stepped onto the jetty.

Cal appeared to be lost in thought, and it wasn't until she put a hand on his shoulder did he realise she was there.

Sitting next to him, she said, 'I take it Bonnie still isn't speaking to you?'

'No. Tara, I, um...' He trailed off as his voice caught, and Tara's unease turned to dread.

Something was very, very wrong.

'What is it?' she asked in a strangled voice, terrified what his answer might be but even more scared not to hear it.

He cleared his throat. She had an awful feeling he was close to tears, and her own eyes prickled in sympathy.

'We can't go on seeing each other,' he said in a rush. 'I'm sorry, but—'

'Wait! *What did you say?*'

'It's over. Me and you, we can't go on.'

'I don't understand. You're *dumping* me?'

'Not dumping as such, but we can't be together any more.'

Tara barked out an incredulous laugh. 'Isn't that what dumping means?'

'It's not like that, Tara.'

'What is it like?'

'I'm trying to explain.' His eyes were damp, but not as wet as hers.

Tears brimmed and spilt over to trickle down her cheeks.

He stared into the distance, refusing to meet her eyes. 'I have to do this. God knows it's the last thing I want, but Bonnie is my daughter and Yvaine is refusing to let me see her. She's using the fact that I broke my promise to Bonnie as the reason, and that Bonnie doesn't want anything to do with me. The only way I can think of to put this right is for us to split up. If I can convince Bonnie that I'm truly sorry...' His voice thickened and he swallowed hard.

Tara couldn't believe what she was hearing, and she stared at him open-mouthed, his face blurring through her tears. She understood, she truly did. Bonnie had to come first. Cal was in an impossible situation. But that didn't make it any less painful. It didn't make her heartbreak any less bearable.

'We can still see each other as friends and colleagues,' he said. He sounded desperate, and Tara choked back a sob.

Shaking her head, in disbelief as much as anything, she said, 'We can't, Cal. Not after what we've done, the things we've said to each other. Oh, God!' She pressed a hand to her mouth to hold in the anguish.

Her heart was being torn out of her chest and slashed into little pieces in front of her eyes. The first time he'd dumped her had been bad enough, but this was way worse. Tara had never felt agony like this. She couldn't breathe. He'd stolen the very air from her lungs.

He was carrying on speaking, as though he could say something to lessen the pain. 'It won't be forever. She'll come around to the idea in time.'

Tara uttered a disbelieving sound. 'That could take months, years even.' Or Bonnie might never accept her at all. Was Cal asking her to wait? To keep their love on ice until his daughter was ready to accept that her father was entitled to a life of his own?

Part of her wanted to do precisely that. She wanted to cling to the possibility that they might one day be together, but what kind of a life would she be living in the meantime if she did? She would be stuck in limbo, halfway between the darkness and the light, a twilight of an existence, yearning for what she couldn't have.

She could far too easily imagine how awful it would be to see him every day, to hear him, to know he was nearby, yet not be able to hold him or tell him she loved him. It would be worse than making a clean break.

With a distraught cry, Tara scrambled to her feet. Cal reached for her, but she brushed him off. He'd made it clear that it was over. That they were done.

Running to the boathouse, Tara knew she couldn't stay here any longer, not without the only man she had ever loved – the only man she would *ever* love.

Chapter 23

Tara fled to the boathouse but Calan didn't follow her. There wasn't anything left to say. He desperately wanted to comfort her but thought it best not to even try. What good would it do apart from giving her false hope?

He remained on the jetty for quite some time, silent tears trickling down his face as he battled with his grief. Once again, he had pushed away the woman he loved, but there wouldn't be another chance. He'd been remarkably lucky to have a second one – a third would be impossible. Tara would never trust him again and who could blame her?

When his tears abated, he returned to the cottage, washed his face, and drove to the village.

Yvaine was even less pleased to see him standing on her doorstep than she had been an hour ago. She'd changed out of her work clothes and was wearing a loose-fitting T-shirt and joggers. She looked tired.

'What do you want, Cal?'

'To talk to Bonnie.'

She shook her head and sighed. 'Didn't we just go over this? The answer is no.'

'I've broken up with Tara.'

The flash of satisfaction in her eyes was brief. She cloaked it quickly, but not before he noticed.

'Can I tell her that? *Please.*'

Yvaine shrugged and gestured for him to go inside. 'Don't expect her to welcome you with open arms though. She's been an absolute nightmare today.'

Cal could well imagine. Bonnie was a happy, chatty child on the whole, but when she had her moments, everyone knew about them.

He'd only ventured into Yvaine's house a handful of times and didn't feel comfortable poking his head into first the living room and then the kitchen, in his search for his daughter. Both rooms were empty, so he called up the stairs. 'Bonnie? It's your dad. Can we talk?'

Yvaine said, 'Go on up.'

His tread on the stairs sounded loud, and he guessed Bonnie knew he was on his way. Hers was the smaller of the two bedrooms at the front of the house, and he knocked tentatively when he reached her door.

'Bon-Bon? It's Dad. Can I come in?'

No answer.

'Bonnie? Please, I want to explain.'

'Go away.'

Cal tapped on the door again, then stuck his head around it.

Bonnie was sitting on her bed, her back resting against the headboard, her arms folded. She shot him a venomous look. 'Go away!'

'I will, after you hear me out.'

Her chin was jutting out and her eyes were narrowed, but despite her obvious show of temper, he could see she was hurting. It made his heart ache abominably to think he was the cause of her distress.

Pushing his luck, he inched into the room.

Bonnie stared resolutely at the opposite wall and her mouth tightened. At least she didn't tell him to go away again, so that was something. Cal gratefully took it as a step forward, albeit a tiny one.

He debated whether to risk sitting on the edge of the bed but decided against it. 'I'm sorry, Bon-Bon.'

'So you said. And don't call me that.'

'Bonnie,' he amended, sadly. He'd called her Bon-Bon since she was born, and although she'd recently begun telling him off for using the nickname in public, she usually tolerated it when they were on their own.

Cal said, 'I should never have made such a promise to you.'

'Duh! Promises should only be made if you intend to keep them.'

'But that's the thing, I *did* intend to keep it. I didn't break it on purpose.'

She gave him a withering look.

'It's the truth,' he insisted. 'I didn't expect to see Tara again.'

Bonnie's stony expression didn't change.

'I used to know her before I met your mum.'

'So? That doesn't mean you could break your promise.'

'No, it doesn't,' he replied slowly. 'But I cared about her very much back then, and when I saw her again I realised I still care about her.'

Was that a chink in Bonnie's armour, Cal wondered hopefully, as she blinked and her expression turned to one of puzzlement.

Then she let out a gasp and cried, '*Princess Tara!* The story was about *you* and *her*! I thought you'd made it up.'

'I… er,' Cal stammered, taken by surprise. He'd forgotten all about that silly tale.

Bonnie was shaking her head, her expression furious. 'She was your girlfriend then, wasn't she?'

'When I told you that story? No, of course she wasn't. I hadn't seen her for years.'

'I don't believe you! You're a liar and I never want to speak to you again. I hate you. I wish you were dead!'

'Bonnie, little one, please don't say that. I love you and—'

'Get out!' she screeched. 'I hate you!'

'You don't mean it,' he pleaded.

'I do. I hate you.'

He really wished she would stop saying that. It stabbed him in the heart every time.

Cal perched on the end of her bed, ignoring her outraged face. 'I've got something to tell you. Tara isn't my girlfriend any more. I told her I had to put you first and that we couldn't see each other again.'

Bonnie glared at him, her enraged expression unable to hide the tears in her eyes. 'I don't believe you.'

He didn't blame her. 'It's true,' he insisted.

Bonnie peered up at him from underneath her lashes, her expression as wary as a red deer fawn. 'Promise?'

'I promise.' This time he intended to keep it. And as he'd screwed it up royally with Tara, it shouldn't be hard.

'Will you keep it?'

'Yes. Cross my heart and hope to die.'

She continued to eye him suspiciously. 'You promise never to see her again?'

Cal sighed. 'You know I can't do that. She lives at the castle, remember? And she works there, too. I have to see her and speak to her as part of my job. But, on Nana's life, Tara will just be a friend from now on, and not my girlfriend.'

'But you do still like her?'

'Yes, I do,' he admitted. 'I like her a lot, but I like you more.'

'Like? I thought you said you love me.' She pouted, but there was a glimmer in her eye.

'Yeah, I do, I suppose. I have to – I'm your father. It kind of goes with the job.' He gave an overly dramatic sigh.

Bonnie stuck out her tongue, then gazed at him solemnly. 'I don't really hate you.'

'I know.'

'I was just disappointed in you.'

'You had every right to be.' He was disappointed in himself.

He should never have made such a promise to her, despite believing at the time that it would be one he could easily keep.

'Calan Fraser, I want a word with you,' Mhairi called.

Cal had been on his way to the castle's kitchen to grab a coffee, having been unable to face anything first thing this morning. He'd drunk several drams of whisky last night after he'd made peace with Bonnie, to try to drown his sorrows.

Yvaine had been pragmatic when he'd informed her that Bonnie had forgiven him, and he assumed it was because she'd already inflicted enough damage. She'd got what she'd wanted, clearly not caring how much he was hurting. Revenge was definitely a dish best served cold, as far as his ex-wife was concerned.

'Calan! I said I want a word.' Mhairi's tone was imperious. He had no idea what she wanted to speak to him about, but she'd used his full name, which was most unlike her, so it sounded ominous.

Mhairi was seated at her desk, the parlour door open. Her expression was unreadable. 'Close the door.'

He did as she instructed, then hovered uncertainly, wondering whether he should sit down. Ordinarily he would take a seat without thinking, but not today. He had a feeling he was about to be hauled over the coals for something, but he couldn't think what.

'You look awful,' Mhairi observed.

Calan felt it. 'Thanks.'

'Sit down before you fall down.'

'I'm OK.'

The look she gave him over the top of her spectacles told him she knew he was lying. 'Have you had any breakfast?'

He shrugged. He hadn't, but he thought it best not to tell her as she would insist on knowing why and he didn't want to lie to her. He hadn't eaten much yesterday either, and the thought of food made him feel sick.

'A coffee would be good,' he said, trying to deflect her.

Not taking her eyes off him, Mhairi rang through for a pot of coffee.

'What do you want to talk to me about?' he asked as her stern gaze settled on him once more.

He was anxious to get this impromptu meeting over with so he could lick his wounds in peace. He'd spent the morning avoiding people, only speaking when it was absolutely necessary. Talking was too much of an effort when all he wanted to do was be alone with his thoughts and his broken heart. God knows how Tara must be feeling, and his gut twisted, knowing she must hate him.

He hated himself. But what choice had he had? Tara was the love of his life, but Bonnie was his confused, upset and hurting young daughter. Maybe if Yvaine hadn't been dragging Bonnie away from her home, her school and her friends, Bonnie would have felt differently about her dad dating.

He would never know.

'Tara came to see me,' Mhairi said, when the silence stretched too long.

Cal froze.

'She wants to relinquish her lease on the studio and the boathouse.'

'*What? She's leaving?*' His stomach clenched and he thought he might throw up. He'd been dreading having to work and live alongside her and not be able to be with her, but her not being at the castle was worse. Way worse.

Mhairi continued, 'She told me what happened. I must say, Calan, that you are a total and utter numpty.'

There was no need for her to tell him what he already knew. 'What did you say?' he choked out, praying that Mhairi had told her that she was in breach of her contract or something. Anything to prevent her leaving.

'I asked if she would remain until I found a suitable tenant to replace her. I don't like seeing empty units. It doesn't create a good impression and it's bad for business.'

Calan's world tilted on its axis. He understood Tara's reasons perfectly, but the thought of her not being here, even though her presence stabbed him in the heart, made him want to beat his chest and howl. He'd only just found her again, and now she was *leaving*?

He knew he was being unrealistic, but subconsciously he'd been harbouring a slim hope that they could continue as friends until he managed to make Bonnie see sense.

'Calan, what were you thinking? I expected better from you.'

'I know I should never have mixed business with pleasure,' he muttered. 'It won't happen again.'

Mhairi uttered an exasperated sigh. 'You really are being dim today. I *meant* I expected you to treat Tara better than you have.'

'I didn't have a choice.'

'Everyone has choices. You decided to allow a nine-year-old girl to make yours for you.'

Calan was astounded. 'You don't understand. Bonnie said she never wanted to see me again and Yvaine backed her up. She's stopped me from seeing Bonnie before, and I couldn't risk it happening again.'

'It wouldn't have lasted.'

'I couldn't risk it. Bonnie means everything to me.'

Mhairi's voice softened. 'I know, but you can't let a child dictate your life.'

Cal didn't want to argue with her, but she'd never had children, so he wasn't convinced she was the best person to give him parental advice. And although he acknowledged there was an element of truth in what she said, he had made another promise to Bonnie and he wasn't prepared to break this one.

'Was there anything else?' he asked, and when Mhairi shook her head he got to his feet.

'I take it you're not staying for coffee?' she observed.

'No, thanks. I'll grab one later.' He felt Mhairi's eyes on him as he walked out of the room, their weight as heavy as the lump in his chest.

Tara woke up with a start. After meeting with Mhairi this morning, she'd hurried back to the boathouse, locked the door and curled up in bed to cry, but she must have fallen asleep. Having not slept a wink last night, she'd been exhausted. She still was, but suspected it stemmed as much from the heaviness in her soul as the weariness in her body.

The meeting hadn't gone as she'd expected. Instead of releasing her from her obligations immediately, which was what Tara wanted, Mhairi managed to persuade her to stay until someone else took over the studio.

As soon as another crafter could be found, Tara would be free to go. She fully appreciated why Mhairi didn't want an empty studio in the craft centre, but how long would it take to find someone to fill her shoes? And what was she supposed to do in the meantime?

Heck, what was she supposed to do when Mhairi *did* find someone? Tara needed to have somewhere else lined up, but that wouldn't be easy without a date to work towards. Neither did she have the heart to look for another place to live. How could she, when it was broken beyond repair? But she had to leave Coorie Castle, there was no question of that.

Her mum! That's what had woken her. She'd been dreaming of her mother's arms around her. And suddenly she wanted her mum desperately. She picked up her phone and dialled.

'Hiya, my love. How are you?' Her mother's cheery voice brought fresh tears to Tara's eyes, and for a moment she couldn't speak.

Her mum said, 'I can't hear you, love. The reception is dreadful. Give me a sec and I'll go outside. I'm in the middle of cleaning the toilet block.' Tara heard rustling and footsteps, and she hurried to compose herself as her mum came back on the line. 'There, is that better? Tara? *Tara!* Can you hear me?'

'I can hear you, Mum.'

'Good. I'd thought I'd lost you. How are you, my sweet girl? How's business? Have you sold your house yet?'

As Tara listened to her mother's rapid-fire questions, she realised it had been a while since she'd spoken to her. Too long, actually. She'd been so wrapped up in her wonderful new life in Duncoorie, that she'd hardly given her mum more than a passing thought. Sending her the occasional snap of the loch or a photo of her latest doll's house wasn't the same as speaking to her.

'Tara? Are you still there? Drat!'

'Calan's back.' Tara's voice was small, barely a whisper.

Her mum heard, nevertheless. 'Calan? *Oh.*'

The 'Oh' spoke volumes. Her mother had seen what a mess Tara had been in when he'd broken up with her all those years ago. Calan was possibly her mother's least favourite person in the world.

There was an edge to her words as her mum asked, 'What do you mean "back"?'

Tara, feeling like a total idiot for letting him break her heart a second time, told her mum everything, and at the end of the sad little tale her mum was crying as hard as Tara.

'You can't stay there,' her mum insisted.

'I have to, for the time being.'

'No, you don't.'

'I can't leave. What about the lease? And where would I go?'

'You'll come to us, of course.'

Chapter 24

What her mum said made perfect sense. Tara could leave most of the contents of the studio in situ, so the place looked as though it was still occupied. And although the craft centre was open seven days a week, none of the crafters worked all seven. One or two studios were always closed on any given day. As long as Tara continued to pay her rent on time, she didn't think Mhairi would be able to complain.

Tara would also keep supplying the gift shop for as long as necessary, until another crafter was found.

The more Tara thought about her mother's suggestion that she stay with her and Toby on the Isle of Wight, the more it made sense. It would give her the physical distance from Cal, Duncoorie and Skye that she craved, although the pain would travel with her. There would be no escaping that.

However, as sorely tempted she might be to shove as much into her car as possible and head south right that second, she couldn't. There was too much to sort out, and she wanted to leave a supply of her bestselling stock in the studio for Jinny to replenish the gift shop with, as and when needed. She also had a commission which was close to completion, and she didn't want to pack it up and take it with her in case it got damaged en route. She may as well finish it and send it off first.

There was also Bonnie's doll's house.

Tara had done so much work on it that it would be a shame not to finish it. What had taken place between Tara and Cal wasn't Bonnie's fault, and if the doll's house helped the child settle into her new home, Tara wouldn't begrudge giving it to her.

Before she got started, she made a coffee and stared at the contents of her fridge, knowing she should make an effort to eat something. But the thought of food made her stomach churn, so she decided not to bother. A couple of skipped meals wasn't going to hurt, and no doubt her mum would try to fatten her up, whether she needed fattening or not.

As Tara changed into her work clothes, she caught a glimpse of herself in the mirror and flinched. She looked awful – pale skin, dark circles under her eyes, a haunted expression. She'd seen that same face staring back at her a decade ago. She'd hoped never to see it again.

Scooping up her hair with her hands, not bothering to brush it, she fastened it on top of her head, grabbed her keys and her phone, and headed to the studio. The sooner she finished, the sooner she could pack and leave. Being here was killing her.

Or it would, if she wasn't already dead inside.

–

Cal couldn't sleep. It didn't matter how exhausted he felt or how much he tried to wear himself out during the day by throwing himself into work, every night since he'd broken up with Tara, he'd been unable to settle, and when he did drop off he woke a couple of hours later, his heart aching, his arms empty.

Tonight followed the same pattern, so he did what he'd done on previous nights – he got up, poured himself a wee dram and stared out over the loch.

But he was even more restless than usual, thoughts whirling around his head, regret and heartache biting deep.

Feeling caged, he got dressed and slipped into the darkness.

The night was still; not a breath of wind stirred the leaves and the only sound was the gentle lapping of the waves on the shore.

He turned away from the loch and the sliver of beach, away from the boathouse and the woman who slept there, and headed towards the castle. He might as well do a quick circuit to check everything was as it should be, then he would head up the mountain, hoping it would help soothe his soul.

However, when he turned the corner into the courtyard, he noticed that the light in Tara's studio was on, and Cal was drawn to it like a moth.

She was inside, beavering away, her head bowed to her task, and he wondered whether she was working late or starting early. Either way, she should have been in bed at this ungodly hour. But then, so should he. It was his weekend to have Bonnie, and he would need his wits about him. This would be the first time he would have spoken to his daughter since he'd told her he no longer had a girlfriend, and he wasn't sure whether she had entirely forgiven him. He'd feared she hadn't when Yvaine had told him not to collect Bonnie on Friday evening as he usually did, but when she explained it was Katie's birthday and there was a party and a sleepover at Katie's house, some of his tension had eased.

Cal continued to watch Tara for a while, drinking in the sight of her until he couldn't stand it any longer, then he went back to the cottage. He didn't go to bed though, taking up residence on the deck and keeping vigil for her return to the boathouse.

When she failed to show by the time the sky lightened, he got stiffly to his feet and went indoors, the early morning chill having settled into his bones. It might still be summer on Skye, but the warmth of the days he'd spent in the sun with her seemed a lifetime ago. The island had returned to her moody, fickle self, and although the day promised to be a calm, dry one, Cal knew there was a storm brewing out in the Atlantic. Before this day ended, the sky would darken, the wind would pick up and squally rain would hide the far shore of the loch.

The weather would suit his equally dark and stormy mood perfectly.

–

'Bloody hell, Tara, what's happened to you?' Jinny demanded when Tara unlocked the studio door on Saturday morning. 'Are you ill? Can I get you anything? Would you like me to fetch Cal? I've just dropped Bonnie off at his cottage because she had a sleepover at mine last night, but I expect you know that.'

Tara lumbered to her stool and slumped onto it. 'No Cal,' she croaked, her voice hoarse from lack of use. She'd barely spoken to anyone since the phone call with her mum, and it was now Saturday.

'Are you sure? It's no hassle.'

'No Cal,' she repeated.

'Tara, hen, don't take this the wrong way, but you look dreadful.'

'I feel it,' she admitted.

'You need to go home and get yourself to bed.'

Tara's laugh was bitter, edged with hysteria. She didn't have a home. Not any more. She'd hoped she could make Duncoorie her home, but Cal had smashed that hope to smithereens.

Jinny was staring at her in alarm and Tara realised she would have to explain. 'Cal and I have split up,' she said.

Jinny pulled up the other stool and sat on it. 'I'm assuming it wasn't a mutual decision.'

'No.'

'Did he give a reason?'

'Bonnie found out about us, which mightn't have been so bad, but Cal had promised her he would never have a girlfriend.'

'Never? That's a bit extreme.'

'Or until she had a boyfriend, at least.'

'Still extreme. What if she's gay? She might never have a boyfriend. He shouldn't have made a promise he couldn't keep.'

'I'm assuming he thought he could keep it until Bonnie was more interested in *her* social life than *his*. And I'm pretty sure that when he made it, bumping into me again was the furthest thing from his mind.'

'Aw, hen, don't take on so. Bonnie will get over herself, and Cal will come to his senses.'

'I'm not sure I want him to. He's hurt me, Jinny.'

'I can see that.' Jinny blew out her cheeks. 'It's not going to be easy with the pair of you living and working in the same place.'

'That's why I'm leaving.'

Jinny's eyes widened. 'You're *not*?! I thought you loved it here?'

'I do. But I can't stay, knowing I could bump into him at any moment. This castle ain't big enough for the both of us.' Her attempt at an American accent was pathetic, and her oblique reference to the song seemed to pass her friend by.

'It is,' Jinny insisted. 'He doesn't have much to do with the crafters on a daily basis, and once you move out of the boathouse and into a place of your own, the chance of bumping into him goes down a lot.'

Tara was shaking her head. 'I've got to. I can't stay here.'

'Where will you go?'

'My mum and stepdad have a caravan park on the Isle of Wight. I'll stay there for a while, until I sort myself out.'

'What does Mhairi say? I'm assuming you've told her.'

'She knows I want to leave.'

'She'll be sorry to see you go. And so will I.' Jinny got to her feet and held out her arms. 'Come here, hen, let me give you a hug.'

Tara rose jerkily from her stool and accepted the hug gratefully, even though it made her cry again. Leaving Duncoorie would be a wrench. She loved it here – the castle, the craft centre, the friends she'd made – but her decision was final. This was her last day. In the morning, she would get up early and go.

She'd debated whether to leave today, because not only had she completed the commission, she'd made loads of miniatures for the gift shop and she'd also finalised Bonnie's doll's house. Once the commission had been collected by the parcel service, all that was left to do was to pack away any of the remaining bits and pieces that weren't already in boxes and load them into the car.

But the journey would take fourteen hours or more, and that was without breaks. Driving on unfamiliar roads in the dark didn't appeal, so she would spend one more night in the boathouse, where she would try to get a couple of hours sleep, then leave at first light.

Besides, she didn't want anyone to witness her departure. She simply couldn't face saying goodbye to anyone else.

Tara read through the letter she'd written, folded it, then slipped it inside an envelope. It was addressed to Mhairi. The castle's owner had been so kind and Tara felt dreadful about sneaking away, but she hoped the old lady would understand. She'd also considered leaving a note for Bonnie, but in the end had decided against it. The doll's house sitting on the table in the boathouse would suffice. She propped the letter against it, guessing it would probably be Cal who found it.

She left nothing for him. All their words had been said. Tara didn't have any more, and if Cal did, she didn't want to hear them.

Edgy and strung out now that there was nothing left to do, she roamed restlessly around the boathouse, running her hand over the worktops, stroking the arm of the chair, and committing everything to memory. She wanted to go for a walk but was scared of running into Cal or Bonnie. Or both.

Hoping she hadn't forgotten anything important, she wandered into the bedroom, checking the wardrobe and drawers yet again.

They were empty apart from the clothes she'd wear tomorrow, and she was about to leave when movement outside attracted her attention.

Cal had emerged from his cottage, Bonnie behind him.

Her heart leapt, banging uncomfortably against her ribcage, and her eyes filled with tears. Would she ever stop crying over this man?

There was a defeated slump to his shoulders, she thought, watching him walk to the Range Rover and supervise his daughter as Bonnie got in and buckled up. She wished she could see his face clearly, but the distance was a little too far.

As he waited, he lifted his head and stared at the boathouse. Tara nearly shrank back in case he saw her, but she realised just in time that the movement might give her away.

She wondered how he was bearing up.

She had no doubt he was hurting, and she had no doubt that he loved her. So how was it possible their love could end like this?

Cal got into the car, and as Tara watched it rumble slowly up the lane, her eyes filled with tears. This was the last sight she would ever have of him.

His departure left her bereft, but at least it meant she could go for a final walk without the worry of bumping into him.

Her keys were on the table, and as she reached for them, her gaze fell on the doll's house and she paused.

Making a decision, she picked it up, careful not to disturb the furniture inside. It might be an indulgence, but she hoped to catch Bonnie's reaction when the child saw it on her father's doorstep.

If there had been any hint of rain in the air, Tara wouldn't have risked leaving it outside, but the sun shone, the breeze was light, and she was as sure as she could be that it would stay fine for the next few hours.

Kneeling, she made certain everything inside the little house was where it should be, then she set off for a final walk around the loch that she had come to love almost as much as the man who lived beside it.

Without Cal's strength, the boat was harder to drag to the water's edge than Tara imagined, and she almost gave up. But with one last heave, it started to shift, and as soon as she had some momentum, she managed to launch it successfully.

Unfortunately, she also got her feet wet, but she didn't care. Her trainers would dry overnight. If they didn't, she had another pair she could wear on the long drive tomorrow.

Tara eyed the oars, dismissing them instantly. Rowing looked like hard work, and although she would have preferred a silent glide across the loch, she could always cut the motor when she reached the other side.

Lowering the outboard into the water, she pulled the starter cord, the way she had watched Cal do it. It took her three attempts and she was starting to worry because *Misty Lady* was beginning to drift, when the engine finally spluttered, then caught and began running smoothly.

Steering the boat towards the middle of the loch, Tara hoped Cal wouldn't be too cross with her for taking it out without his permission, but she had an undeniable urge to revisit the place where she and Cal had reconnected, where they had made love on Skye for the first time. It would always hold a special place in her heart, and she would never forget it. The opposite bank of the loch was where she'd been the happiest, and the desire to say farewell to it had hit her the moment she'd stepped onto the beach.

She'd only intended to walk to the end of the jetty, but once the idea of borrowing the boat had entered her head, the decision had been made. She wouldn't be out long, and with any luck Cal wouldn't realise she'd borrowed it at all. Anyway, she hoped to be back in time to witness Bonnie's reaction when the child spotted her doll's house.

With her gaze fixed on the opposite shore, Tara felt an overwhelming sadness. As she drew closer to it, the tears she'd been trying to hold back welled up and trickled down her face, as she sobbed her despair into the uncaring sea.

Chapter 25

At first, Cal didn't spot the doll's house sitting by his front door. His mind was on the boathouse, wondering whether Tara was in it, as he'd noticed that the studio lights were off. And when he did see the doll's house, it took him a second to understand what he was looking at.

His daughter knew what it was immediately, leaping out of the car and dashing towards it as soon as he brought the vehicle to a halt.

'Daddy! Daddy! Look!' She crouched down to peer at it. 'It's just like my house.'

'So it is.' He looked towards the boathouse again, part of him expecting to see Tara.

She was nowhere in sight.

'Shall we take it inside?' he suggested, glancing at the sky. Clouds were building to the west and the wind was picking up. It wasn't raining yet, but it would do soon, even before the storm arrived.

Being very careful, which wasn't easy with Bonnie dancing around excitedly, Cal gently picked up the house and carried it into the cottage.

'Can you move that out of the way?' he asked, indicating the tablet and documents on the table. Then he set it down and stepped back to examine it. Tara had done a brilliant job. On the outside, it looked exactly like Yvaine and Bonnie's house.

'Can I open it?' Bonnie asked.

'Absolutely! It's yours.'

The interior was just as wonderful, and the attention to detail was astounding. Bonnie thought so too, as she exclaimed over every little thing, pointing out this and that, and picking up various items to show him.

'Tara is very clever, isn't she, Dad?'

'She certainly is. We'd better go and thank her,' he suggested. The thought of seeing her made his heart leap, and a desperate yearning filled his chest.

Bonnie's expression became wary. 'Do I have to?'

'No, you don't. But one of us should, it's only polite. She's put a lot of work into this.'

'I didn't ask her to.'

Disappointed with his daughter's sudden surliness, there was a hint of rebuke in his tone when he replied, 'I asked her. I thought it might be a nice keepsake.'

Bonnie relented. 'Tell her I said thank you.'

Cal recognised that this was as good as he would get for now. 'I won't be long,' he said. Bonnie didn't respond.

Leaving her to play with her little house, Cal headed down the track to the beach. His heart was thumping and he had no real idea what he would say to Tara, apart from 'Thank you'.

Should he ask how she was? Or would that seem patronising?

As his feet hit the shingle, he faltered. Perhaps it might be better if he sent her a note instead. Or a card; the gift shop had some nice ones. He might even persuade Bonnie to sign it, although he wouldn't hold his breath.

He was about to turn back when he realised something wasn't right, but it took him a second or two to figure out what was wrong.

Misty Lady was missing.

Great. That's all he needed. Some thieving scabby bawbag had nicked his damn boat.

He stared over the water with narrowed eyes, trying to spot it. A few vessels were still on the loch, and he scrutinised them. Some were obviously not his – too big, wrong colour, wrong shape – and all of them, except one, were high tailing it towards the shore ahead of the encroaching storm. Having no idea when his boat had been stolen, he realised it could be anywhere by now, and may have been taken out to sea.

Cal concentrated on the speck near the far shore, but although his eyesight was good, it wasn't *that* good. He needed a pair of binoculars.

He dashed back to the cottage to fetch them and found Bonnie at the window. She'd been watching him, and when he hurried into the hall, lifted his binoculars from the coat peg where they usually lived and shot outside again, she followed closely behind.

'Wasn't Tara in, Dad?'

'I don't know. I didn't get that far. The skiff is missing.'

'Where has it gone?'

'I think someone might have stolen it.'

'That's not fair!'

'No, it isn't.' Cal came to a halt on the shingle and raised the binoculars. As he scanned the water, which had grown considerably choppier in the few minutes it had taken him to fetch the binoculars, he adjusted them to sharpen the image.

The sea was grey, with racing flecks of white, the water whipped up by the wind. Angry clouds scudded overhead, and the mountains on the opposite shore were shrouded in mist. He could see the rain coming, purple and iron-grey columns darkening the water.

Cal felt a twinge of alarm, and hoped whoever had stolen his boat wasn't still out there. Things were about to get nasty pretty quickly, and the skiff wasn't built for rough weather.

Thinking he must have imagined seeing a small vessel on the far side of the loch, he was about to give up searching when he saw something.

Was that it? Concentrating hard, he adjusted the lenses again, trying to get a clearer view. The waves were higher now, hiding the vessel, so he could only catch brief glimpses of it now and again before it disappeared into the troughs.

Feeling certain it was *Misty Lady*, he gripped the binoculars hard. Even if it wasn't his boat, it was in danger, and that was a job for the coastguard.

'Can you see it, Dad?'

'I think so.'

'Can I see?' She held up her hand for the binoculars, but he didn't answer.

The rain had reached them, and although the first drops were only a smattering, Cal knew he and Bonnie would soon be soaked to the skin.

'Why don't you go inside before you get— Oh, God!'

'What?'

'It can't be! She wouldn't!'

'*What, Dad?*'

'It's Tara.'

Bonnie glanced at the boathouse. 'Where?'

'On the loch. She's taken *Misty Lady* out.'

'But you said there's a storm coming.'

'There is, and it's nearly here.' He lowered the binoculars, grabbed his daughter's hand and began to run. 'We've got to go.'

'Where?' Bonnie panted, as she hurried to keep up.

'You are going to the castle. I'm going to see Mack.'

'Why? What's—?'

'I haven't got time to answer questions,' he replied, barging into the cottage and grabbing his waterproofs, phone and the car keys. 'Get your coat,' he instructed, dialling Mhairi's number as he charged outside again, Bonnie hot on his heels.

Mhairi answered on the second ring.

'Call the coast guard,' he yelled, the strengthening wind snatching at his words. 'Tara has taken *Misty Lady* out.'

Mhairi didn't argue. She knew as well as he did what that could mean. 'Will do.'

'I'm going to Mack's. Can you have Bonnie?'

'Drop her off on your way.' She hung up, and Cal made another call. 'Mack? It's Cal. I need your help.'

—

Tara's teeth chattered as she fought with the rudder. Although she was aiming the boat in the right direction, the waves wanted to take it in another. She also suspected that the tide was going out, and slowly but surely the little boat was being pulled out of the relative shelter of the loch and towards the open sea.

'Relative shelter' was a relative term, because the waves were higher than she thought possible, whipped into white angry peaks by the worsening wind. The troughs between them were even worse as the distant shoreline disappeared from view each time the boat sank into one.

And every time it did, she feared she was about to be swamped.

The boat was slowly filling up as waves sloshed over the side. Driving rain didn't help either, and with each minute that passed, Tara grew ever more fearful that she wouldn't come out of this alive.

If she'd realised there was a storm on the way, she never would have taken the boat out. But it had been so calm and so peaceful. The calm before the storm. She knew now where the phrase came from.

Tara had been psyching herself up to go back to the boathouse, having cried herself into a strange surreal calm of her own, when she'd noticed that the sea had become choppy, the boat bobbing more than it had previously. The wind had picked up, and when she'd glanced at the sky, a darkness above the mountains had struck a chord of worry. It was only then did she appreciate that the weather on Skye truly could turn in an instant. And it was at that point she started to become scared.

It had taken her several tries to get the outboard going, but once she did some of the tension eased a fraction. She had power therefore she could get back to safety. She hoped. But chugging across a millpond was vastly different to battling waves higher than her head, and she was worryingly sure she wasn't making much headway in the direction she wanted to go.

However, that wasn't the worst. In her eagerness to deliver Bonnie's doll's house, Tara had forgotten her mobile phone. She couldn't call for help, and no one knew she was out here. There was a very real possibility she might die if she was swept out to sea.

When the engine spluttered and cut out and she failed to get it going again, the possibility became a certainty.

Terrified, freezing, soaking wet and filled with despair, Tara began to shout.

But it wasn't 'Help' she shouted. It was Cal's name.

–

The Range Rover slid to a halt in a scatter of gravel, and Cal was out of the door and reaching for his waterproof jacket a split second later. He'd made the short trip from Duncoorie to Mack's place in record time, but despite only speaking to Mack mere minutes ago, the man was already there, readying the boat.

Cal waved and Mack held up his hand, so Cal hung back, not getting on board just yet.

When Mack gave him a thumbs up, Cal released the boat's two mooring ropes and jumped down onto the deck. Mack was already in the cockpit with the engine running as Cal joined him at the helm, and when the boat moved away from the quay Mack pulled back on the throttle and engaged the thrusters.

In less than a minute, the quay was behind them, obscured by the driving rain. The boat's navigation lights were lit, and as soon as it reached open water, Mack also flicked the searchlight on.

'I don't get to use this very often,' he said, his eyes on the radar screen.

As well as radar, the boat was equipped with sonar and GPS, but Cal knew it wouldn't be easy to detect a small wooden boat in heavy rain. What he was depending on was Mack's expert knowledge of the winds and the tides in the loch. If anyone could find *Misty Lady* and her precious cargo, it was Mack. He hadn't needed an explanation. His friend knew the danger that Tara was in better than anyone.

Cal clapped a hand on Mack's shoulder and shouted to make himself heard over the engine and the howling wind. 'Thanks, mate.'

'We haven't found her yet.'

'We will,' Cal was certain of it. To think otherwise was, well… unthinkable. He had to believe they would find Tara safe and well. *He had to*.

'Where do you think her starting point would have been?' Mack asked.

'Due west of the boathouse. I believe she would have tried to moor up on the other side in the shallows.'

'I'm assuming she wouldn't have gone out if the weather had already turned, so she would have been caught out either when she was still there or on her way back. Can you give me a guestimate of where you saw her?'

'A quarter of a mile north of where she'd started, and a few hundred yards from shore.'

Mack nodded, then began muttering to himself. Cal caught a few snippets – wind speed, drift, tide, rate of knots – but he didn't interrupt. Mack knew what he was doing.

'I reckon I know where she could be, there or there-abouts,' he announced and changed course slightly. 'If we get ahead of her and turn our backs to the tide, we'll have a chance of netting her. The last thing I want is to miss her. We'll take a zig-zag line because her location depends on how well she can steer that little boat of yours. Not that your piddly motor will be much use in this weather. What?' he asked as Cal let out a groan of despair.

'She mightn't be able to use the motor. The damned thing keeps cutting out. Oh, God!' He felt like gnashing his teeth and wailing, and it was with difficulty that he held himself together. If anything happened to her, he didn't know how he would carry on.

When they found her – he had to say when, not if – he was going to throw himself on her mercy and beg her forgiveness for being such an idiot.

He'd tell Tara he loved her and wanted to spend the rest of his life with her, and he hoped she would forgive him. He wouldn't blame her if she didn't, because he could never forgive himself for putting her through such heartache for a second time.

Please, please, let her be safe.

Please.

Chapter 26

Noise filled Tara's head. All she could hear was the wind and the slam of the waves against the boat. All she could feel was the rain and the spray soaking her already sodden body. Her feet sat in the freezing puddle at the bottom, and she couldn't feel her fingers. She kept having to look to check they were still gripping the sides. Her hands were pale and dead in the false gloaming, as though they belonged to a ghost.

How long had she been on the loch? She wasn't sure, but it couldn't have been more than a couple of hours, could it?

She didn't think night was approaching just yet, despite the heavy, lowering cloud. The thought of being out here in the dark terrified her even more than she already was.

Her voice hoarse from shouting, she tried again. It was little more than a whisper. 'Cal.' Would his name be the last word on her lips?

The boat rose, a wave lifting it, tilting the stern so high she thought it would topple backwards, before it slammed down to sink into the watery chasm that opened underneath.

Tara screamed, a harsh guttural cry, expecting icy water to close over her head.

Miraculously, the boat stayed afloat. But for how much longer?

Blinking tears and raindrops out of her eyes, she squinted into the distance, desperate for a sight of land.

The loch was only two miles wide, but it may well have been an ocean. If there were any lights on in the castle or the village, she couldn't see them. But maybe she was looking in the wrong direction.

Or was she?

Tara blinked again and narrowed her eyes as she peered into the murk, keeping her head still as the boat turned. That was definitely a light. It pierced the gloom in a single beam, then disappeared as a wall of water reared up to obscure it.

Filled with dismay, Tara craned her neck. She wanted to stand up for a better look but knew it would be fatal. Her grip tightened on the sides of the boat, and she gritted her teeth, pain flaring along her jaw.

Then she saw it again.

Was it closer? She couldn't tell.

A new noise filtered into her consciousness, a low grumbling rumble, mechanical rather than natural, and a shape behind the light emerged out of the lashing rain.

'Help! Help!' she screamed. She wanted to jump up and down and wave her arms, but she had to trust they had seen her.

When the beam caught her and held, she knew they had.

Sobbing with relief, fresh tears cascaded down her face to mingle with the rain and the spray.

But as the sound of the engine increased as her rescuers grew nearer, she began to worry that they hadn't seen her after all and she was about to be run down. Then the vessel turned sideways on when it was still some distance away, and the engine noise decreased.

Now that the light wasn't shining directly into her eyes, Tara could make out a figure on the deck.

'Tara! Can you hear me?'

The voice was achingly familiar, but it couldn't be.

'Here!' she shouted back. 'I'm here.' It ended on a sob.

'I'm going to throw you a rope. Do you think you can catch it?'

It really did sound like Cal, but that was impossible. She must be hallucinating. The cold was affecting her mind, making her imagine things.

'I'll try,' she called, through teeth that chattered so hard she feared they might shatter with the force of it. The thought of releasing her hold on the boat petrified her. She couldn't feel her hands, and she was afraid they would be too stiff. But when something landed with a heavy thud inside the boat, Tara dived on it instinctively, and she didn't realise she was clutching the rope until she'd wrapped her hands around it and was holding it with the same death grip as she'd held onto the sides of *Misty Lady*.

'Tie it to a cleat,' the man yelled, but she hesitated. She had no idea what a cleat was.

'Tara, hurry! Tie the rope off.'

'I don't know what to do,' she wailed.

'You *do*! Remember the first time we went out in *Misty Lady*? You saw me tie a rope to a metal horn on her side? Tie the rope to that.'

'Cal? *Cal!*' She was shrieking now, unable to believe it. It hadn't been her imagination – it *was* him on that boat. 'Is that really you?'

'Yes, it's me. Now, *please* tie the rope.'

Tara felt around for one of the metal horns, and when her fingers encountered one, she wrapped the rope around it in a figure of eight. She wasn't sure how secure it was, but it would have to do.

He called, 'Hang on, we're going to pull you in.'

Tara clung to the sides once more as the boat moved beneath her, and she prayed for nothing to go wrong. Not now, not when she was almost home and dry.

She was still clinging on for dear life when Cal dropped into the boat and knelt beside her.

'Here.' He placed a life vest over her head, then helped her to her feet.

She swayed as the boat rolled underneath them, and his arms immediately came around her.

'Thank God you're safe,' he said, his mouth against her ear. 'Let's get you aboard. I'll help you reach the ladder and Mack will help you climb it. OK?'

'OK.'

He gave her a squeeze. 'Atta girl.'

Unsteady, her legs trembling, Tara shuffled towards the other boat's ladder, Cal still holding onto her. Guiding her feet onto the bottom rung, he grasped her legs as she heaved herself upwards.

Terrified she would fall, it took a gargantuan effort to reach the top, but Mack was waiting for her as Cal promised, and he ushered her into the relative shelter of the cabin. But no sooner was she inside, he abandoned her.

She stood there shivering, and watched anxiously as Mack threw another rope over the side. Worry for her own safety faded. She now worried for Cal's instead. What if he fell overboard, or—?

Tara's legs gave way and she dropped to the floor, trembling violently. This was all her fault. How could she have been so stupid! Burying her face in her hands, she sobbed uncontrollably.

Then Cal was on the floor beside her. He took her in his arms, cradling her as Mack draped a silver foil blanket over her before throttling up the engine.

'It's OK, you're safe,' Cal soothed.

'I'll let the Coast Guard know they're no longer needed,' Mack said, 'and request an ambulance instead.'

Tara's breath caught in her throat and she raised frightened eyes to Cal. 'Are you hurt?'

'It's not for me, it's for you. We'd better get you checked out.'

'I'm fine.'

'Let the experts be the judge of that. You could be suffering from hypothermia.'

'I'm OK,' she insisted, then promptly burst into noisy tears again. 'I'm sorry, I could have got us all killed.'

'But you didn't. We're fine.'

'Your poor boat.'

'My boat is also fine. Mack is towing her back as we speak.'

The knowledge didn't make Tara feel any better. Aside from her physical discomfort, her heart was breaking. Her stupidity had put the man she loved in danger. Mack, also. She would never forgive herself.

Still shivering, as much from shock as the cold, it took her a while to realise that Cal was shaking too. He was racked by deep shudders as he clung to her, and she abruptly realised he was crying.

'I thought I'd lost you,' he muttered, over and over again. And Tara wept with him because, despite his presence, *she* had already lost *him*.

'I don't want to go to hospital.' Tara was adamant. She was sitting in the back of the ambulance that had been waiting for her when Mack's boat had returned to its mooring, and feeling mortified at the mayhem she'd caused – the coast guard, the ambulance, Mack having to take his boat out in such dreadful weather...

She was reminded just how awful the weather was when a gust of wind buffeted the side of the vehicle, making it rock.

'Can't you make her go?' Cal asked one of the paramedics. He was in the ambulance with her, looking on anxiously.

'Not really, and in Tara's instance I don't think she needs further medical attention. She's cold, but she isn't hypothermic.'

'Does that mean I can go home?' she asked. Although exactly where 'home' was, wasn't clear.

The boathouse would have to do for today. She would see how she felt tomorrow. Despite being keen to get away from Duncoorie, if she didn't feel up to the journey she'd wait another day until she left for the Isle of Wight. Even though she'd spent the last twenty minutes convincing everyone she was fine, she wasn't. The cold had seeped so deeply into her bones she didn't think she'd ever be warm again. She felt so weak that the thought of walking from here to Cal's car was daunting, and she was so tired that if she slept for a week it wouldn't be long enough. And her heart was still in shreds, the pain more acute and much longer lasting than anything today had caused.

Eventually, the paramedics were happy to relinquish her into Cal's care, and he led her to his car and sat her in it with the engine running and the heater on, while he went to speak with Mack. He was back before long, and as he slid behind the wheel she saw how drawn he looked. This afternoon had taken a toll on him, too.

'OK?' he asked, his expression wary.

She nodded, too weary to speak, and they drove back to Coorie Castle in silence.

When the car pulled up outside the boathouse, Tara took a deep breath. 'Thank you,' she said simply.

He blew out his cheeks. 'You're welcome.'

It was an effort to get out of the car. She may have stopped shivering, but every muscle ached and her hands throbbed. The main reason for her distress, though, was that she was acutely aware this would be the last time she would see him.

Cal, however, appeared to have other ideas. He had exited the driver's side, walked around the bonnet and was waiting to escort her to her door.

'I'm coming in with you,' he said, his tone brooking no argument.

Tara was too tired to object. She unlocked the door to the boathouse and stepped inside, her movements stiff and sluggish.

Cal took the keys out of her hand. 'Go have a hot shower. I'll make you some food.'

'I'm not hungry.' The shower sounded good, though.

'I'll make you something anyway.'

Tara shuffled into the bathroom and turned on the shower before peeling off her wet clothes. Her skin was prickling with goosebumps, and while she waited for the water to heat up, she examined herself in the mirror.

It wasn't a pleasant sight. Her hair hung in damp rats' tails, her face was white, and the skin around her eyes looked bruised, the eyes themselves haunted. She looked exactly how she felt.

It took her a while to wash her hair. Her arms were leaden, and halfway through she was forced to sit down in the bottom of the cubicle, the hot water sluicing over her bowed head and shoulders as she cried quiet tears.

Cal might have risked his life to rescue her, but she was wise enough not to read more into that selfless act than it warranted. She knew he loved her, that hadn't changed. But neither had his reason for breaking up with her.

He must have popped home, because when she emerged from her bedroom having dried her hair and changed into some fluffy pyjamas, he was in a dry pair of jogging bottoms and a sweatshirt. He was also stirring something on the hob.

A delicious smell hit her nose, and her stomach rumbled.

'Better?' he asked when he saw her.

'Yes, thanks. Are you OK?'

'Yeah.'

'What are you making?'

'Chicken and vegetable soup. It's quick, filling and nutritious. And I already had it in my freezer.'

Tara lurched over to the table and sat down. 'Where's Bonnie?'

'With Mhairi at the castle.'

'Does she know what's happened?'

He shot her a keen look. 'She was with me when I noticed the skiff had gone.'

Tara's eyes flew open. 'The doll's house!'

'Don't worry, we came back before it started to rain. It's sitting on my dining room table. Bonnie loves it, by the way. She says thank you.' He smiled. 'I love it, too.'

There was a pause, and his gaze locked with hers. Then, still looking at her, he slowly moved the pan of soup off the heat and said, 'I love *you*.'

Tara screwed her eyes shut as a fresh wave of misery hit her. 'Cal, don't.'

When she opened them again, he was still staring at her.

He said, 'You're right. Now isn't the time.' He turned away, his attention returning to the soup as he lifted the handle and poured it into a couple of bowls.

She was surprised he was eating with her, but didn't say anything, drawing her bowl nearer when he placed it on the table.

Her appetite abruptly deserting her, Tara ate without tasting, forcing it down, knowing she needed to eat if she was to feel better by the morning.

Cal didn't join her at the table. He ate his soup standing at the counter, and when they had finished he cleared away the dirty dishes.

'Go to bed,' he told her. 'You look done in. I'll see you in the morning.'

He wouldn't, she thought as she climbed into bed. She intended to be long gone by the time he got up. There was no point in dragging this out. It would be better for both of them if she slipped away quietly.

As she closed her eyes and sleep claimed her, the last memory she had of Cal was hearing the boathouse door softly click shut behind him.

—

Mhairi was waiting in the parlour, and as soon as Cal entered she hurried towards him. 'Thank goodness you are safe!' she cried, opening her arms to give him a hug.

He hugged her back, inhaling the scent of Chanel. 'Where's Bonnie?'

'I told her you'd found Tara, and that you are both safe and well and back on dry land. She's in the library, playing solitaire.'

'I didn't know she knew how to play solitaire.'

'She didn't. I taught her this evening. After I taught her how to play poker.'

'You didn't!'

Mhairi smirked. 'I did. She's good, too. We played for Scrabble tiles.'

'You could have actually played Scrabble instead.'

'Where's the fun in that?' Her head cocked to the side. 'You look dreadful.'

'Don't say that. It isn't good for my confidence.'

'It's true. Was it bad out there?'

'It's been better.'

'Whisky?'

'Please. I think I need one.'

'How is Tara? I know you said she was safe and well when you phoned, but that doesn't tell me how she is.'

'She's leaving – tomorrow, I think.'

'Ah. I see. I understood she was staying a while. I'd hoped you would have enough time to sort yourselves out.'

'I'll speak to her in the morning, try to persuade her to stay. She's asleep right now.' He wasn't going to try to persuade her – he was going to *beg*.

'I'm not surprised. She must be exhausted after her ordeal. She was very lucky.'

'She was.' Cal took a mouthful of whisky, savouring the warmth. Tara's brush with death had chilled him to his core. Today could so easily have ended in disaster.

'Do you know why she took the boat out?' Mhairi asked.

He shrugged, pretending he didn't, even though he had a reasonably good idea. The loch was their special place, and the memory of her lying in his arms naked under the sun hit him with such force it made his chest ache.

'Hmm. At least there's no harm done,' Mhairi said.

The door burst open and Bonnie bounded in, shouting, 'Is my dad back yet?' When she saw him, she flew into his arms, buried her head in his stomach and burst into tears.

'There, there,' he soothed. 'No need to cry. I'm safe and sound.'

Bonnie sniffed loudly, and Mhairi handed her a clean handkerchief. She always had at least two about her person.

After Bonnie had blown her nose and mopped up her tears, his daughter looked up at him, her expression unreadable, and said in a rather scoffing tone, 'I knew *you* would be OK. It was *Tara* I was worried about.' Then her little face crumpled again. 'I'm sorry, Daddy. I didn't mean it when I said I wished you were dead. And I didn't want Tara to die either.'

'I'm pleased to hear it. Thankfully, we're both all right.'

'Bonnie and I have had a little chat,' Mhairi said. 'Would you like to tell your dad what it was about?'

Bonnie hung her head, and Cal gave Mhairi a questioning look.

'Mhairi told me I was being selfish,' Bonnie mumbled. 'That you had to have someone to look after you when I'm with Mum.'

'And…?' Mhairi prompted.

'That it was wrong of you to break your promise, but you shouldn't have made it in the first place. She called you a numpty.'

Cal raised an eyebrow.

'You are,' Mhairi said. 'What else, Bonnie?'

'I like Tara. If you have to have a girlfriend, I'd prefer it to be her, rather than someone I don't know.'

Cal heard Mhairi's voice in Bonnie's words. 'Do you mean that, or are you just saying it because Mhairi told you to?'

'Mhairi didn't tell me to say anything. She told me to go away and think about my actions and how sad you were.'

'Was that before or after she taught you to play poker?'

'Before. Does Tara play poker?'

'I don't know.'

'Can I go and ask her?'

'Not right now, she's asleep. I'd better get back and check on her.' He met Mhairi's eyes over the top of his daughter's head.

Mhairi's expression was solemn. She was as aware as he of the dangers of the loch and how things could have been much worse.

'Is she your girlfriend again?' Bonnie asked.

'If she'll have me.'

'She will.'

He loved his daughter's confidence. Cal, on the other hand, wasn't so sure. 'Do you mind?' he asked.

'A bit. But Mhairi says that's selfish.' She pulled a face. 'Being selfish isn't nice.'

Mhairi pointed at the door. 'You can thank me later,' she said to him. 'Now, go home. I need a cup of cocoa.'

'Fetch your night things,' Cal said to Bonnie after he'd thanked Mhairi for looking after her and had taken Bonnie back to the cottage. 'We're spending tonight in the boathouse. I don't want to leave Tara on her own, not after—' He stopped.

'Could Tara have died?' she asked, her eyes wide.

Cal was tempted to gloss over the danger Tara had been in, but he didn't want to minimise how treacherous the loch could be. It was like any other wild place on Skye – it had to be treated with respect, so he decided to be truthful. 'Yes, she could have.'

'But you saved her.'

'*Mack* saved her,' Cal corrected.

'Oh, I thought you did.' She sounded disappointed, and so was he. He would have liked to have hung onto his superhero status for a while longer.

Bonnie brightened. 'Can I make him a thank-you card?'

'I think he'd like that.'

'Shall I make one for Tara?'

'You definitely should. Tara's only got one bedroom, so I bagsy the couch. You, young one, can have the floor.'

'That's not fair!'

Calan's smile was wide as he carried a bundle of bedding from the cottage to the boathouse.

Bonnie, to his amazement, had accepted Tara as his girlfriend – with a few home truths from Mhairi. Now all he had to do was to persuade Tara to forgive him and give him another chance – for a second time.

He feared it wasn't going to be easy.

Chapter 27

Tara awoke slowly, taking a long time to surface from a very deep slumber. As she lay there, her eyes still closed, the memory of the awful events of yesterday cascaded through her mind in a terrifying kaleidoscope. Her limbs were heavy, and she felt like she'd gone ten rounds with an Olympic boxer. She was aching in so many places that it was probably easier to list the places which *didn't* hurt.

She was wondering what the time was and how soon she could be on the road if she heaved herself out of bed now, when she froze.

She wasn't on her own.

Someone else was in bed with her.

Cautiously, she opened one eye, then the other and very gently turned her head so as not to disturb—

Bonnie? The child was curled on her side, her hair fanned across the pillow, her breathing even and deep.

Tara rubbed her eyes and looked again.

Bonnie was still there, which begged the question, where was Cal?

She managed to get out of bed without waking the little girl and shuffled in a rather ungainly manner into the corridor.

She found him in the living area.

He was sprawled on the sofa, a cushion under his head, one arm dangling, sound asleep.

Tara studied him: the way his hair was sticking up, the stubble on his jaw, his long limbs. He looked younger in repose, the man he used to be superimposed on the man he had become. Her heart ached for the love that had slipped through her fingers for a second time. *Or had it?*

Yesterday he'd told her again that he loved her, and she believed him, but it didn't alter the fact that he had to put Bonnie's happiness first.

Tara glanced back at the bedroom where his daughter lay sleeping, and wondered whether Bonnie had forgiven her dad, or whether sharing a bed with Tara had simply been preferable to sharing the couch with Cal.

Cal's eyes were open.

Startled, Tara put a hand to her chest, her pulse hammering as his amber gaze bored into her.

He cleared his throat. 'How did you sleep?'

'Better than you, I suspect.'

'Is Bonnie awake?'

'No. Why is she in my bed?'

'Because she couldn't settle on the sofa.' He sat up, running his hands through his hair, making it stick up even more.

'I'm not surprised. It isn't big enough for both of you.'

'I was on the floor. I didn't think you'd appreciate waking up to find *me* in your bed.'

'I don't think Bonnie would have approved, either.'

'Oh, I don't know…'

Tara frowned. Moving away from the doorway, she took several steps towards him before halting. Something was going on, but she wasn't sure what.

'When I was out looking for you, Mhairi had a chat with Bonnie,' he said. 'About me and you.'

'And?'

'Let's just say, Bonnie isn't going to hold me to my promise.'

'She isn't?'

He smiled. It was tentative and there was a wariness in his eyes. 'No.'

'What if Bonnie changes her mind?' she asked, the words catching in her throat.

'I don't think she will, but if she does, it won't alter anything between us. I love you. I always have, and I always will. Please give me another chance – give *us* another chance.'

She thought he might be close to tears, but he wasn't the only one.

It took everything Tara had not to fall into Cal's arms. She desperately wanted to forgive him but was terrified of being even more hurt than she was already, and she didn't think she could. She was numb. Exhausted. Frightened he would break her heart again. Once had been bad enough. Twice was unforgivable. And although she understood his reasons, she hated herself for resenting them.

Cal's father hadn't been able to help being unwell, but Cal should have told her. She would have waited, however long it took. As for Bonnie – what mother would use such a flimsy excuse to prevent a father from seeing his child?

Tara was fairly certain she knew why that was. Yvaine was still in love with Cal. Her reaction when she'd confronted Tara in her studio proved it. Yvaine had made it her mission to ensure Cal broke up with her. She'd succeeded, and it had nearly cost Tara her life.

Wearily, her heart aching more than her body ever could, Tara shook her head. 'I love you, Cal, but I can't do this.'

He paled and the anguish in his eyes almost made her change her mind. But she had to remain strong.

'I'm going to get dressed, then I'm leaving,' she announced, surprised how calm she sounded. The car was packed. The outfit she intended to travel in was the only thing left in the wardrobe. She could be out of here in a matter of minutes.

'Tara—'

'Stop,' she hissed, keeping her voice low, not wanting to wake Bonnie. 'I'm leaving, and there's nothing you can say to make me change my mind. We're over, Cal. We've been over for a decade. Getting back together was…' She didn't know what it was. But she did know she wished she'd never set foot on Skye.

Calan turned away, to stare through the picture window. Yesterday's storm had blown itself out and the loch was calm once more. She would miss it. Heck, she'd miss the little boathouse, her studio, the castle and the friends she'd made. Most of all, she would miss Cal, and she knew she would love him for as long as she lived.

Quietly she retrieved her clothes from the bedroom and retreated to the bathroom to dress. With a splash of water on her face and a quick brush of her teeth, she was ready.

Cal hadn't moved.

'I've left a note for Mhairi,' she told him. 'Please see that she gets it.'

'I will.' He still had his back to her, and she was thankful she couldn't see his face.

She said, 'Thank you for saving my life when you could so easily have lost yours.' Not waiting for a response, she whirled on her heel, snatched up her bag and her keys, and ran for her car before she crumbled.

Tara had crossed the bridge between Skye and the mainland before she managed to stem her tears. But no amount of distance could repair the damage to her heart.

'Daddy, are you crying?'

Cal jumped, and hastily swiped at his eyes with his arm. 'Hay fever,' he fibbed.

'Where's Tara?'

'She's gone.' He was struggling to believe she'd walked out of his life, and he'd never see her again.

As he'd heard her car start up, he'd considered chasing after her. There was only one road off the island, and if he put his foot down he might catch up with her. But he had Bonnie to consider, and by the time he found someone to look after her, Tara would have had too great a head start. After she crossed Skye Bridge, she could go anywhere: back to Edinburgh perhaps, or Glasgow where she had grown up, or to the other side of the world.

The pain of her loss stole his breath. His heart was as raw as an open wound, and he felt utterly sick with grief.

Bonnie said, 'I'm hungry. Will she mind if you make me breakfast? Could you make pancakes, and we can take some to the studio for her.'

Cal pressed his lips together as he struggled to compose himself. 'She's not at the studio. Bon-Bon. She's left Duncoorie for good.'

'Why?'

'Because.' What could he say that would make sense to a nine-year-old?

'That's a silly answer. Didn't she want to be your girl-friend?'

'No.'

'Why not?'

He rubbed a hand across his face. 'Can you please stop asking so many questions?'

Bonnie pouted. 'My teacher says you learn best by asking questions.' She plopped her backside onto the sofa, her expression serious. 'Is that why you were crying?'

'I wasn't crying.'

'You were. It's wrong to lie.'

'OK, I was crying, but I'm not now.'

'You're still sad.'

Cal was beyond sad. He was devastated. He didn't blame Tara for leaving. The blame lay entirely with him. Ten years ago, he'd been swayed by his mother's entreaty that no one should know how ill his dad was, but he should have confided in Tara. Instead of thinking it would be better for her if he ended it, he should have talked it over with her, laid his cards on the table and let her decide.

Cal snorted. At least he'd explained his reasons this time. However, he should have stood up to Yvaine and her ridiculous insistence that she allow their daughter to call the shots.

He'd blown it for a second time. How could he have been so stupid? He'd had a second chance at happiness with the woman he loved, and he'd messed it up.

'Dad, I'm hungry.'

Cal forced his thoughts away from his misery. 'Get your things. We'll go back to the cottage and I'll cook you those pancakes.'

As he slipped his feet into his boots, he remembered the letter Tara had left for Mhairi. Tenancy agreements and studio lets were his remit, so he opened it in case there was anything he needed to know, and his chest constricted when he saw her handwriting.

He scanned it quickly and was about to put it in his pocket when he noticed she'd included a forwarding address. She was going to the Isle of Wight.

Suddenly, he knew what he had to do. He had to go after her.

First though, he had to find someone to look after Bonnie. He reached for his phone. 'Yvaine? Hi, something's come up and I need to bring Bonnie back.'

'Is she OK?' Yvaine's voice was filled with worry.

'She's fine. I've got to go somewhere, that's all. And she can't come with me.'

'I'm at Lenn's house, in Portree.'

'No problem. I'll drop her off on the way.'

'On the way where?'

Before he could reply, Bonnie shot into the living room. 'Is that Mum? Mum, Dad almost died yesterday.'

'*What?*' His ex-wife's screech made Cal flinch. 'What happened?'

'It's nothing,' he said. 'We'll be there in forty minutes.'

However, when Cal pulled into Lenn's driveway and Bonnie saw her mother waiting for them, she scrambled out of the car, launched herself at her and broke into noisy sobs.

Yvaine gathered her up and glowered at him. 'Tell me,' she demanded.

Bonnie got in first. 'He went out in the storm to rescue Tara,' she wailed. 'Mhairi said Tara could have died, and Daddy could have died too.'

Yvaine pursed her lips and turned her attention back to Cal. 'You'd better come in.'

'I haven't got time.'

Her expression turned from annoyed to horrified. 'Is Tara OK? She isn't in hospital, is she?'

He shook his head. 'She's fine.'

Bonnie sniffed, 'She's gone. She told Daddy she doesn't want to be his girlfriend, and now he's really sad. Mhairi said I was being selfish.'

'Go inside,' Yvaine said. 'I'll be there in a minute.' She waited until Bonnie was out of earshot then said, 'You need to explain.'

Cal didn't have time for this, so he made it quick, finishing with, 'She's gone to the Isle of Wight, to her mother's, and I'm going after her.' He stared defiantly at his ex-wife, sick of letting her call the shots. If she wanted to make a thing of this, she'd have to wait. He had a six-hundred-mile drive ahead of him and the love of his life to win back first.

Yvaine surprised him by bursting into tears.

At a loss, he eyed her uncertainly, wondering whether he should give her a hug or call Lenn.

'You almost died,' she cried, her face in her hands.

Cal froze in shock. She didn't still love him, did she? Oh, hell!

'But I didn't,' he replied. 'I'm still alive and kicking.' He stepped towards her, then hesitated. 'I'm sorry, Yvaine.'

She dropped her hands and sniffed. A wry smile appeared on her tear-streaked face. 'For not dying?'

He huffed out a breath. 'For everything. For not loving you enough, for not trying harder to make it work. I really did care about you. I still do.'

'But you don't love me.'

Filled with deep regret, he shook his head and repeated, 'I'm sorry. I never meant to hurt you.'

'I know.' She swallowed and looked away. 'You can't help who you fall in love with.'

'You can't,' he agreed sadly, his heart going out to her. He'd made such a godawful mess of everything.

She said, 'We never should have got married.'

'No.'

Yvaine brought her gaze back to him. 'I always knew you didn't love me the way I loved you, and when I realised why and that she'd come back into your life, I kind of flipped.' Her eyes bored into him and he shuffled uncomfortably. This wasn't easy to hear but he owed it to Yvaine to listen as she continued, 'I'm sorry for being such a cow. It was wrong. I suppose I wanted to get back at you, and I was also cheesed off by your attitude toward Lenn. He's no threat to you, Cal. You'll always be Bonnie's father.'

'Are you happy, Yvaine?'

She looked surprised at the question. 'I am. I love Lenn with all my heart. He's a good man, and he thinks the world of Bonnie.'

'I'm glad. You deserve to be happy.'

'As do you. Go get her, Cal. Persuade Tara to come back to Skye.'

That was precisely what he intended to do – *if* he could convince her to give him another chance.

Tara woke feeling even more exhausted than when she'd gone to bed. Her back ached, her shoulders and arms were in agony, and her hands felt like claws from gripping the steering wheel for hours on end. To add to her list of woes, her eyes were dry and gritty, her neck had gone into a spasm, her head pounded, and her hips and legs felt like they belonged to an eighty-year-old.

But those physical woes were nothing compared to the emotional ones.

Tara's heart had been torn out of her chest, and the gaping hole was a throbbing, pulsing agony. Each time she thought of Cal, pain so intense that it made her gasp shot through her. Yet, not thinking about him was as impossible as not breathing.

Damn him! It had taken her years to get her life back on track after the last time he'd broken her heart. She had an awful suspicion she mightn't get it back on track at all this time.

Snippets of yesterday's long drive floated into her head – the endless motorway, the sun in her eyes as she headed south, the tears on her cheeks, then the safety of her mother's embrace, and the feel of her cool hand on Tara's clammy brow as she tucked her into bed.

A clock on the nightstand told her it was only seven a.m.

Maybe she would stay here for the rest of the day. Tomorrow, as well. What was there to get up for?

Then she guessed that her mum wouldn't allow her to slip back into her old ways. And neither should she. She'd survived having her heart broken once; she could survive it a second time. But she vowed never to let it happen again. No more falling in love, and no more relationships. How could she give herself to another man whilst she loved someone else? Her love for Cal wasn't going to go away. But even if it did and she found herself able to love again, she wanted a man who was prepared to go to the ends of the earth for her, who would fight tooth and nail for her, instead of letting her walk out of his life with barely a murmur.

Reluctantly, she forced herself to get out of bed, smiling sadly when she saw that her cases had been brought up. Goodness knows where she would put the rest of her stuff, but no doubt she'd find a spare corner to store it in until she felt up to making doll's houses once more.

She staggered to the bathroom on stiff legs, and hoped she'd feel better after a shower. Unsurprisingly she didn't, although she did look marginally more respectable with her hair freshly washed and clean clothes on her back.

Despite having consumed very little food yesterday, Tara didn't feel hungry. Aware she should eat something, she ventured downstairs to head for the kitchen, but paused in the hall when she saw a vehicle pull up in front of the office. She noticed the make. Her heart clenched, missing a beat before thumping again as it caught up with itself.

Tara gave herself a shake. There must be thousands of black Range Rovers in the country, and quite a few with similar number plates. Cal was going to haunt her for quite some time to come, and although there might be fewer triggers here on the Isle of Wight, there would inevitably be some. She would never escape them completely, just like she would never escape her memories. Huh! Even the guy getting out of the car looked like him.

Tara caught her breath, her heart hammering. The guy didn't *look* like Cal. It *was* Cal.

She saw him stretch, glance around, and then head inside the office.

Rooted to the spot by indecision, Tara didn't know what to do. She put a hand on the newel post for support, breathing in short gasps, and sank onto the last but one stair, her legs unable to bear her weight. Her treacherous heart leapt, joy sparking through her, but she quickly dampened it, beating it down with the pain he had caused her not once, but twice.

Closing her eyes, fearing she was about to pass out, she inhaled slowly, held the breath, then let it out. On the third repetition, her eyes snapped open as she heard the front door open, and saw her mother enter the hall.

Cal was with her.

Her mum was livid. 'He won't leave without speaking to you. Should I call the police?'

Tara hauled herself to her feet. Her voice unsteady, she said to Cal, 'Say what you've got to say, then go.'

He glanced at her mum, looking worried. And so he should. Her mother wasn't a woman to be trifled with. He also looked haggard, exhausted and dishevelled, and Tara assumed he must have been on the road all night.

To his credit, he didn't ask to speak to her alone. Or maybe he sensed that her mother intended to stay put.

With another cautious glance at her mum's resolute face, he said, 'Tara, I've been an idiot. I love you with all my heart and I should never have let you go.'

Her mum snorted. 'Yet you managed to *let her go* twice.'

'I know.' Cal's cheeks glistened. His eyes were on Tara and she realised he was crying. 'If I could spend eternity making it up to you, I would.'

'It's OK, Mum. I can take it from here.'

'No police?'

'Not yet.'

'I'll be in the office if you need me.'

Tara waited for the door to close, then said, 'I'm not sure an eternity would be long enough.'

'You're right. I don't have eternity, but I do have the rest of my life. I want to spend it with you.' He got down on one knee, and she gasped. 'I don't have a ring to give you, just my heart. But you've already got that. It's yours.

It's always been yours, and it always will be. Marry me, Tara. *Please*. Let me show you how much I love you.'

She stared at him as he balanced awkwardly on one knee, his expression pleading, adoration in his eyes, and she knew he meant every word.

Could she bring herself to give him another chance? Ten years ago, she would have said yes in an instant. A week ago, her reply would have been the same. Now, though…

But if she didn't, she had a feeling she might always regret it. He *was* fighting for her. He hadn't allowed her to walk out of his life. He was here, now, begging her to be his wife. And when she imagined all the years to come, years without Cal in them, she didn't like the look of them one little bit.

'Yes, I will.'

He didn't appear to hear her at first. He looked puzzled, a frown creasing his brow. Then his face lit up with the widest of smiles, and he got to his feet and walked slowly towards her.

Tara's heart skipped a beat and thousands of butterflies took flight in her tummy. She was shaking from the force of her love for him, and as she looked into his eyes, he gently took her face in his hands and kissed her.

Epilogue

'My teacher is Mrs Phillips and she's nice but strict and she's got a wee dog called Chico. She showed us pictures and says he's really naughty.'

Bonnie hadn't stopped talking since Cal had brought her to the castle for her weekend visit. He'd collected her from Yvaine and Lenn's house in Portree after school today, and he looked somewhat shell-shocked.

Tara guessed he'd already heard it all on the journey and was now getting to hear it all over again because Bonnie wanted to share her news with Tara.

After her flight to the Isle of Wight and Cal's subsequent proposal, Tara had returned to the castle and had moved back into the boathouse. She may have agreed to marry him, but they hadn't told Bonnie yet and didn't intend to for a while. It had been Tara's suggestion they keep the news under wraps for the time being, to allow Bonnie to get used to her dad having a girlfriend, as well as her move to a new town and new school.

Bonnie hadn't finished. 'I sit next to Shannon. She likes caramel ice cream and she lets me borrow her gel pens. Mum said she can come to tea next week and I'm going to invite her to my birthday party. I'm not going to invite Helga because she said my hair is silly. It's not silly, is it, Dad? Lenn said if I don't like the colour of my bedroom,

I can pick another one. I think I want pink. Or purple. Or gold. What colour would you have, Tara?'

Tara was breathless just listening to her, and was wondering how to respond when Bonnie cried, 'Can I go see Giselle, Dad? She said I can help her look for sea glass tomorrow.'

'You most certainly can.' The relief on Cal's face made Tara giggle.

Bonnie shot off in a blur of long, thin legs and flying hair, and Cal collapsed onto the sofa.

'She's only been here five minutes and I'm worn out already.' Smiling indulgently, he added in a heartfelt tone, 'Thank heaven she's settling into her new school. I was so worried she wouldn't.'

Tara sat beside him, and his arm automatically draped around her shoulders. 'I know you were.'

'I could have cursed Yvaine when she told me she was taking Bonnie to live with Lenn, but I don't think it's worked out too badly.'

Autumn term had started five weeks ago, and it was seven weeks since Bonnie had said goodbye to her home in Duncoorie. There had been tears, but not as many as Cal and Tara had anticipated.

'Would you like to join us for supper?' Cal asked.

'Don't you and Bonnie want to spend some time together?'

'Bonnie won't mind if you hang out with us.'

'Is that what I'm doing?' she asked, nibbling his ear. 'Hanging out?'

'Driving me crazy, that's what you're doing,' he growled. 'I'll make you pay for that.'

'Promise?'

The look he gave her sent delicious shivers down her back. She knew she would have to wait until Bonnie went home on Sunday, but she didn't mind. The wait would be worth it.

Skye in autumn was beautiful, an isle of mist and golden grass, russet bracken and navy water.

It was early morning. A clear dove-grey sky, streaked with pale apricot, promised a fine day ahead, perfect for kicking through the recently fallen leaves in the woodland.

Tara made a mug of coffee, and still wearing her pyjamas but with the addition of a padded jacket, she thrust her feet into a pair of trainers and headed to the end of the jetty to drink it.

She wasn't surprised when she was shortly joined by Cal. He'd also brought a mug with him, and they sat in comfortable silence to enjoy the peace of the morning. A heron moved through the shallows, lifting one foot carefully before slowly placing it down with barely a ripple, its beady-eyed gaze trained on the water. A flashing stab of its beak indicated that it'd caught a fish, and Tara watched in fascination as it ate its breakfast.

'I love it here,' she murmured, resting her head on Cal's shoulder.

'Skye gets under your skin, doesn't it?' There was a smile in his voice.

'I couldn't imagine living anywhere else.' Tara absently fingered the gold heart-shaped pendant at her throat, remembering when Cal had given it to her. She'd kept it in her jewellery box, unworn and unloved. It had resurfaced when she'd unpacked the car after she returned from the Isle of Wight, and finding it had seemed prophetic somehow. She'd worn it ever since.

'So I couldn't tempt you to leave?' he teased.

'Absolutely not!'

'Not even for a week?' He smiled down at her.

'For a holiday? Where do you have in mind?'

'I think it's time you met my parents.'

Tara's eyes widened with mischief. 'It must be serious if we're at the meeting the parents stage.'

'It must be.' He was grinning, but then he sobered. 'Mum still feels awful for what happened when we were younger. She blames herself.'

'What happened, happened.' Tara was philosophical. 'At least we found each other again.'

'And I'm never letting you go,' he vowed, kissing her deeply.

'Ew!'

At the sound of Bonnie's voice, Tara hastily dragged her lips away, mortified. Cal, however, didn't seem perturbed.

The child sat down on the jetty beside her father, her nose wrinkling. 'You're as bad as Mum and Lenn. They're always kissing. I'm never having a boyfriend if that's all you do.'

Tara stifled a snigger, and Cal shot her a look. 'I'll hold you to that,' he warned his daughter. 'No boyfriends ever.'

Bonnie kicked her legs, staring over the water. 'Helga's got a boyfriend. His name is Charlie and he's got a ferret. I like ferrets but I don't like Charlie. He brought it into school for show-and-tell, and it bit Mrs Phillips. After Giselle has taken me to look for sea glass, can I go see Katie?'

'You can.'

'Yay!' She jumped up and scampered back up the jetty.

Cal met Tara's eye. 'I think it's time I told her we're getting married,' he said, scrambling to his feet and jogging after her.

Tara hitched in a breath, then blew it out slowly.

It seemed an age until he returned, but it couldn't have been more than a few minutes.

'How did she take it?' she asked, anxiously.

'She was fine. Said "OK", and that was it.'

'Really?'

He sat beside her. 'She wasn't bothered in the slightest. Not even when I told her you would be moving into the cottage.'

'I am, am I?'

'Have you got a better suggestion?'

Tara didn't. Living in Cal's cottage sounded wonderful.

'By the way,' he added, 'she'll only let us get married on one condition.'

Tara's heart sank. She should have guessed there might be something. 'What is it?'

'Bonnie insists on being a bridesmaid and she wants to choose her dress.' Cal looked worried, as though this might be a deal-breaker.

'Is that all?' Tara began to giggle. 'Heck, she can choose *mine* if it makes her happy.'

'Yeah, I wouldn't mention that to her if I were you. She'll have you walking down the aisle in a mermaid's outfit.'

'I don't care what I wear as long as we get married.'

Cal got to his feet and held out a hand to haul her upright, clasping her to him. 'I don't have the words to tell you how happy you make me or how thankful I am that you came back into my life. I love you, Tara, always and forever.'

His eyes brimmed with adoration, and she melted, marvelling at how deeply this wonderful man loved her.

And she loved him. More than he would ever know.

Acknowledgements

I had so much fun writing this book! In fact, this much fun shouldn't be allowed!! But, as usual, I didn't write it all by myself. Well, I *did*, but other people had an input too. Emily Bedford, my editor, helped me polish it, as did Alicia Pountney (actually, they did most of the polishing), Cath Mills for the moral support, Valerie Brown for her eagle eye, and Simone Groombridge for her unwavering championing of every one of my books. And I really must thank Head Design for the stunning cover art. It's probably my favourite yet.

Behind the scenes, my husband supplied the tea and biscuits to keep me going, along with lots of cheering. He nagged a bit, too – mostly when he knew I should be writing but caught me scrolling the internet, watching video clips of cats playing with balls of string.

Mum, thank you. Without you, I wouldn't be a full-time author and doing what I love for a living.

And finally, you, my lovely reader, for taking the time to read my story – you have my eternal gratitude.

Lilac xxx